A Wedding to Die For

The Fourth Something to Die For Mystery

Radine Trees Nehring

ST KITTS PRESS   WICHITA, KANSAS

PUBLISHED BY ST KITTS PRESS
A division of S-K Publications
PO Box 8173 Wichita, KS 67208
316-685-3201 FAX 316-685-6650
stkitts@skpub.com www.StKittsPress.com

The name St Kitts and its logo are registered trademarks.

This novel is a work of fiction. Any references to real people and places are used only to give a sense of reality. All of the characters are the product of the author's imagination, as are their thoughts, actions, motivations, or dialog. Any resemblance to real people and events is purely coincidental.

Edited by Elizabeth Whiteker
Cover illustration by Cat Rahmeier
Cover design by Diana Tillison

First Edition 2006

Library of Congress Cataloging-in-Publication Data

Nehring, Radine Trees.
  A wedding to die for / Radine Trees Nehring.-- 1st ed.
    p. cm. -- (The fourth Something to die for mystery)
  ISBN-13: 978-1-931206-01-3 (pbk. : alk. paper)
  ISBN-10: 1-931206-01-5 (pbk. : alk. paper)
  1. McCrite, Carrie (Fictitious character)--Fiction. 2. Ozark
Mountains--Fiction. 3. Elderhostels--Fiction. 4. Older women--Fic-
tion. 5. Eureka Springs (Ark.)--Fiction. 6. Weddings--Fiction. 7.
Widows--Fiction. I. Title.
  PS3614.E44W43 2006
  813'.6--dc22
                                    2005037987

Praise for the
Something to Die For Mysteries

"Readers will delight in Carrie McCrite, a spunky heroine who faces danger and finds love."

—**CAROLYN HART**, author of the
Death on Demand and Henrie O mysteries

"Nehring's delightful novel features history and romance with murder thrown in. A winning combination and fun read."

—**PATRICIA SPRINKLE**, 2005-06 President of Sisters in Crime; bestselling author of the Thoroughly Southern mystery series

Advance Praise for
A Wedding to Die For

"Nehring's novel redefines the cozy mystery and overturns misconceptions about age, murder, foreigners, and romance. If you've come to love Carrie McCrite's independent pluck, spirit, and evolving relationship with co-sleuth Henry King, this novel is 'to die for.' If you're new to the series, welcome to high entertainment that's thought-provoking, tender, funny and chilling."

—**CROW JOHNSON EVANS**, internationally acclaimed musician, song writer, author, and performer; board member, The Writers' Colony at Dairy Hollow in Eureka Springs, Arkansas

"I'm a big fan of novels that are true to a local community and region—those that capture a sense of place and really let me feel the area's pulse. That's exactly what Radine Trees Nehring's superb mystery series does."

—**JOE DAVID RICE**, Arkansas Tourism Director

Acknowledgments

The Crescent Hotel in Eureka Springs, Arkansas, is, happily, a very real place. My deep thanks go to owners Elise and Marty Roenigk for giving Carrie McCrite, Henry King, and their friends permission to romp about in this magnificent and historic building. We had a wonderful time there!

Other locations in Eureka Springs, except for Bubba's Barbecue, the Bavarian Inn Restaurant, and St. Elizabeth's Catholic Church, are fictionalized.

An important source of information on all things floral, including details about what it's like to own a flower shop and "do weddings," was Beverly Gibson of Gibson Gardens—Greenhouses, Nursery, Florist—in Gravette, Arkansas.

My thanks for information about historic buildings goes to Beverly Tetterton, Special Collections Librarian, New Hanover County Library, Wilmington, North Carolina, and thanks also to my good friend and fellow author, Ellen Elizabeth Hunter, for finding Ms. Tetterton for me, as well as supporting me via e-mail during the writing of this novel.

Law enforcement information in Eureka Springs came from Detective Shelley Summers and Patrol Officer James Loudermilk.

Additional information was added by members of the Gravette Police Department, including Chief Trent Morrison, Sergeant Lonnie Ash, and Officer David Smith.

There are other areas where I needed extra help and the following people (in reverse alphabetical order) filled the gaps for me:

My niece, Jennifer Weiss, who shared up-to-date information about having babies in the 21st century.

Raymond Waier helped explain what's on the shelves of the bottle shop in the Crescent Hotel.

Sun, who guided me around the New Moon Spa.

Mary Jean Sell, part-time Eureka Springs City Clerk, shared information about the workings of city government there.

David Rowe helped with his knowledge of the Spanish language.

Larry Rahmeier, treasured brother-in-law, practices law in Claremore, Oklahoma. Over the years I've learned something about his work. (You'll see why that's important later.)

Donna Patrick was married in The Crescent Hotel and told me about her wedding.

Tom Monie, former coach, helped me get to know Cody Wells. Tom's knowledge of sports and insight into the life of this seventeen-year-old boy were a tremendous help.

RoAnna McDaniel and Misty Moyer, Wedding Consultants, shared ideas about wedding planning.

Ron Lerchen, Crescent Hotel bellman, showed me guest rooms you'll now see in the pages of this book.

Bob and Sandy Kelley, Shelter Insurance in Gravette, explained what happens after a building sustains bomb damage.

Dr. Jeff and Lou Honderich helped me fix Carrie's cut face and told me about Charlie's needs as a "preemie."

Dr. Arthur and Crow Johnson Evans's trips to India and familiarity with the people there were a help throughout the book.

To all of the above mentioned: Guys, I may have gotten it wrong, but, if so, it sure isn't your fault! Goodness knows you tried. Besides, sometimes a fragment of imagination manages to bend facts in a work of fiction.

Forever thanks to cover artist and dear sister-in-law Cat Rahmeier, who enhances every book I write.

Continuing gratitude goes to my husband John Nehring, and to editors Laurel B. Schunk and Diana Tillison. These three stand with me every day.

THANK YOU, ONE AND ALL!

Dedication

To members of the Spavinaw Authors Guild critique group who walked the road with me while this book was being written. Special thanks to regular members (talented writers all), Janelle Engle, Crow Johnson Evans, Lucia C. Greer, Mary McKee, John Nehring, Ray Waier and Gayle Williams.

Prologue

The woman's figure twirled faster and faster, ivory satin skirts flaring, veil blowing across her face like a cloud. She was a blur now, her gown and veil growing darker as she spun. Darker, until they were the color of...

Carrie popped up in bed as if some backbone spring had snapped, jerking her to a sitting position. She shook her head, trying to dislodge the image of a bride who danced in a wedding gown that changed from ivory to the color of blood.

No, no! It wasn't real, *it wasn't,* as she'd reminded herself twice before when—in her dreams—the terrible bride danced.

The image disappeared, replaced by a new fright when a rattling crash came from her front hall.

FatCat?

She'd only begun to mull that possibility when a streaking motion brought the cat out of her basket and into a flying leap aimed at Carrie's lap. The collision shoved

Carrie back against the headboard before FatCat bounced away from flailing arms and slid off the bed, pulling the white down comforter after her.

Carrie turned on the bedside lamp and stared at her cat, whose face said clearly that a peril-impelled leap into forbidden territory—Carrie's bed—should be welcomed by any human with an ounce of sense.

So, FatCat hadn't been the cause of the noise. *What, then?* Carrie reached out and turned the lamp off. Right now, darkness felt safer than light.

For a moment she contemplated December, when she would be a bride, and strong, fearless Henry King—former cop, her love and her new husband—would occupy this room with her.

If only...

Stop it! *If only* was a useless supposing, and she wasn't about to call Henry. He'd come, of course, leave his bed and come down the path in the woods to look through her house while she cowered under the covers.

So! She'd take care of whatever it was by herself, just as she'd been doing here at her home in Blackberry Hollow for nearly six years.

Carrie listened in the darkness. After a few minutes of monitoring, hearing nothing but her own heartbeat, she pushed the remaining covers aside and slowly, quietly, slid out of bed, dropping her feet into wooly slippers as soon as they reached the floor. She picked the comforter up and shoved it back in place, resisting the temptation to wrap its sheltering softness around her head and shoulders.

Carrie shivered when she realized the comforter wrapping would make her look like a ghost...a fat Halloween ghost.

She almost, *almost,* wished she hadn't said no to keeping a sawed-off shotgun by her bed. Henry wasn't keen on the idea either, though he agreed with the county sheriff that the best firearm a woman alone could have for protection would be a shotgun with its barrel sawed off 1/8" outside the legal minimum. The shotgun idea had come up when they found supplies for a meth lab hidden in the woods on the far side of Blackberry Hollow.

"Very few people, high on drugs or not, will argue against a shotgun pointed in their direction," the sheriff had said. "And even if you can't shoot well, you'll have a hard time missing anyone who's close enough to be inside your home when you use a shotgun. Besides, a shotgun's usually not strong enough to blast through a wall and kill somebody in the next room."

After consideration, she'd decided not having a gun would be safer for her than having one, even if it was "impossible to miss your target" with a shotgun. She couldn't face thinking about all the things that could go wrong with any gun meant to maim or kill. She wasn't a gun person, and she wouldn't feel safer if she saw a gun by her bed every night. Its presence would bring only fear.

The orange numbers on her clock winked from 3:59 to 4:00 a.m.

Everything was absorbed in quiet darkness except for the clock face and the soft glow of the night light in the hall.

Then another crash came from outside her bedroom door. Carrie swallowed a shriek and grabbed the phone, putting her finger on the button to speed-dial Henry's number.

Henry was living in his daughter Susan's house, just a few hundred yards away through the woods. He would come very quickly, and he would bring a gun.

She stopped, her finger frozen on the button.

Oh, for good garden seed! She didn't need to call Henry. She knew what the sound was now; in fact she'd heard it several times before, but never in the dead silence of night. One of the suction cups holding her stained glass sun catchers in the hall window had come loose, that was all. Well, maybe two of them. There had been two crashes.

Carrie reached for her robe, padded across the room, started down the hall. She'd check the sun catchers just to be sure.

It was easy to tell. Even in the dim night-light glow, she could see that a stained glass angel was missing from its place on the square of window pane. Maybe it had fallen to the table first, teetered for a while, then dropped to the floor. Two crashes.

Carrie flipped the light switch and bent to pick up the angel, sighing with relief when she saw that it hadn't broken. Her sigh turned into a squeak of fear when she stood up and looked back at the window.

The angel's clear plastic suction cup with its hook was still stuck fast to the pane.

How on earth had the angel fallen?

Carrie slipped the angel's halo back on the hook, noticing that it was very difficult to get the metal circle over the deeply curved wire. What made it bounce off that wire?

Fear jerked down Carrie's spine. To satisfy herself she needed to search the house, and do it at once.

Praying Psalm 91 for protection, *There shall no evil befall thee, neither shall any plague come nigh thy dwelling;* and forcing boneless legs to move, to lift her feet, take steps forward, Carrie inspected every corner in her home. With shaking hands she opened all closet doors, though her breath caught in her throat each time a door latch clicked.

FatCat came along, staying right at her heels.

At last she shut the final door. Except for the angel, all looked normal, undisturbed. No windows were open, no exterior doors unlocked.

But the angel...? What had happened to it was impossible. It had to have help, some kind of help, getting off that hook.

Carrie returned to her bed but, as number after number rolled past on her clock, she didn't sleep. Nor did she shove FatCat to the floor, even when fur tickled her cheek and the purring that sounded like a motor scooter engine rumbled on and on until dawn.

The image of the bride dressed in red had been bad, but it was only a nightmare. She could wake up from nightmares.

The angel was different. How did that heavy piece of stained glass get off its hook?

The answer was too easy. By itself, it couldn't have.

Chapter 1

There were things to discuss. That's why Carrie took a peach pie out of her freezer and turned on the oven. Her friend, Eleanor Stack, said discussions with men always went better if you were feeding them. Eleanor believed food was a panacea for many things. Feminine wiles? Maybe, but one might as well use every available tool.

When the oven reached 375 degrees, Carrie took the frozen pie out of its box and removed the aluminum pan, fitting the still-frozen crust into her own heat-proof glass pie plate before she stuck it in the oven. The rim of the crust with its machine-made crimps would be soft in the time it took her to pour a glass of iced tea. She bet that was something Eleanor didn't know.

As soon as the tea was ready, she opened the oven door and lifted the pie out. She used her fingers to make scalloped pinches all around the softened edge of the crust, just as she'd watched her mother do all those years ago. With the point of a knife she wrote "I Love Henry" on top, leaving the machine-stamped center hole as the "o" in Love.

There. The factory-made edge crimps were gone, the pie was personalized. She approved the result and put "I Love Henry" back in the oven to bake.

She'd never told Henry she made the pies she offered him, and he was probably smart enough to understand where they came from. He did say once that he thought she made better pies than Eleanor. All she'd done then was look at her plate, murmur, "Thank you," and scrape up the last bit of sugary juice from the slice of cherry pie she'd just finished eating.

Come to think of it, maybe he'd said she *served* better pies than Eleanor. That was probably it. Serving was different from making, and Henry never lied about anything.

As for Eleanor...Carrie had no idea whether her friend guessed the source of the pies she served or not. She didn't really care, and if Henry hadn't figured it out yet, he would soon enough. In a couple of months they'd be living together.

That was the reason they had things to discuss. It was time to talk about their wedding. Though Henry asked her to marry him three weeks ago at the Elderhostel in Hot Springs, and she'd said yes, they hadn't made any real plans yet. She knew what *she* wanted, she just didn't have a clue to what he had in mind. It was time to find out.

Three hours later Henry had come, they'd talked—more or less—and he'd left for Roger and Shirley Booth's dairy farm in the valley. He and Roger got together every month to work on the agenda for the next Rural Water Board meeting, and today Shirley had invited Henry to have supper with them after the planning session. She'd included

Carrie too, but Carrie declined. She needed time to make wedding plans and figured, after talking things over with Henry, she could settle down and get started.

Ha! Henry had no plans. He promised to think more about it, had a piece of pie, kissed her, and left for the Booths'.

The one thing she did find out was a huge surprise. Henry had a half-sister. She'd asked him, very cautiously, about inviting relatives to the wedding. He never talked about his parents or family—indeed, seemed to avoid the topic. But now that she was going to be his wife, Carrie thought it was time to know more. At first he'd insisted that his daughter Susan was his only living relative. He had no aunts or uncles, no cousins, nieces or nephews.

Then, finally, he admitted there was a much younger half-sister, saying it so reluctantly that Carrie was bewildered. What's more, he added that he had never seen this sister and had no idea where she was.

After a conversational dragging session—Carrie asking question after question while Henry answered in monosyllables—she'd learned that Henry's dad left his mother for a much younger wife, Elizabeth MacDonald, when Henry was already a married adult. The father's second marriage produced one child, a daughter named Catherine MacDonald King. Henry "supposed" that had been around thirty years ago, which meant his half-sister and his daughter Susan were nearly the same age. He insisted he knew nothing at all about this young woman, the product of a marriage that had split his family.

But, Carrie thought, how could he possibly resent Catherine now? He obviously knew nothing about her, and the poor girl didn't choose her parents or the facts surrounding her birth.

Carrie wondered whether the half-sister could be anything like Henry. She pictured Henry's black hair, brown eyes, and square jaw on a woman. Well...maybe not quite that. But with both of his parents dead, it was now high time the two siblings met. She was going to do her best to find Catherine.

Finding her could be a wonderful wedding present to herself as well as Henry. She would give them both a sister.

As soon as Henry left she sat down at her computer, logged onto the Internet, and began a search for Catherine.

Chapter 2

On Saturday morning Carrie rushed home from the grocery store and dumped the sack of magazines she'd just bought on the couch in her living room. After she put her groceries away she hurried back to the couch, plopped down, and began turning pages.

An hour later the last bridal magazine slid out of her fingers and joined seven others on the floor. There was not one word in all those pages about a mature bride. Not one picture. Not one hint!

What now? She'd opened her mouth, insisting to Henry that she was, at last, going to have her very own perfect wedding. No standing up before a judge in the court house as she'd done over thirty years ago with Amos. (And that was when the Tulsa court house also held the county jail.) No! This time she was going to have it all. Frou-frou. Fancy. Maybe even white! Hadn't someone said white was now supposed to be okay for older women who'd been married before?

She'd decided only minutes after she said yes that she and Henry should make wedding plans before telling others about it. Then they'd invite friends and family to come and share their day. It would be so romantic, so polished.

Surprise! Henry had very different ideas. Last night he'd finally given in to her repeated requests that he tell her what he honestly wanted in a wedding. She should have known. He'd prefer getting married in the Spavinaw County Court House (*same kind of court house scene, different groom, no jail*), where wearing jeans would be fine. They'd exchange simple vows before a justice of the peace.

"We'll be together, that's what matters," he said.

She wanted more, and after the conversation dam broke and she finished explaining it all to him, she was almost sure he understood. At least he'd been kind enough not to ask, "Well, why did you want to know how I felt, then?"

So, now it was time to get really serious about wedding plans.

When she'd begun to think about planning early this morning, she realized she hadn't the slightest idea what went into creating the frou-frou part. Still, she knew she didn't want to turn her wedding over to a hired planner who designed dozens of similar weddings every year. This was just for the two of them, their families and special friends. It was something she wanted to do by herself.

So, where to start? Bridal magazines of course. She'd bought eight of them when she was at the grocery store, rushed home to turn pages eagerly, note pad and pen at the ready.

And all, *all* she'd seen during this past hour were hundreds of tall, pipe-cleaner thin models with smooth, unlined faces and perfect bosom curves rising above elegant satin and lace gowns. They had waists. They had hair in every color but grey. They were certainly not *the mature woman*. Phooey, they were barely even adult.

She'd seen wedding cakes that cost over a thousand dollars, enough diamonds to sink a ship, flowers sufficient to stock that ship—the Queen Mary of course, with all her ballrooms.

She hadn't seen anyone remotely resembling a short, round woman in her sixties who yearned to be a real bride.

And the lists! Every magazine had a sample "to-do" list. Every one of those lists began months and months before the wedding date.

Carrie looked down at the blank note pad, picked up her pen, and doodled a frowny face with tears dripping from the polka-dot eyes.

It was the first week in October. Henry, who would prefer to get married tomorrow, had said last night that yes, he'd wait until December if having a fancy wedding meant so much to her. Two months. Not even enough time to make a list, according to what these magazines told her.

She should have known these magazines were meant only for young people. They made it obvious the mature bride was supposed to be invisible.

So, was it going to be another plain suit like she'd worn when she married Amos? Her mother said even then she was too old for the fancy stuff. "After age thirty a woman is beyond satin and lace," Momma had said. Huh! What about now? Now she was *really* mature, and Amos had been dead over six years.

She hadn't cared about the plain suit back then, because both she and Amos accepted their marriage as a convenience, not romance. He needed a companion and hostess for his increasing social responsibilities. After living with her parents all her life, she wanted a home of her own. She wanted children. Well, she got the home, and a couple of years later she had her son Rob. Now she hoped Rob would give her away when she married Henry, and she'd planned to ask Henry's daughter Susan, who, like Rob, was thirty-one, to be her only attendant.

She'd dreamed of a real wedding—flowers and a bridal gown and saying *I do* to the man she loved.

Well, forget it. There would be no fancy wedding.

All she felt like doing now was crying for lost dreams, but that's when the darn phone rang.

"Carrie, it's Shirley. Do you mind if I come up to your place for a bit? There's something confidential I want to ask you about, face-to-face."

Not even wondering what Shirley's question might be, Carrie said, after a tiny sniffle, "Sure, come ahead, I'm at home the rest of today. I was just getting ready to clean house, and I already have the grocery shopping done."

Carrie looked at her clock. It would take Shirley about five minutes to drive up to Blackberry Hollow from the Booths' dairy farm in the valley. She hurried to the kitchen, set out instant coffee, put on water to heat. Thank goodness she'd bought cookies this morning. She got her prettiest plate, fitted it with a paper lace doily, arranged cookies. She couldn't fool Shirley into thinking the cookies were home-made, but at least they'd look nice. Hurry, hurry. Napkins, cups and saucers...Shirley always served home-made but at least Carrie's offering would be well-presented.

She heard Roger's old truck rumble onto her lane and

smiled as she headed for the door. So Roger had parked his truck behind Shirley's car again.

The Booths' on-going contest about who parked where, and what vehicle blocked another, was familiar to everyone who knew them. Once, in revolt, Shirley had ignored moving Roger's truck so she could get to her car and simply drove the truck off for a full day of errands and appointments. She came home to learn that the truck-less Roger had taken her car into town to pick up two dozen bags of special feed for his favorite cows. Unfortunately one bag split as Roger moved it onto her back seat. Friends who rode there even now, a year later, crunched against dusty bits of cattle cubes that were still sliding out from under the seat.

And all this in spite of the fact that Roger and Shirley owned acres and acres of flat valley land where there should be plenty of room to park a fleet of cars *and* trucks.

Shirley looked unusually serious as she came through the door and headed automatically for the kitchen table. Carrie cut her off, saying, "Let's sit in the main room and have refreshments. Take a seat and I'll bring a tray." She'd decided serving Shirley in a more formal location might help redeem store-bought cookies.

Shirley turned toward the couch and that's when Carrie remembered the magazines. No, no! Why, oh why, had she wanted to play like they were ladies having tea?

Quick, think. How to explain? A possible wedding for Rob? Wouldn't work. Shirley knew quite well he'd just broken up with the woman he'd been dating for over a year. Big-mouth Carrie had told all her friends how disappointed she was about that.

Rob gave no reason, just mentioned the end of the relationship a couple of weeks ago. Too bad. Since both Jane

and Rob were professors at the University of Oklahoma—
Jane in art history, Rob in archeology and natural history—they'd seemed like a perfect match. Evidently they
weren't.

Shirley was turning magazine pages when Carrie came
in with the tray. Well, what did she expect? And she hadn't
thought of one single explanation for having eight bridal
magazines in her house.

Shirley, however, could think of one, very easily, it
seemed. She looked up and winked. "You and Henry finally decide it was time? I'm more 'n glad. He's a good
man and you two belong together."

So Carrie put down the tray, sat on the couch and,
freed from reserve by Shirley's question, talked.

"He asked me at the Elderhostel we went to in Hot
Springs, and I guess we could have gotten married right
away, but there were our children, and all of you...and...
and..."

Now tears began streaking down her cheeks. Silly, but
she just couldn't hold them back any longer.

"And I wanted a real wedding, but I'm too...t-too old
and too...well, just l-look at those brides."

Shirley scooted closer and put her arms around Carrie.
"Yep, a mite exposed, aren't they, at least on top? We'll put
more of a top on your dress, and..."

"*My* dress?"

Shirley moved back on the cushion, grinned, and said,
"For sure, but can we hold off about that for a minute?
This news makes what I wanted to ask about easier. Where
are you and Henry going to live?"

"Uh, well, that is kind of a problem, because of the extra house, you know. Susan's keeping the house she inherited from her aunt JoAnne because they're thinking about

living here some day. Besides, she and Putt knew Henry
needed a home, so having him move there from where he
was renting seemed the perfect solution. They didn't want
to rent to people they don't know, and this way they can
use the house when they visit.

"We figured, after we're married, we'd have to divide
our time between that house and mine until Putt and
Susan decide what to do. But we aren't sure how, or when,
to tell them."

"Do you think Susan and Putt would consider Roger,
Jr., as someone okay to take Henry's place in JoAnne's
house?"

"You mean...?"

"Yep, Junior has finally come to his senses, at least so's
his dad and I would put it. He's moving back home. Seen
enough of the big city and is ready to work with us on the
farm. That means we can continue dairyin' and won't have
to sell out and move to town just 'cause we can't do some
of the heaviest work any more. Junior is single still and
he's our neat one, lives like a monk. He'd take good care
of that house.

"'Course we have plenty of room down at our place,
but he's dead set against living with his folks. So, renting
JoAnne's house from Susan is what I came to ask about, to
see if there might be any possibilities after the first of the
year, and if you thought I'd dare to ask her about it. It's
close by, and there aren't any other houses available around
here that would do. We'd otherwise have to build on our
land or get a mobile home.

"Besides, I been wondering if you and Henry might...
if you might be needin' only one house soon."

"Why did you think that? We haven't said anyth..."

Shirley laughed. "Well, since you two came back from

that Elderhostel, there's not been such longing looks, not from Henry, at least. You don't give away much, Carrie, but he sure does, and he's been looking more, well, more content, lately. Either there's a wedding coming up or you are...are...you've come to some agreement."

Instead of crying now, Carrie giggled. "How wonderful for you that Roger, Jr., is coming home. Oh, Shirley, I know Susan will okay the change, especially after she hears her dad and I are getting married. And if...that is, *when* Henry and I share a bedroom, there'll be plenty of space here in this house for the two of them and baby Johnny whenever they come for a visit.

"Of course I can't say yes, as it's not my decision, but it sounds like a perfect solution to me." She put her arms around Shirley's thin, bony form and hugged her back. "I'm so glad for you!"

"That's all right, then. I will ask her.

"Now, about this wedding. When is it to be? Have you made any plans yet?"

"Henry wants to go to the court house but I never had a real wedding, and, and..." She heard her voice saying the words, rushing through them: "And I'd like a minister, a dress, and flowers, and a cake, and friends, and a Christmas wedding, and all of it, but Shirley, look at me, just look at me, and look at them." She pointed toward the magazines. "*Look!*"

"Never you mind about that, those bride models make no difference to your wedding. I do think we need to get Eleanor in on this right quick, though. She knows about such things, has married off her three, plus one niece. She'll have good ideas. We'll all have a grand time together, and I can make the dress if you get the fabric and findings."

Shirley looked out the window into the autumn forest. She began talking to herself as if Carrie were no longer there. "I think cream color. Lace and satin, a simple, straight dress with a bit of a v-neck edged with lace. Long sleeves. Skirt down to the ankles. I can picture it, and I can make it."

"You really can make such a dress?"

Shirley looked back at Carrie, seeming surprised to find her still in the room. "Of course. I made our eldest daughter's wedding dress, didn't I? This'll be much easier; oh, the fancies that girl wanted! I'll show you the pictures the next time you're over.

"The three of us will do it together, almost like being girls again. Just to think..."

Her voice faded. After a moment of silence, she sat up straighter and was all business. "You get on that phone now and dial Eleanor. I know she's home by herself; she said yesterday Jason would be away most of today doing Kiwanis stuff.

"Go ahead, call her. I'm gonna look at your magazines and have one of these special fancy store-bought cookies while you use the phone. Then we'll get busy."

Chapter 3

As soon as Eleanor arrived and heard the news, she spent quite a lot of time babbling superlatives and hugging Carrie. Then she and Shirley sat on the sofa together and began paging through Carrie's bridal magazines, yammering away, holding up pictures to share, pointing, making all three of them laugh like loonies.

I've never seen Eleanor or Shirley act like this, Carrie thought as she watched and, for the first time, pictured what her friends might have been like as teenagers.

Then all at once the laughs faded as Shirley and Eleanor began finding possibilities where Carrie had seen none. They said things like, "Look, here's an idea," or, "What do you think about this? If we shortened the hem"—or cut, or let out, or subtracted or added—"it could work." After every new idea, they eyed Carrie speculatively.

Eventually she noticed they were talking about her in the third person. "This would fit her short frame if we..." Or, "Here's a neckline that would complement her oval face."

She began to feel like an object called *The Bride*.

When the two women had finished designing her dress to their satisfaction, they went to work on a location for the wedding.

Meanwhile Carrie huddled silently in her chair, wondering how things had gotten out of hand so quickly. Twice she'd tried to offer an idea, and once attempted a question, but the excited chatter rolled right over her as if she were no longer relevant.

"What about the Crescent Hotel in Eureka Springs?" Eleanor asked. "Have you seen it since the restoration? It's a fabulous place, just dripping with Victorian atmosphere. They do lots of weddings, information in the lobby says so, and there's a really good restaurant, too. I remember the gardens below the hotel from last spring. They're beautiful, though of course we'd be there in winter. What do you think, Shirley?"

"Ummm..."

Neither of them paid any attention when Carrie cleared her throat and said, "I..."

"Jason and I drove over to Eureka a couple of weeks ago to eat at the German restaurant there and have a look at some of the places we hadn't visited recently. We'd heard that the Crescent restoration work was about finished and decided to stop by. I know it was a grand place when it opened back in 1886, and believe me, it's elegant again, though it retains a look of antiquity, if you know what I mean. Nothing new sticks out at you. It smells old too— old wood, maybe old cigars. Not a whiff of new paint or lumber.

"Oh, hey!" Eleanor was warming to her topic and she hopped to her feet, standing before them to draw a large square in the air. "They have this wonderful conservatory, all glass windows and white paint, very *frou-frou*. It would be just perfect for a winter wedding!"

Frou-frou? Carrie perked up.

"Have you seen it yet? It's so...so *wedding-cakey*. A confection in white paint and glass."

She flopped on the couch again, landing with such force that Shirley bounced and Carrie shuddered on behalf of the springs. "I wonder if they have any openings for weddings in December? What date did you say you wanted, Carrie?"

Carrie didn't answer but neither woman seemed to notice.

Shirley said, "Crescent Hotel. Yes, well...maybe, if'n you don't mind about the ghosts."

"Ghosts? Yes, we heard about those when we were there. Four of them, I think the concierge said. They even have ghost tours in the evening, but no one takes any of that seriously, do they? Jason and I figured it was just another way to bring in money-spending tourists, and the Victorian setting with all its antiquity lends itself to that kind of thing."

Shirley said, "I don't know...what if someone actually saw a ghost? Wouldn't that sorta dampen things for the folks? Besides, it'll be December. Could have snow or ice, and the whole area is nothing but a bunch of mountains and switch-back roads."

Both women fell silent. Carrie assumed they were thinking about ghosts and snow and how those might intrude on their plans. Well, let them go ahead if they were having such a good time at it. Then she, and she alone, would decide what to do, even if someone's feelings got hurt. It really was silly for Shirley and Eleanor to rush ahead making plans like this, to take the ball and run with it, as Henry would say, when it was her wedding, *all* hers!

Still, Shirley's ideas about a wedding dress had sounded interesting—best she could tell from what had been discussed, at least.

Finally Eleanor broke the silence. "No one could really *see* a ghost. They're all in the imagination."

Shirley frowned but said nothing and, for a minute, neither did Eleanor.

Carrie was just opening her mouth to tell them she liked the idea of being married in Cooper Chapel at Bella Vista when Eleanor conceded. "I guess you're right. It would put a kink in wedding festivities if someone thought they saw a ghost, especially since the main ghost is supposed to be a bride. And besides, we'd all have to spend at least one night there getting things ready, and also stay the night after if it's an evening wedding. I guess you'd never be quite sure...about ghosts *or* weather.

"Too bad, though. Carrie and Henry could have had their wedding night in one of the Crescent's fancy bridal suites. All of those are furnished with genuine Victorian antiques. One was open for inspection when we were there."

She wiggled her shoulders and raised her eyebrows. "Oooo, was it elegant! Huge king-size bed. So sexy." She hesitated, glanced at Carrie, sucked in her breath, and said, "Or romantic, if you prefer. Well, anyway, whatever you're in the mood for." She turned toward Shirley.

Carrie saw a sly look pass between her two best friends and suddenly wished she was anywhere but here. She eyed the copy of Ellen Elizabeth Hunter's latest mystery novel lying on the table beside her. What would they do if she threw that book at them?

Suddenly she felt like laughing hysterically and wondered why, since her face was hot and she was sure it was from anger. For good garden seed! They were talking about her wedding night as if it were on a dinner menu.

But Eleanor wasn't finished. "Had a down comforter for tucking over our two love birds—just in case they don't keep each other warm enough, that is—and such beautiful sheets! There's even a hot tub in the room. Can't you just imagine...?" Eleanor's voice faded into silence as she and Shirley turned to smile at Carrie. At long last they seemed to expect her to say something. Instead she ducked her head and pretended to brush lint off her slacks.

Suddenly Carrie wanted to rush down the hall to her bedroom and slam the door really, really hard like some furious teenager. These two had taken over everything to do with her wedding *including* her wedding night. That was surely something only she and Henry should be concerned with.

And she was concerned.

For one thing, what would she wear? Sexy nighties definitely did not seem her style. She'd freeze in those wispy things she saw in the Victoria's Secret catalogue, not to mention...not to mention that she'd look like a lace-wrapped bundle of lumpy and very mature female flesh.

So, what was wrong with wearing a flannel nightie and socks on your wedding night if it was cold?

Finally Eleanor broke the silence, changing directions in a flash. "Nope, you're right, Shirley, not the Crescent, too many negative vibes. So, do you think our Methodist Church in Guilford? It has an attractive sanctuary, lots of pretty stained glass."

The heat in Carrie's face was becoming unbearable and she exploded out of her chair. "The Crescent Hotel is perfect, and since I'm only working at the Tourist Information Center part-time now I'll be free on Monday. I'll drive to the hotel then and see about arrangements. Do you two want to come? Shirley, can you get away from the farm for a few hours?"

Both women stared at her, then began to nod. All at once the matter seemed to be settled.

As soon as she'd shut the door behind her friends, Carrie wondered if—coming from rebellion as it did—a decision to have her wedding in the Crescent Hotel might not turn out to be a big mistake.

In fact, everything to do with fancy wedding dreams was conspiring against her: pictures of young and skinny brides, friends taking over planning, Henry wanting to get married right away instead of in December, and now the place where the wedding was going to be held was said to be full of ghosts.

It wasn't that she believed in ghosts, and the red bride was just a dream. A brief frown crossed her face, then a laugh began deep inside and bubbled out, almost choking her. Suddenly she was laughing wildly, giggling until tears dripped down her cheeks.

Ghosts! They could all be in the wedding party. Wait until she told Henry about it.

Her laughter faded. Maybe telling him wasn't such a good idea. It sounded pretty silly when she stood back and looked at it with his sensible mind.

Still, she was eager to see that hotel.

She picked up the phone and punched in Henry's number while she pictured wispy cloud-like creatures bouncing along in time to a wedding march.

Henry's rumbled "Hello" was the most comforting

sound she'd heard all morning.

"Hi, it's me. Finished with your house cleaning yet?"

After he assured her he had, she said, "Well, I'm not done, just starting now, but this is a touch-up weekend. So, here's an idea. Eleanor and Shirley just left and Eleanor talked about a German restaurant over in Eureka Springs that she and Jason tried out a couple of weeks ago. It sounds really good. Have you heard of it? The Bavarian Inn?...

"No, I hadn't heard about it either, but wouldn't it be fun to drive over there for an early supper today—my treat? We'd see fall color on the way; those mountains are always beautiful when the leaves begin to turn...

"Wear jeans? Of course you can. Things are never fancy in a tourist town, wear whatever you like.

"I'm going to make a sandwich now, then get on with my cleaning. How about picking me up at 2:00? That way we'll have time to look around the town before we eat. For one thing, Eleanor says the restoration at the Crescent Hotel is quite interesting. I'd like to see it...Okay, great. I'll be ready." She dropped the phone in its cradle.

Henry was such a sweetheart. She almost wished they could move up the wedding date. She was so eager to introduce him to his sister, Catherine—if she could find her. How surprised he would be!

FatCat came from the bedroom, pausing to watch a cardinal land in the viburnum bush outside the hall window. Following the cat's gaze through the sun catcher-bedecked panes took Carrie's thoughts back to the night of the angel's fall.

There were many reasons to be glad she and Henry would soon be married.

Chapter 4

Carrie seemed lost in her own thoughts as the miles rolled past, but Henry barely noticed. His own mind was occupied with a growing suspicion about the reason for this trip. He hated being suspicious, but sometimes the old law-officer feeling came back. Couldn't stop it.

Suspicion hit him with a nagging mental twinge that jerked to life whenever a human who was important to him said or did anything out of order. Trouble was, important could mean all kinds of relationship degrees ranging from crime suspects to, to, people he loved.

Order was important to Henry, always had been. When something didn't fit his idea of order, well, there it was, bang. Suspicion. It was another of those mind scars police work left you with: a lack of trust in fellow humans. And when the fellow human who'd awakened the suspicion was Carrie, then, no matter how insignificant the reason might be, he still suffered the familiar twinges. It was a royal pain in the tail.

Plainly, she was concealing something from him.

He hadn't figured out why yet, but it had to do with this sudden trip to Eureka Springs, and he needed to settle his innards by figuring out what was going on.

Carrie had never before said a word about an interest in historic hotel restoration or being fond of German food, and just last week they'd talked about taking a trip to see the fall color toward the end of October. Now was too early for a fall color trip. This was the Ozarks, not New England.

But here they were, headed for the "Little Switzerland of the Ozarks," Eureka Springs.

Henry scanned the steep hills rising ahead of them as they began the switch-back curves on the last leg of the drive. There was some color but none of the blazing maple reds that would make it really outstanding later. Soft yellow and muted green swept over the hills, spiked only by darker pine trees. That was all.

So far Carrie hadn't seemed to notice the landscape as it rolled up and down on either side of the highway. She was staring straight ahead, answering his few attempts at conversation absently or not at all.

He spotted a scenic turn-out and pulled into it, stopping by the guard rail and turning off the engine. That got her attention.

"Why are we stopping? This isn't a particularly pretty view—not yet anyway."

"No, it isn't. So, tell me Carrie, what's going on here? And don't you dare say 'nothing,' because I'm a trained observer, remember? We're not here for the fall color, and what's with the German meal and seeing a fancy hotel restoration? I don't mind going joy-riding with you on a whim, but..."

"Wedding."

"*Wedding*? There's going to be one, right? I'm going to take you as my lawful wedded wife, and all that legal-sounding cr... Um, those words." He'd barely avoided using one of the old, raw, policeman terms. Carrie was trying hard to edit the last remaining bits of squad-room language out of his conversation.

"We're going to have our wedding here, in Eureka Springs, not Cooper Chapel in Bella Vista."

"Here?" That was an odd twist. Did she mean they were getting married now—eloping?

Reason took over. They didn't have a marriage license or suitcases with clean clothes. He grinned without realizing it. Carrie had none of that fancy underwear or the stuff brides always wore on their wedding night.

"It's not funny." She lifted her hand and began twisting a curl around one finger. "This morning Eleanor and Shirley just grabbed my...our wedding and planned it right out from under me. They decided it would be in Eureka Springs, and..."

"Well, for heaven's sake, Carrie, it's not like you to allow them to do that. You've got definite ideas, *good* ideas. How did they get so involved?"

"Because I wanted a real wedding dress."

"Hmmm." This was getting away from him, getting very deep. He was lost and didn't know what to say, so he started the engine, waited for an RV to pass, and pulled back on the highway while Carrie turned to stare out the front window again.

Women! What was it with women? He had no experience with weddings, had thought the fancy goings-on when he and Irena were married happened just because she and her family were part of that high society crowd back in Kansas City. Sure, he'd been to a few weddings before and after his own, but never paid much attention to form and substance, hadn't thought about how they got put together. Back then he usually had too much to drink anyway, didn't notice stuff.

And he hadn't seen Susan's wedding. He sure wished he could have, but this miracle daughter didn't come into his life until she was a thirty-year-old woman with a husband and son already in place.

Not Irena's child. His former wife, Irena the icy, had seen to it she was never bothered with motherhood. No, Susan had been the result of a one-night-stand that happened when he was mature enough to know better. Fittingly, he'd been shut out of Susan's early life, including her wedding. Didn't even know when and where it was, where she was, until...until Carrie...

His eyes felt damp. Blast it, *oh, blast, blast it!*

Susan had been lost to him until Carrie, doing very good detective work on her own, discovered he had a daughter and brought the two of them together in November of last year. And now it was his turn for a wedding. He and Carrie were going to be together. *Really* together, and there had to be a wedding to accomplish that.

He wished he'd insisted on the court house.

She wished she'd gone along with Henry's idea of getting married at the court house. They'd probably already be married. Her face felt hot again as she tried to picture it. Stupid, she'd never been subject to hot flashes.

Married. Wedding night. Oh golly, it had been so long, and there'd never been much going on with Amos, anyway. All of Amos's passion had been expended during his heralded work as a defense attorney. She'd always been amazed and grateful that they'd managed to create their son.

And now it was so many years later. What did mature men and women...do? She and Henry had been close before, very close, but this would be the real thing. What, exactly, would go on under that down comforter Eleanor described? Anything?

Henry's voice broke into her frowning speculation. "You're going to have to help me now. How do we get to that hotel you want to see? I've never been there. Where do we turn?"

Fortunately Carrie did know the answer to that question. She gave him directions as they twisted and squirmed their way through narrow, car-jammed streets, past crowded sidewalks and people who crossed from one side to the other without looking. Antique shops, massage parlors, bed-and-breakfasts beckoned from both sides of the street and people followed their call. Evidently it didn't matter to any of them that peak color season hadn't arrived yet; and they were having too much fun to bother about cars trying to get past. Once Henry was forced to back into an alley while a tourist trolley stuffed with people clang-clanged its way by.

Henry said nothing as he concentrated on making headway through the crowds, and Carrie was afraid to break the silence lest he end up side-swiping some car creeping past them in the opposite direction, or worse, put a care-free pedestrian in the hospital.

She hadn't realized he'd have to cope with all this traffic, but they were here now. She'd give the hotel a polite look, proclaim it wrong for some reason or other, and go back home to call the folks at Cooper Chapel.

Finally, a sign appeared: *Crescent Hotel, Built 1886.* Behind the sign was a park full of chrysanthemum color, centered by a gazebo at the end of a raised walkway. The walk led to a white-painted room that extended from the ground floor of the main building. The hotel itself, a five-story narrow-windowed structure built of crowned stone, certainly looked imposing. It had been sited on a ridge-top, possibly the highest point in Eureka Springs.

Henry threaded the car into a loop drive between the hotel's imposing entrance and a fountain centered by a crescent moon sculpture. There was a throaty honk behind them and, as Henry moved forward, the double bronze and wood entry doors of the hotel flew open. Propelled by a torrent of fancy-dressed young adults flowing behind them, a bride and groom burst out and ran head-long down the stairs. They tumbled into the stretch limo that had pulled in after Henry, disappearing in a cloud of swirling white tulle. As soon as Henry's car was out of the drive, the limo slid around the circle and was on its way, accompanied by shouts, laughs, rowdy phrases, and a forest of waving hands.

Suddenly Carrie felt like crying. Those people were all so very young, and...and silly. She wondered what they found hilarious about a wedding. Was it because of too much champagne?

Henry pulled into one of the few remaining spaces in the parking lot. Did the majority of these cars belong to wedding guests or hotel guests? Carrie wondered how many people the hotel had room for. Surely they would be completely booked through the end of the year, and no doubt too busy to fit in even one small, sedate December wedding.

Thank goodness for that, she thought.

Chapter 5

They walked toward the hotel slowly, holding hands. Henry, who had never been one to think much about old buildings, either to admire or dislike, couldn't help admiring the look of strength about this one. The stone work was sturdy and sensible looking, had obviously served well for over a hundred years. Nice design and not especially fancy, except for those dog-house windows, chimneys, and pointed roof extensions on the top floor.

He looked down at Carrie. She was staring at the front of the building with an intensity that seemed peculiar, and gave him an itchy feeling. What was it about this place? She'd turned quiet again, shutting him out of her thoughts.

He went back to his own study of the building as Carrie's increasingly slow steps brought them closer, and he matched his pace to hers. He hadn't paid much attention to the entrance area earlier. Understandable. All that wedding party folderol and limousine honk-honk distracted him. Now he noticed red carpeted stairs, a lot of shiny brass, and highly polished wood doors. There was even a uniformed man to open the doors. White columns rose to support long balconies on each floor. The crescent moon fountain out front splashed freely. It was early in the month. Temperatures here probably wouldn't hit freezing for two or three more weeks, thus silencing the fountain's music.

Elegant. Maybe too elegant for Henry King, the cop from Kansas City. Made him think about his society wife, Irena, again. *Former wife.* He'd had more than enough up-pity-crust nonsense when they were married.

His ever-alert senses brought him back to the present. He'd picked up movement at the top of the building, and flicked his gaze to the top windows just as Carrie's hand jerked out of his. She stopped walking, and he heard her gasp as she pointed up.

"Look there Henry, *quick*. There. Did you see her? In that arched dormer? A woman in a red dress. Was it a wedding dress? Did you see her?"

He had seen a flash of red. "Yes, I saw something. Maybe that Arkansas flag blew in front of the window, or it might have been a hotel guest wearing red. Surely not a wedding dress, wouldn't that be...?" He looked at her face, and his words faded to an uncertain murmur because she looked, of all things, frightened. "Wouldn't that be odd? Unless she's Chinese or something? Some reason like that."

He sputtered into silence and put an arm around her. What was the deal here? Did she have weddings so much on the brain that she'd imagined the woman in red was dressed as a bride? He'd never known Carrie to be afflicted with a run-away imagination, and even if it was someone in a red wedding dress, well, that might be unusual, but he couldn't figure out why it would be frightening.

He sidetracked into wondering what Carrie planned to wear for their wedding. She'd said something about wanting a real wedding dress which was—he couldn't figure this one out—supposed to be what got Eleanor and Shirley involved in the first place. Had they suggested she wear red, was that why she was acting so strange?

But it still didn't make sense. Carrie never wore red and her friends knew it. She was a former redhead, probably the reason she avoided the color. He knew something about redheads because his father's oldest sister had been one. She'd displayed increasingly orange-red hair until her dying day at age 95. Aunt Jenn wouldn't wear red, wouldn't have the color in her house, or even put up red Christmas decorations, come to think of it. He spent a moment remembering his aunt. She'd been an odd duck, but that made her all the more appealing to a young boy, and even to the adult Henry.

Now the frightened look on Carrie's face had been replaced by a simple frown. Better. Still not good.

"A bride is not unusual for this hotel, Henry. It's known as a place for weddings, and Eureka Springs as the wedding capitol of the South." She hesitated a long moment, then said, "This is where Eleanor and Shirley want us to get married." She looked back at the front of the building and continued, speaking so softly he almost didn't hear her. "I suppose that's...that's why the bride in the red dress is here. She's getting married."

"Carrie..." He stopped. He couldn't think of a single thing to say, though he wanted to comfort her, erase her silly fantasy about some woman dressed in red.

And as far as having their wedding here? Why the dickens did Eleanor and Shirley think this place suited Carrie or him? Suited *him*? Shoot, they wouldn't have been thinking about him at all. He looked down at Carrie. Did this place suit her? She was hardly wild with enthusiasm.

This might be an okay place if a person lived in Eureka Springs, but why travel all the way here for a wedding, especially in December? He and Carrie had driven more than fifty miles over curving, mountainous roads that sometimes had drop-offs into valleys right next to the edge. If there were snow or ice, travel would be hazardous, if not impossible. They'd be stuck wherever they were when a storm hit.

He almost sighed aloud, but silenced his "whoosh" just in time. He didn't want to make a disturbing sound while Carrie was on edge.

Maybe she had wedding nerves. Maybe even older brides got those. He'd read about it once, a long time ago. Wedding jitters. Come to think of it—might have been the grooms who were supposed to get jitters.

Whatever. He thought this was a pretty dumb place for their wedding, but it obviously wasn't going to be up to him. Men didn't decide these things. Women did. Women tended to get goofy over weddings. If Shirley and Eleanor were planning their wedding here, then those two sure *were* goofy. Well, so what, Carrie could just say no, and that would be the end of it.

Now he knew the real reason for their trip. They had come so Carrie could scope out this place. She probably wanted to see what Eleanor and Shirley were talking about so the idea could be squashed before things went too far. At least he hoped that's what it was.

But why hadn't she confided in him? And why such nerves over seeing—or imagining—a woman dressed in red through the hotel window?

The red bride. Carrie wanted to shake her head back and forth, back and forth, hoping to erase the images of the woman from her dreams and from the window above her just now, but stopped the motion as soon as she sensed Henry's concerned gaze. He was probably thinking that this was not like her and he was right. It was ridiculous. She didn't believe in visions or ghosts or premonitions. What was *wrong* with her? Was it pre-wedding jitters? That was ridiculous too, people her age didn't have those. She was too old for jitters. Too old...

You're only as old as you feel.

That was the whole problem. Seeing all those young, beautiful brides in the magazines, seeing the wedding party spill out the entrance here—all of it made her feel like everyone's grandmother. And she had wedding dreams that obviously didn't fit grandmothers.

Nonsense, Carrie McCrite. You're acting more like a silly teenager than a grandmother—imagining fantasies about some woman in red, thinking up problems. Now stop it! You can have the kind of wedding you want; it's your decision after all, no matter what Shirley, Eleanor, or anyone else says. You're the BRIDE. Brides take charge. Get ready to enjoy that.

She lifted her chin, grabbed Henry's hand, and stalked toward the hotel entrance. Might as well get it over with. Maybe they'd even see a perfectly ordinary woman inside who was wearing a red suit, or blouse, or red something; and phooey, who cared anyway.

She said a tiny, silent prayer. *Guide me here, God. I*

seem to be in a silly muddle over an event that is supposed to bring only happiness.

The polished wood doors led to a lobby full of more pol-ished wood, most of it very dark. Carrie and Henry stood together and stared at elaborately patterned teal carpet, gold-medallioned burgundy wallpaper, black wood, and Victorian carving.

"Oh, my." Carrie's words were an echoing whisper.

"Kind of dark, isn't it?" Henry said, also speaking softly in the hope that no hotel employee would overhear him. She didn't respond, so he cut off his next comment—that the place smelled kind of like wet dog. At least it wasn't the smell of remodeling, of new paint and lumber. That would seem out of place among all this look of settled and elegant age.

He knew about the smell in elegant old buildings be-cause he remembered being in a historic home and mu-seum back in Kansas City that smelled like this hotel. It also held a few smells better forgotten. Except he couldn't forget.

The museum caretaker's skull had been smashed from behind by at least three blows with a heavy, irregular ob-ject.

The place closed at 2:00 on Saturday. It didn't open again until Tuesday morning. It was August, and hotter than Arizona. The main part of the museum and histor-ic home were climate-controlled, but not the workshop where the caretaker had been killed. The M.E. said the weapon might have been something like a small heavy statue, but they never located anything to fit the wounds.

The attendant who opened on Tuesday and discovered the body had turned out to be the killer. Did a convincing job of throwing up all over the place after she found him, making one more smell to deal with. Fresh death is nothing like death left to steep in humidity and heat for two and a half days.

"It was a horrible mistake," she told Henry when he and his team finally confronted her. "I thought he was a burglar."

True, the man didn't usually work late on Saturdays, but he'd been in the shop making repairs to an antique banister. He probably wanted to have it back in place by opening time on Tuesday. The attendant was the only one they found who could have known he was working late on those repairs, and anyone else going to the workshop would have had to either go past her station at the entry or get in through the loading dock. The loading dock doors had an alarm programmed to be on from 5:00 Friday until Tuesday morning at 8:00. The control to that alarm was at the attendant's desk, and she'd said when Henry first arrived on the scene that the alarm had been connected all weekend. Later she changed her story to say she'd found it off when she got to her desk on Tuesday.

Henry had asked why, if she thought there was a burglar in the building, she hadn't called the police right away rather than take matters dangerously into her own hands and attack the presumed intruder by herself. He remembered her answers clearly.

"I wasn't rational. I was so frightened that I acted on impulse." (Lots of tears here.)

What had she hit him with?

"I, I can't recall. I just grabbed something, his hammer, maybe?"

Why had she hit him more than once?

(More tears.) "Oh, dear, I just don't know. I must be

blanking the awful experience out." (Psycho-babble.)

Why no 911 call after she saw that he was dead?

"I knew he was dead, didn't I? It was too late for help, and besides, he didn't have any relatives, no one to notify. I was terribly upset, you can understand I wasn't thinking rationally. I went right home, took a sleeping pill, lay down on the couch. I wanted to forget the whole thing, pretend it would go away like a bad dream and things would be normal on Tuesday."

That lie was transparent to anyone in law enforcement, and even the jury didn't buy it, no matter how sweet she looked, no matter how many tears and hankies there were, no matter about the psychiatrist's testimony.

She was in prison only two years.

A number of small but valuable pieces had turned out to be missing from the museum's storage room. She said the caretaker undoubtedly stole them to sell, but that bird didn't fly for Henry. The caretaker, according to all who knew him, was a good-hearted bachelor who kept to himself except for functions at his church. There was no evidence of extra money anywhere, and the museum and the church had been his whole life.

The attendant, on the other hand, was used to luxury. Henry could tell that from one look at her apartment. She'd cut back on an elaborate lifestyle after her husband died but, in fact, once moved in Irena's crowd. They knew each other slightly. Irena's wry comment, "Silly woman, none of us really liked her," told Henry a lot. Besides, there were those unexplained deposits in her bank account.

Henry figured she killed the caretaker because he discovered she was stealing museum pieces for wealthy collectors and made the mistake of confronting her when they were alone. A small bronze statue was one of the missing items and Henry still thought it had been the murder weapon. What's more, since they never found the piece, he was sure she sold it to a private collector the weekend of the murder, thus getting rid of evidence and gaining money at the same time.

She'd been such a little thing, no bigger than Carrie. That was undoubtedly why the caretaker hadn't worried about sitting down at his work table and turning his back on her. In Henry's experience, killers—especially those who commit their crimes on impulse—rarely look evil or dangerous. Could easily be someone like that woman, someone as innocent-looking as Carrie.

He shoved the unpleasant thoughts and memories aside and went back to observing the hotel lobby.

They were walking past a fireplace area on their right, a black and gold registration desk, left. An ornately carved sofa and chairs with burgundy velvet upholstery faced the fireplace. Did people sit on those?

Enormous wood columns, looking like they'd come from an Egyptian temple, supported ceiling beams high above them. Copies of 1880's gas lanterns offered a warm glow of light.

Henry suddenly felt horribly out of place in his jeans and windbreaker. He wondered if Carrie also felt underdressed in her own jeans and quilted jacket.

She didn't act like it, there was no more hesitancy in her step. She led the way down an open lobby hallway to their left. They passed a bottle shop and Henry saw familiar names like Absolut, Seagrams Crown Royal, Chivas Regal, and other top-shelf stuff. Old, terrible friends of his and all too appealing right now. He shook his head. He was through with that forever—for Susan and Carrie's sake, as well as his own.

They ended up in a wood-floored dining room with crystal chandeliers and leather-upholstered arm chairs carefully positioned at a multitude of white-clothed tables. Because it was late afternoon, there was no one in the room but a young girl putting silver and elaborately folded napkins on the tables. Henry bet hamburgers and shakes weren't on the menu here.

Carrie still hadn't said a word, and now she reversed direction, striding purposefully back toward the main lobby. A small round table topped with a wedding cake stopped her. He watched her extend a finger cautiously and touch the cake. "Fake," she said and, after a short inspection, took a business card from the table. She put the card in her pocket and headed toward a hall extending south from the lobby.

Curious, Henry stopped at the wedding cake table and saw two stacks of cards. He picked one up. *Tiffany Albright, Wedding Consultant, Sales Manager.*

Oh-oh.

Was Carrie developing some interest in this place? He'd better watch what he said until he knew for sure.

He couldn't help feeling that coming on this trip with Carrie had been a mistake. He should have no part in her decision about where to hold their wedding. He just wanted to show up at the right time, say the proper words, put it all behind him. Then they could begin life together as a normal married couple.

Too bad Carrie hadn't waited to come here with Eleanor and Shirley, leaving him out of it. He understood why she wanted to come today, but suspected he'd been included in the trip more for expediency than affection. And now something about this place was beginning to give him the creeps.

Henry put the card back on the table next to the stack for another consultant named Melissa Donley and turned to follow Carrie down the south hallway.

Which was empty. Where had she gone?

Ah, a gift shop. She loved looking at postcards. He walked in to find a rack of postcards and lots more, but no Carrie. She'd been only a minute ahead of him, so where the dickens had she gotten to?

An important-looking stairway with ornately carved railings and finials was across the hall from the gift shop. He looked up and down. No one on the stairs but a woman in uniform carrying a stack of towels. There was an elevator, but surely Carrie wouldn't have taken it without telling him. He hurried past the stairway, came to a cross hall. Also empty. Lots of doors opening off it, every door closed.

Only one more possibility. A group of people bobbled into view, laughing and talking as they left some kind of party room at the south end of the main hall. Bucking the tide of humanity now moving around him, Henry hurried toward the entrance. She must have gone in there.

Chapter 6

Carrie hurried along the south hallway, eager to see the last part of the hotel's ground floor and be off to dinner with Henry. The building was elegant, no doubt about that, but she wasn't a fan of Victoriana, and nothing she'd seen so far made her want to get married here. She wondered where they usually held weddings. Lobby? Crystal Dining Room? The gardens and gazebo would be good locations, but they wouldn't work in December.

Her hand found the wedding consultant's card in her pocket. She'd show that to Eleanor and Shirley, proving she'd been here and had taken the place seriously. Then she'd tell them there was no need to make Monday's trip. She and Henry would be married closer to home.

Planning a wedding was still a problem though, and her thoughts were busy pondering that while her feet carried her along the richly colored hall carpet.

She passed a stairway with black balusters and huge carved ball finials on its newels. *Impressive* and *heavy* were words that registered as she looked up, though most of her thoughts were still involved with wedding puzzles. She was also planning how she'd explain her decision about this place to her friends. She'd been the one who insisted, just this morning, that the Crescent Hotel would be perfect. Once again, she'd spoken too soon!

Come on, Carrie, forward march, might as well look at all of it.

More burgundy walls, more dark doors. Then she saw bright light ahead of her and, at the end of the hallway, came into a room made entirely of windows and sunlight.

Let there be light! The conservatory!

The minute Carrie got inside the doorway, happy shivers began wiggling up and down her spine. This was *it,* a fairy-tale kind of place. Eleanor had called it "wedding-cakey," and Eleanor's description wasn't as ridiculous as it had sounded back at home. Not ridiculous at all, in fact.

Suddenly Carrie felt like spinning in a circle of joy, copying what Julie Andrews had done in that meadow during *The Sound of Music.* She felt like daisies and puppies, like fudge brownies with ice cream. She felt like a *bride.*

Henry, where was Henry? He had to see this place.

Forget stupid ghosts and snow. Here in the bright sunlight of a winter afternoon was where they would be married. No wonder Eleanor had thought of this. Carrie suddenly wanted to hug her friend. She *would* hug her, and Shirley, and Henry, and...

Remembering what was expected of a mature female, Carrie cut off a joyous bounce and decided skipping was also out of the question. She walked sedately into a room so full of light that she blinked.

A woman in a pink suit stood at a table on the far side of the room. She looked up and smiled at Carrie.

"Hello. May I help you?"

Henry walked into the party room and squinted until his eyes adjusted to the brightness. Almost every surface in the room was white, with the exception of a highly polished wood floor. The walls were full of windows, white-painted, multi-paned and arched at the top. Even the furniture was white, and all of it glowed in late afternoon sunlight.

The remnants of a party were scattered everywhere, and as Henry scanned table surfaces he understood why. The reception for the bride and groom they'd seen must have been here. Ropes of pink and white flowers swooped and swirled above windows and over tables scattered with dirty crystal and silver. Uniformed caterers hurried through clean-up, lifting chafing dishes and platters holding bits of unrecognizable goo onto a rolling cart.

And there stood Carrie in the middle of it all. Her back was toward him and she had some kind of conversation going with a woman working at a round table in the center of the room's south wall. The woman, who looked as if she was about to wilt inside the shell of her crisp pink suit, manipulated the top layer of a wedding cake into a ribbon-covered box as she talked. Tired though the woman might be, she occasionally glanced up and smiled. Was it because Carrie had introduced herself as a potential wedding customer?

Henry pursed his lips, blew a puff of air. He'd had no idea marrying Carrie would get to be such an involved process. He hadn't pictured a process at all, but a simple saying of words, then a welcoming of Carrie into his arms and his life.

Well, forget all this planning stuff, he could take the pleasure of putting his arms around her right now, and hang what anyone else thought. He walked quietly across the floor and, winking at the woman in pink, put both arms around Carrie from behind, linking his hands chastely under her breasts.

The woman was saying, "December? Oh, I am sorry, we're fully booked during December. How about January?"

Carrie had just begun to think—*hmmm, begin the new year with a new life?*—when an upward flicker of interest in Ms. Albright's eyes warned her. Before she could turn to see what was going on, Henry's arms appeared across her mid-section and she felt the warmth of his body against her back.

The rush of love bubbling inside surprised her with its intensity. Suddenly she wanted Henry to help her make wedding plans, not Eleanor and Shirley. After all, he was the groom, it was his right. They should be doing this together, though she knew he'd prefer a simple courthouse wedding. But—now that he had seen this room...

Tiffany Albright's flicker of interest turned to a full smile beamed at Henry. "And I just bet you're involved in this wedding. I'm Tiffany Albright, wedding consultant. Welcome to the Crescent Hotel. Are you making arrangements for your daughter?" She dusted off her hands and wiped them on a napkin as she studied their faces. "Or granddaughter?"

For a minute the senior-citizen doubts re-surfaced in Carrie's head, but then she lifted her chin. "No, it's for us. I'm the bride, he's the groom."

Ms. Albright recovered quickly and re-applied her big smile as Carrie made introductions. That meant Henry got involved in shaking hands and Carrie was standing by herself again.

The woman said, "Well, how exciting, and you've certainly chosen the right place to get married."

Carrie thought: *Right place because this is an old hotel and she thinks we're old folks? She's probably under thirty, and that means we look ancient to her.*

The consultant glanced around the room. "I'm through here until the decorator for this wedding comes to pick up her stuff, and I'd sure like to sit down for a few minutes. Let's go to the lobby and talk. I have my daily planner with me. I don't dare be without it in this busy season. Would you believe we have another reception here in just four hours? Thank goodness Melissa, our other wedding consultant, is doing that one."

As the woman crossed the room to get her planning book, Carrie looked up at Henry and said, "Isn't this a beautiful room? Don't you think it would be a good place for our wedding? It's so...happy...joyous."

She felt her brow scrunch as she willed him to understand. "We could stand together in front of those windows, we..." Emotion surprised her again, shutting her words down. Now she wanted to throw herself back into Henry's arms and just stand there with him. He *had* to see that this was the perfect place. She waved her arm in a circle and found her voice. "Look around, Henry, can you picture it?"

Henry had been biting into the lone remaining mint he'd taken from a silver shell dish on the table next to him. He stopped with the mint clamped in his teeth and it cracked in half, leaving pieces in his fingers. He studied her while he chewed the half remaining in his mouth. "It is very...nice, very white. Getting married here is fine with me. Y'know, these mints aren't good at all. Could you make some of your special fudge if we're going to have candy at our wedding?"

When they were following Ms. Albright down the hall, Henry brushed his fingers across the back of Carrie's neck—briefly, lightly, electrically. January seemed ages away.

"Please call me Tiffany," Ms. Pink Suit said as she indicated a place for Carrie next to her on the burgundy velvet sofa and pointed Henry into a matching chair. "Now, what did you have in mind? Do you want to be married here in the hotel, or elsewhere, with your reception here? A wedding in Thorncrown Chapel, perhaps? Do you know it?"

"I like that white room, the conservatory," Carrie said. "What dates do you have open? We'd rather not wait until January." She looked at Henry and grinned, then turned back to Pink Suit.

"How is the planning usually worked out? I've never planned a wedding. I do need help, but I don't want to turn everything over to someone else. I want to take part, since we're doing this for our families and closest friends. I need guidance, that's all. I hope you understand."

"Of course," Tiffany said smoothly, and Henry figured she'd dealt with brides much more difficult than Carrie.

"How many people will you be inviting?"

"Well, we don't know for sure. Let's see..."

Henry could tell she was counting, and he counted too. The Booths and the Stacks, maybe the Bruners, all from along their road. Then Susan and her family. Carrie's son Rob. Rob had just broken up with his girlfriend, so that meant he would be coming alone. Wouldn't that be all?

"About a dozen," Carrie said as Henry thought, *Not more than ten.*

"We have a Storybook Wedding Package that sounds right for you," Tiffany said, pulling a sheet of paper from the back of her date book and handing it to Carrie. "This is a general outline only; you can adjust it as you wish. The cost printed there"—she pointed with her pen—"includes a two-night stay for the bride and groom in one of our parlor suites, and two hours in a private reception room, with the Crescent Conservatory where we just were as one of your choices. You might also look at the Veranda Room on our fourth floor as a possible location."

"What's on the fifth floor?" said Carrie. "We saw a woman dressed in red in a dormer window up there."

"Red?" Tiffany looked startled. "How very odd. That's the hotel owners' penthouse suite. But...you couldn't have seen anyone there today because they're away at a hotel convention." Then she repeated, "Red. How odd."

After a thoughtful pause she was all business again, and pointed back at the sheet of paper. "Now, as you see, this package includes cake and punch for up to twenty-five guests, plus champagne or sparkling grape juice; and keepsake glasses, mints and nuts, and the minister. How does that sound?

"You can take care of decorations yourself, or we'll be glad to give you the names of local florists we work with. Since people have such varying ideas, we don't include flowers or other decorations in the package, and you'll want to choose your own bouquet, of course. If you'd like to serve food, arrangements can be made with our restaurant manager. We supply white tablecloths, dinnerware, and serving pieces."

Carrie looked at the paper, then handed it to Henry.

"What you offer looks fine, but how about dates? We had planned on getting married over the Christmas holidays because the holiday gives our children time off without penalty."

The consultant didn't even blink at the word *children*, probably understanding that both of them had been married before. "I am sorry, we simply have no openings remaining in December. In fact, we're over-booked."

Silence.

Henry said, hesitantly, "Would Thanksgiving be...?" He looked at Carrie.

Relief washed over her. "Well, yes, of course, Henry, that *would* work. Thanksgiving is good. Very good." She reached over to squeeze his hand. "Thank you."

"Ummm." Tiffany was turning pages in her book. "I don't think...oh, wait, let me call Melissa." She pulled out a cell phone.

"Missy, what did the Heathertons decide? Oh, hey, that's great. I have a maybe for then. Wait, I want to be sure. Just a mo."

She looked back at them. "Is Friday afternoon, the day after Thanksgiving, okay? We've had a cancellation."

Henry and Carrie nodded in unison.

"That's fine, Missy. Wait, I'll verify names."

"McCrite-King," Carrie said, spelling their names.

Tiffany spelled into the phone. "I'm writing them down for the Friday after Thanksgiving. Um..." Her eyes evaluated Carrie and Henry. "Mature couple. Storybook Package, I think. In the Crescent Conservatory. Got it?"

There was a pause. "Yes, Dunnigan-Bates went okay except for Bates dropping his cake down the front of Dunnigan's dress before he got it to her mouth. She shrieked like a steam locomotive and clutched at her bosom as if he'd stabbed her. They'd chosen the soft icing, and the stuff smushed everywhere. A lot of it went straight down her cleavage."

Tiffany Albright began giggling. "If that dress hadn't been so unbelievably low-cut, it wouldn't have...you know."

Tiffany looked at Carrie and choked the giggles off with a cough.

"Ah, well, just part of the game. And now, dear heart, I'm beat. Going to spend the rest of the weekend with my feet up, doing nothing. Good luck tonight. See you Tuesday."

So it was settled. A few questions to answer, forms to fill out. Carrie wrote a check, and the count-down to Thanksgiving had begun.

Carrie and Henry grinned at each other, then looked up to see Tiffany Albright watching them placidly. Henry figured she was used to seeing goofy grins on the faces of her clients.

Well now, this wasn't going to be as bad as he had imagined. He began to think about soft cake icing going down the front of a bride's dress.

As soon as the pink suit disappeared down the hall, Henry said, "The young man wasn't as clumsy as Ms. Albright thinks. In fact, I'll bet he did it on purpose. Why don't you plan for that fancy cleavage front on your dress? Then we can have soft icing on our cake too, and I'll figure out how to get icing off you if we have the same kind of accident."

For a minute all she could do was stare at him, then a picture of the possibilities flashed into her head. She said, "Quick, elevator. We're supposed to see the Veranda Room on the fourth floor."

If only the elevator was empty.

As soon as they were inside she faced him and lifted her arms to circle his neck.

Fortunately the elevator was old and moved very slowly.

Chapter 7

"It's stopping," Carrie said, pulling back from Henry's kiss and trying to see around him.

"Um hm."

She heard the elevator door open, heard a feminine squeal of surprise, heard a man laugh.

Henry's left arm slid away from her waist and reached for the elevator buttons. There was a pause, his arm came back, and the door closed. Before it shut off outside sound, she heard the man say, "Well, don't y'all mind us now, we'll be right glad to use the stairs while you..."

The elevator started down.

Henry's mouth covered hers again, but not for long because she couldn't control the giggles. By the time the door slid open on the first floor they were both laughing.

A couple stood in the hall at the foot of the stairs, their backs turned, looking—or pretending to look—in the gift shop windows. Carrie wondered if they had just walked down from the fourth floor. She cut off a final bubble of laughter and whispered "shhh" to Henry, pointing at the couple. At least they didn't turn around.

Henry punched the "4" button. By the time the door was fully closed he had turned to face her again and his lips were on hers, warm and possessive. She felt his tongue brush against her lips. Oh, my. No one had ever kissed her quite like that before. Then his fingers slid under her jacket, teasing the front of her shirt, tracing gentle spirals around and around.

She leaned, breathless, against the elevator wall. If only...

"Let's try one of those parlor suites right now," he whispered, his voice low, compelling, husky. She could feel his breath tickling her curls.

"Hunh-unh," Carrie said, wondering if he knew how much her body wanted her to say *yes*. "Not until after 'I do.'"

"Why, Carrie? We've both been married before and, as Ms. Pink Suit pointed out, are old enough to be grand-parents—or even great-grandparents—though she didn't mention that part. Surely taking advantage of what's within reach for us now would be good."

An eternity passed. "Cara...? We *are* engaged."

"Hunh-unh," she said again, realizing she had to pull back before she weakened and followed her feelings, and his, to their natural end.

Willing her body into compliance, she slid away from him, though, at the moment, it seemed one of the most difficult things she'd ever accomplished. "Dear, dearest Henry, I have to practice what I preach. That's important to me."

The elevator hummed at them and slid to a stop on the fourth floor.

"Well…okay," he said, his voice sounding almost normal. "Then let's find that Veranda Room, give it a brief inspection, and go eat. I'm hungry."

As they left the elevator he added, "In more than one way, woman, in more than one way."

Carrie managed a smile. At the moment she didn't feel capable of saying anything.

After a walk down another hall with burgundy walls and patterned teal carpeting, they found the Veranda Room, a long and currently empty space on the front side of the hotel. It would be well suited for a large group seated to view a wedding, but that wasn't what Carrie pictured now. In fact, almost as soon as she'd seen the conservatory, wedding plans had begun to form inside her head.

Their friends and family would stand with them. They'd talk together, sharing cups of punch maybe, or—if it was really cold—hot cider. Then, at the right moment, she and Henry would step in front of a minister on one side of the room to say their vows, while everyone else remained almost close enough to touch. After the ceremony they'd eat a buffet dinner at round tables on the opposite side of the room. It would be perfect.

Henry interrupted her thoughts. "Let's see what's out there." He pointed to a door on the other side of the Veranda Room. Rays of western sunlight glowed through the glass, creating tawny stripes across a bare oak floor.

Carrie followed him along the sun-paved path and out onto a large open deck. At first all they could see was the grove of trees at the edge of the hotel parking lot. As they walked closer to the railing, the parking lot itself came into view, and then the circle drive and *porte cochere* marking the building entrance.

Henry put a protective arm around her shoulders

when they reached the railing and looked down.

While they watched, a green van pulled around the drive and stopped. Even though the van was four floors below, it was easy to tell that, under a new-looking polish job, the paint on its roof was splotchy and faded.

"Someone's been taking good care of that old Dodge," Henry said, as a small man with dark honey-toned skin and heavy black hair got out of the driver's door and headed toward the back of the van.

Before he could get the rear doors open, a late model white van rolled quickly in behind him, and Carrie gasped. For a moment she thought the newcomer was going to crush the little man between the bumpers, but he slipped sideways just in time. The white van stopped so close to his rear doors that it would now be impossible for him to open them.

A large woman with big blond hair slid out of the white van, and the man from the green van walked toward her, saying something. He spoke so quietly that his words couldn't be heard from the fourth floor. His gestures were clear, however. He was asking the white van's driver to back up.

There was no problem understanding the woman's words. "No. Get out of the way, you heathen devil-worshiper, and quit trying to horn in on my flower business. Take your family back to India where you belong. You're not welcome here in Eureka Springs. *Now, move out of my way.*"

The man started to speak, but the woman turned, walked around the back of her van, and disappeared from view, going, Carrie assumed, through the front door of the hotel.

The little man stood for a moment, then opened the

driver's door and got back in his van. Carrie thought he might start the motor and pull up, but all remained quiet below, and nothing moved.

Then Big Blond Hair re-appeared, accompanied by Tiffany Albright. Each woman carried an open box full of what looked like curved strips of clear plastic. Carrie was sure they were the clips she'd noticed in the conservatory when she inspected flowers used for the afternoon reception. The pink and white garlands had been secured to tables and window ledges with plastic clips and pins that were almost invisible. Carrie thought the idea incredibly clever, even something she might like to copy for her wedding and reception.

Tiffany looked at the green van but said nothing, and after the boxes were stowed away, she and the big-haired driver disappeared into the hotel again.

"Wonder what's going on between that blond and the driver of the green van?" Henry said. "Some kind of friction over business competition? Her words were sure ugly."

Carrie had started to agree when the passenger door of the green van opened and a woman, smaller and darker than the man, got out. What stopped Carrie's reply was the woman's clothing. She wore a bright red sari.

Of course it had to be coincidence, but Carrie didn't want to see any more women dressed in red.

At least it wasn't a wedding gown, and this woman was very real—no dream phantom.

Impulsively she said, "Henry, let's go down there. We need to plan flowers for our wedding, and I'll bet we're seeing two of the florists who might be available. Besides, maybe that woman in the white van won't be so rude to those folks if she knows we're watching. And...let's take the stairs this time. Probably quicker than the elevator, anyway."

She started to smile up at him, but the smile vanished because he was looking at her so seriously. A twinge of worry flicked through her brain. She shouldn't have mentioned the elevator. What happened there wasn't something to make light of. Had she hurt his feelings?

Not knowing what to say, she looked out over the parking lot and noticed the couple who'd been staring in the gift shop windows when the elevator opened on the lobby. They were walking toward a car.

At last he spoke. "About the elevator, Carrie. I, I guess I forgot. You know, forgot—for just a few moments—my age, or something like that. We could have been in our twenties again. Young. That's how I felt."

He reached over, ran a finger down the side of her cheek to her chin, tilted her face up until he was looking into her eyes. "Carrie, I wish we could go back to that young time and have it together."

He looked so sad that she hugged him, in spite of the fact that the couple who had seen them in the elevator was out there in the parking lot, maybe looking at them right now and thinking, *Again?*

"Henry, I felt that way too." She stepped back and winked. "And that makes our age pretty insignificant, doesn't it? Hey, who says we can't have it all?" She tapped his chest with her finger. "You just wait until our wedding night, Henry King, you just wait."

That got a smile. She looked back toward the parking lot where the couple she'd seen earlier was, indeed, staring up at them. If only they knew what she'd just promised.

For good garden seed, what *had* she just promised? Talked herself out of a comfortable flannel nightgown and bed socks, for one thing. She was back to imagining her own lumpy bundle of female flesh wrapped in ridiculous lace and nylon. *Oh, Carrie, you'll never learn there are times when it's better to keep your mouth shut.*

They reached the lobby just as the bouffant blond went past them toward the entry door pulling two full trash bags behind her.

"Guess the flowers are now garbage," Henry said. "Too bad they're being wasted."

"True," Carrie said, already re-considering her idea about copying the afternoon's floral design. "But there's not much you can do with flowers pulled apart and woven into ropes except put them in the trash."

"Or compost," Henry said.

"Or compost. But somehow that female doesn't look like the type who makes compost."

Big Hair had stopped in the lobby to say a few words to Tiffany, which meant Henry and Carrie reached the hotel entrance before she did. The doorman was out front talking with the woman in the red sari, so Henry held the door open for the florist and her two trash bags.

She tugged the bags through, snorted a brief thanks in Henry's direction, then clopped down the steps, bouncing the bags behind her while she called to the doorman, "Can't I get a little help here?"

The doorman nodded graciously to the woman in the sari and went to take the garbage bags. While he lifted them into the back of the white van, its owner walked around to the driver's door. She stopped to shout toward the green van. "Move that thing. Can't you see you're in my way?"

This time the green van's motor started. It pulled out

and, as the white van swept past it and disappeared over the edge of the hill, came back around the circle to its original parking slot. Carrie read the name painted on the side aloud: *Artistic Floral Designs.*

"Henry, can you wait a few more minutes to eat? They're probably bringing in flowers for this evening's wedding, and I'd like to see what they offer. Besides, I guess we don't really have to go to that German restaurant, we can always eat here."

The small, dark couple began carrying boxes toward the Crescent Conservatory, but the boxes all had closed tops, so it was impossible to tell what the contents might be. Since Tiffany Albright was no longer in sight and therefore couldn't introduce them to the couple, Carrie felt hesitant about barging in on their work.

On the other hand, as a stranger, she could walk in the room when they were almost finished and take a peek. If she liked what they'd created, she'd get their business card. If she didn't—well, she was just one more tourist wandering around the historic hotel.

She explained her reasoning to Henry; he nodded and then went to sit on the velvet-upholstered sofa across from the registration desk. She joined him, and they began watching lobby activity.

The registration desk was busy checking people in, and several drop-in room seekers were turned away. There was, it seemed, no space left in the hotel for anyone without a reservation. Henry said, "Guess we couldn't have gotten a room here anyway."

He took her hand and squeezed. She squeezed back. For the moment, that said enough.

Members of the wedding party began arriving. They were easily identified, since each of them carried a long clear plastic garment bag holding either a peach and rust-colored gown or dark suit. They lined up for room keys, then disappeared.

The bride came, accompanied by her parents and another couple—probably an aunt and uncle—who were in charge of toting an enormous bag holding the wedding gown.

Finally the lobby grew quiet. Henry stood and, reaching out, took Carrie's hands, pulling her to her feet. "I'm tired of sitting," he said. "Let's go see what's in back of the hotel." Together they went across to French doors opening off the lobby and stepped outside.

The doors led to a covered porch holding a row of white wooden rockers, all empty, since the air had grown chilly. The porch overlooked a formal garden and a wooded area beyond. Garden beds displayed bronze mums outlined with what looked like rows of pansies, but details were muted, since sunset created deep shadows all along the back side of the hotel. There were paths winding through the wooded area, some of them ending far below at the edge of a road with marked parking spaces along its side.

While Carrie and Henry stood watching, a white vehicle of some sort appeared on the road below and parked. Carrie supposed it held tourists who were coming to see the Catholic church next to the road. The hillside was so steep that the church entry from the upper level led through its bell tower, and that feature alone attracted many tourists.

She heard doors slam, then two people, both dressed in dark clothing, appeared on one of the paths leading up to the hotel. Nope, not tourists going to the church. Both of the people had hoods pulled up over their heads, and Carrie couldn't be sure if they were male or female. The pair didn't come to the porch but disappeared along a stone walkway leading around the south end of the building.

"Let's go for a walk before we check on the wedding decorations," Henry said.

"Just what I was thinking."

They went down steps to the garden and turned south. As they walked, gaps in the foliage allowed views of the street and some of the parking area by the church. Carrie pointed and got a nod from Henry. The white vehicle they had seen was a van.

Bright light gleamed through the conservatory windows, highlighting spots of floral color along the path. High above them two dark figures leaned against a railing in the gazebo, standing just beyond reach of the light.

Henry took Carrie's arm as they circled around the end of the gazebo on the uneven stone path. When they arrived at the stairs to the walkway connecting the conservatory and gazebo, he asked, "Shall we go up?" speaking more loudly than necessary. "I'd like to see what that gazebo is like."

They climbed and went along the walkway, managing to act surprised when they came on the mystery couple. In unison they said, "Good evening," getting answers so soft that Carrie thought she might have imagined them. She still couldn't tell the gender of either person. Both of them had their heads down as if they were studying the floor. But why stand out here in the cold at all?

Spying? She suspected it was the white van florist and a companion, spying on the Indian couple. How stupid and melodramatic that seemed. But then, the blond woman had said incredibly stupid things and obviously knew nothing about the Hindu religion. Carrie didn't know much; she just remembered enough from a comparative religion class in college to realize that, though Hindus—like Christians, Muslims, and Jews—varied in religious practice within their general faith, most saw God as one. That God might have many faces, but they were all parts of the One. She sighed. Once more, prejudice had been fed by ignorance and a personal agenda which, in this case, seemed to be nothing but professional jealousy.

She and Henry went back down the stairs to the path and continued along it to the entry drive and front door of the hotel. Once inside, they turned toward the conservatory.

As they walked along the hall, Henry said, "Curious place to be on a chilly night."

"They're spying."

"I thought that, too."

The conservatory door was closed, but when Carrie tested the knob it turned, so she opened the door and they walked in.

"My word," Henry whispered. Carrie was speechless.

The people from Artistic Floral Designs certainly lived up to their name. Delicate white wicker window boxes filled every window sill, sixteen of them in all. Each container held what looked like peach snapdragons mixed with ruffled white-bordered ivy and sprays of delicate white heath aster. A few small rust-colored leaves were tucked among the ivy and flowers. Matching garlands framed the French doors opening on the gazebo walkway.

That will be a perfect place for us to stand in front of the minister, Carrie thought, *outlined by flowers.*

White baskets with ribbon-woven handles were at the center of all the room's tables. They displayed the same type of arrangements as the window boxes. The cake table was still on the south wall, but now a circle of flowers outlined its top. Matching ribbon-trailing nosegays, pinned a foot apart, caught the bottom of the tablecloth in graceful scallops.

The woman in red was on her knees by the cake table, gathering the fabric gracefully in one hand, holding the last nosegay ready to be pinned over the gathers. The man also had his back to them and was closing and stacking boxes, undoubtedly getting ready to carry them back to their van.

"Excuse me?" Carrie said. Both the man and woman turned at once. The women gave a cry as she dropped the nosegay, and the gathers she'd been pleating fell apart.

"Oh, golly, I'm sorry," Carrie said, "I didn't mean to startle you."

"No, no, my fault," the woman said in unaccented English. "It's just that we've had...difficulties, and..."

Her husband interrupted her, "And we are always careful to guard our designs until members of the wedding party arrive, it's just good sense." His words held a light touch of what Carrie would have called cultured Oxford English.

"Yes, it does make sense," Henry said. "Can't be too careful. Actually, the reason we're here is that Carrie and I...oh, I'm forgetting my manners. This is Carrie McCrite, I'm Henry King. We plan to be married here."

"We are Chandra and Ashur Mukherjee, Artistic Floral Designs of Eureka Springs." The man took two cards from his pocket, handed one to each of them.

"I'm glad to meet you," Carrie said. "I think what you've done here is beautiful. I want something like it for our wedding. We don't live here, but can drive over to see you and make plans if..."

Suddenly Carrie was yanked off her feet as Henry yelled, "GET DOWN," and fell against her, dropping them both to the floor.

At the same instant she heard a sharp crack, breaking glass, and a cry from Ashur Mukherjee.

Chapter 8

For a tick of seconds there was nothing but breathless silence. Then Henry, whispering from his place on the floor beside her, asked, "You okay?"

"Yes. What...?"

He raised his head higher, said aloud, "Are both of you all right?"

She heard stirring, a clicking that might be shards of glass falling on the floor. From behind one of the tables Ashur Mukherjee said, "Yes, we are fine. I was sprayed with glass, but we're not hurt."

At the moment Carrie didn't have enough strength to hold her head up, so she put her cheek against the floor, ignoring dust and what were probably tiny flecks of food. At least the flecks weren't crawling.

A chorus of only two words sang inside her head. *Thank God. Thank God.*

Henry said, "Thank God. I saw the muzzle flash but that wouldn't have been enough warning if the shooter really intended to hit one of us. I'm sure whoever's responsible is long gone, but stay down until I turn the lights off and can check outside. We're in a fish bowl right now."

His knees swished across the floor, and Carrie found enough strength to lift her head and watch while he reached for the light switches and the room went dark.

As soon as the lights were out, Henry was on his feet, running. He shoved the French doors open and burst out onto the walkway. She heard his steps fade as he ran toward the gazebo.

Henry!

Stay with him, keep him safe.

It had probably been a revolver. They wouldn't want to leave a cartridge behind. Henry's eyes searched the darkness, looking for unusual shapes or movement.

The gazebo was empty, no surprise. Those two were smart enough to hightail it out at once. He listened, heard a powerful engine start up far below. In less time than he would have thought possible the smooth hum faded away. Sure hadn't sounded like a van, but it was too late to chase after it now, and finding tire tracks on that concrete would be a miracle.

He jerked in surprise when a second set of lights flashed on and another engine, more van-like, came to life. That sound followed the first engine around the hillside, but its throaty rumble faded more slowly. What the...? He hadn't noticed anything but the white van earlier. Coincidence? Huh!

Blast it, he should have paid more attention to everything, especially that pair dressed in black. He should have tried harder to engage them in conversation, should have leaned against the railing with them, stayed until they said or did something that hinted who they were. Surely there couldn't have been any danger for him or for Carrie, gun or no gun. They were only after the florists.

Probably.

He swore in disgust. He had ignored the uneasiness, the warning twinge he'd felt when he saw them out here in the approaching darkness.

He'd let himself grow complacent, allowed his mind to separate from the nagging suspicion that was a police officer's best weapon. He was too darn eager to enjoy his civilian life and the fun of being, for the first time ever, really close to a loving woman. And he wasn't a cop anymore. Or was he? Would it ever be possible to get away from that life? Could he ever become just plain Henry King, a man making plans to take a wife...his Cara, his little love? Was it possible for him to turn his back on the world's evil?

He knew better. There were too many crazy people out here in the darkness. And Carrie was as aware of that as he was.

He started back toward the conservatory, thinking that having dinner anywhere was probably out of the question now.

It didn't matter. He wasn't hungry.

She was starving. The second wedding consultant, who introduced herself as Melissa Donley, appeared while Carrie helped a weeping Chandra out of the darkened conservatory. After looking at them, eyes narrowed, for a few moments, the woman roused herself and began, "What...?" but Carrie cut off the question by asking...no, *telling* Ms. Donley to have the restaurant prepare hot tea and something for them to eat. It was not a time to mince words. They all needed sustenance.

The consultant gave her a startled look and opened her mouth in what Carrie was sure would be a protest. But then, glancing again at Chandra and over at Ashur, who had bits of glass sparkling in his hair, she nodded and disappeared toward the kitchen. Some kind of food would be forthcoming.

Carrie was sure Ms. Donley didn't yet know about the destruction in her wedding reception room, but at least she recognized an emergency when she saw one.

So far, few people at the hotel were aware of any problem, but, in the nearby gift shop, the attendant had heard the shot and shattering glass. When she came out to check, Carrie sent her to explain the emergency to the desk clerk and see that the police were called. A bellman appeared, and Carrie asked him to guard the conservatory doors, keeping everyone away.

So, she'd done all she could until Henry came back.

She asked the bellman where they might sit privately until the police came, and he pointed to a small room around the corner from the conservatory entrance. It was outfitted as an office, but had obviously once been a guest room with an attached bath. Carrie took Ashur to the bath tub, had him kneel, bend over the edge, and close his eyes. Then she used a hand towel to flick the larger pieces of glass out of his thick, black hair, finishing the job with his comb. For the first time she noticed that there were streaks of white in the black and thought of Henry's black hair going grey. She pictured the waves over his ears and imagined reaching up to brush those waves back with her fingers.

Ashur asked, "Is that all?"

She jerked back to the present, said, "All done," and handed him the comb.

She'd already seen grey in the heavy rope of hair caught in a bun at the back of Chandra's head. Perhaps this couple was older than she'd thought.

Before leaving the bathroom Carrie dampened a face cloth in cold water, went to Chandra, and gently wiped her face. Then she pulled up another chair.

Chandra's tears had stopped, and for a moment the three of them sat in silence. Carrie had no idea what the other two were thinking, but she spent the quiet time in prayer, asking for guidance from God and praying that Henry, wherever he was, was wrapped in safety.

Finally, feeling it was time to carry on, she said, "Someone has been bothering you. This is not a new thing." She didn't put it as a question.

Ashur tightened his lips and said nothing, but after she'd blown her nose, Chandra said, "Yes, that's true. It's been happening for some time. First it was little things, then it got bigger and bigger. Our tires were slashed, and not long after, someone painted a cross on our shop window with words warning people not to shop at a heathen business. The police can do nothing, because so far there is no evidence to say who's doing this. But now I'm frightened. They've gone too far.

"I wanted to hire a private detective to find out the truth for us, but Ashur wouldn't do it. Maybe, after this..."

She glanced at her husband.

Ashur said, "We shouldn't do that. We don't want to make trouble. When they see we are not caving in to intimidation, they will stop. We are taught to be responsible before God for loving service to our fellow man. Suspicious spying on people doesn't sound like loving service to me."

"You carry that ideal too far," Chandra told him.

Ashur put an arm around his wife, lifted his chin, and said, almost defiantly, "We have been in the United States for thirty years. We are citizens, we love this country. We raised our children here, and now we have a business that has grown large enough to support all of us. We belong here as much as anyone else. We will stay here."

"Yes," Chandra said, echoing her husband's defiant tone. "But we will always have our skin color, always be Hindu, always appear 'different.' We cannot change those things. I will not stop wearing the sari because it makes me look different, or because our religion isn't understood by most Americans. I agree with my husband that we won't move away simply because of a few who now say they fear dark-skinned terrorists. Where would we go? The people who bother us, they are the terrorists."

Tears began running down her face again. "This has never happened to us before. People have all been friendly, there has been room here for many differences. It is so wrong that this happens. And our children suffer, too."

Ashur struck his forehead with the heel of his hand and jumped to his feet, obviously agitated. "Oh, no! Our son and his wife are at the chapel finishing arrangements there. The chapel is mostly glass—they will not be safe."

Carrie quickly understood the possible peril. She asked, "Thorncrown Chapel?"

"Yes, yes. The wedding is to begin there at seven. These days we let the children do church preparations because my son's wife, Heather, is fair-skinned and Christian. That way, no one is offended."

Carrie hurried to the registration desk and told the clerk to phone the chapel and let the younger Mukherjees know what had happened at the Crescent. "Is the chapel outside city limits?" she asked. When the clerk replied that it was, Carrie said, "Then would you notify the sheriff's department of the shooting here and request a deputy for the chapel? Tell them a wedding is about to begin there, and that we don't think anyone in the wedding party is a target, but want to be sure no one shoots into Thorncrown from the darkness as they did here at the Crescent.

"And please," she added, "be sure the Mukherjees' son knows his parents are okay. We're in the small office near the conservatory. If you need us or there have been any problems at the chapel, would you let us know?"

The woman nodded. She might wonder what authority Carrie had to ask all this, but following human nature she responded to the firmness of someone who sounded sensible and knew how to give instructions.

Before Carrie left the lobby, the desk clerk was already talking to the sheriff's department. Fortunately there were no hotel guests close enough to hear.

Carrie had just reached the office door when Henry slipped in from the conservatory. At the same time, a waiter pushing a cart with enough food and drink for a dozen people appeared. The wedding consultant, Melissa Donley, followed behind the cart.

Henry told Melissa what had happened, and Carrie added information about precautions being taken at the chapel. Considering the awful circumstances, Carrie thought the woman took everything pretty well. She wanted to go at once to see the damage and begin clean-up for the reception, but Henry explained they couldn't do anything until the police gave the okay.

It was 6:15. The wedding would begin at 7:00. Carrie figured they had approximately an hour and a half to get ready for the reception unless the wedding could be delayed. Weren't weddings often late starting?

Carrie asked Melissa that question. "Any extra time will help us," she said, then realized she'd just added Henry and herself to the emergency repair crew.

Melissa nodded and hurried out to get in touch with the minister, putting him in charge of delaying the ceremony as long as was gracefully possible.

The waiter set platters of finger food, a water pitcher, and a large urn of hot tea on the desk. Carrie wondered if they were seeing the same things that would be served to the wedding guests later that evening.

While they drank hot tea and nibbled who-knew-what, she asked the Mukherjees gentle questions—as much to keep their minds occupied, she told herself, as to learn anything important.

"The white florist van, that belongs to a competitor?"

"Yes," Ashur said. "Owen's Flowers. The business is run by half-sisters, Jan Owen and Sonya Wells. They were both born in this area, and their father, Russell Owen, started the flower shop business here many years ago. He was a good businessman and did well. As he earned more money, he bought land in and around Eureka Springs whenever he found it at a low price. After a number of years he was able to begin selling his land at a huge profit. People wanted it to build motels, restaurants, shopping centers, and tourist attractions."

"But the flower shop stayed in business?" Carrie asked.

"Yes. His daughter Jan worked with him there from the time she finished school and took over when he died. The younger half-sister, Sonya Wells, joined the business about a year ago. She had divorced her husband and returned to Eureka Springs to help out at the family land and investment company as well as in the flower shop. One of our current employees lost her job with them when the sister came back home." He hesitated, then added, "They have always been good florists."

"Are they the ones harassing you?"

"It would be impossible to say."

Chandra spoke up. "No, not impossible. When we see them and no one can hear, they say terrible things to us, and sometimes the words sound like what was painted on our shop window. They must be the ones doing this."

Carrie asked, "Which sister did we see this afternoon?"

Ashur answered. "That was Jan, the older one, the one who has been here all along. She was devoted to her father and never married."

Chandra said, "About four months ago I had just finished putting out arrangements for a party at a motel near here and was leaving the parking lot when I saw Jan Owen going in a side door of the building. I knew that door was supposed to be locked. I decided to return and check things. By the time I parked and walked across to the motel all was quiet, and the door to the party room was secure. But, when I went in, I found everything we had prepared smashed on the floor. People at the motel said they weren't paying attention to what was going on in the room. No one admitted to seeing or hearing anything or anyone out of the ordinary.

"But Jan could have had a key. Sometimes the motels loan us keys to their meeting rooms when we are providing decorations for an event. I am sure they do the same for the Owens. It would be easy to have a copy made."

Ashur shook his head and, looking toward the plate of food in his lap, said, "With all the weddings and other events in Eureka Springs, there is plenty of work for both of us. We are not trying to rob them of customers. Besides, they are wealthy from land sales, and if people like our designs better, well, that's business. People are free to buy what they like. Never will everyone have the same tastes, though. There will always be those who prefer what Owen's Flowers creates. I think the Owens just don't like people from other countries, people with dark skin."

"You said you came to the United States thirty years ago?"

"Yes." He took his wife's hand, lifted his chin, and began to tell Carrie their story.

It's as if they're already old friends, Henry thought.

This was not a new phenomenon. Carrie could break down barriers between other people and herself faster than anyone else he knew. What might otherwise be separating walls of race, culture, class, type of job, or even entertainment preferences disappeared like magic before her open kindness and lively interest in those she saw as "all God's children." Not only was it a charming and, as far as he was concerned, lovable trait, it was also very useful when the two of them were helping people in trouble.

As they seemed to be doing right now.

In fact, it looked like they were headed into what Carrie's son called their Ma and Pa Kettle detective work. He hoped they weren't and willed Carrie not to get tangled in this couple's problems. The two of them should be concentrating on plans for their Thanksgiving wedding.

All they really needed to do here was tell the police what they'd seen, then they could go home. They weren't obligated beyond that.

He looked toward Ashur, who was saying, "The caste system has been outlawed in India for many years, but old ways die hard. My family owns vast rice holdings, Chandra's family worked in our household. When I wanted to marry her, well...my father is of the old school. We decided to emigrate to the United States to be free of the old ways.

"I had read about rice being grown in Arkansas, and of course I knew the business, so we came to this state. For a number of years we lived in Jonesboro and I worked for Riceland. But we had always wanted a business of our own.

"In Jonesboro, after our son and daughter were in school, Chandra did flower arranging for a florist part-time. Her designs were in much demand. When we heard of the many weddings and opportunities here, we got the idea to come and open a flower shop. So we moved and began our business.

"We had also heard Eureka Springs was a place where all people, all types of political thought, all religions, got on well. For several years that was so. But now..."

He stopped, shrugged, and said no more.

While Ashur talked, Henry ate. He'd filled his plate almost automatically when the waiter urged food on him.

Now he glanced down to see that the plate was empty. He hadn't a clue what that fancy rolled-up stuff or the puffy bite-sized things were, nor what was inside those tiny sandwiches. The only thing he'd been able to identify was the shrimp, which had been skewered on, of all things, carved toothpicks. What he saw on his plate now was a stack of carved toothpicks. They looked like miniature table legs.

He ought to save those, show them around back home. Well, come to think of it, the Stacks might have seen such fancies. They were used to posh restaurants when they lived in Ohio and probably ate at a few places here in Arkansas that Henry hadn't even heard of. Still, in all the fancy places Irena and her family had frequented—with Henry tagging along in his role of devoted husband when he wasn't on duty—there had never been carved toothpicks.

Whether Eleanor and Jason had seen such things or not, he could bet Shirley and Roger Booth hadn't. He'd take some home to show them. He'd also mail one to his daughter, Susan.

Oh! Come to think of it, maybe Susan and the Booths would see the same kind of toothpick at his wedding. His and Carrie's. Ha! That would be posh, indeed.

He'd have to ask Carrie what all these tricky-looking food bites were. They tasted pretty good. And he'd also ask her if they couldn't have the miniature table-leg toothpicks at their wedding reception.

He had just reached out to put more of the baby sandwiches on his plate when two uniformed police officers appeared in the doorway.

Chapter 9

Carrie looked up at the two crisply uniformed men in the doorway and realized she'd never seen so much as a photo of Henry in a police uniform. In spite of her brave words on the deck outside the Veranda Room, she felt a heart-twisting surge of regret about missing so much of his life.

When Henry stood to greet the officers, she tried to picture him dressed as they were. She liked what she saw.

What she imagined.

The men introduced themselves as Sergeant Lonnie Trent and Officer Kurt Gibson. Henry told them about the shooting and, more simply and clearly than she ever could, what the two of them had seen in the gazebo a few minutes before the shot came through the conservatory window. He finished by mentioning that he had been with the police department in Kansas City for many years, omitting the fact that he retired as a major heading the CID.

Sergeant Trent, however, asked about his rank and experience, and then requested Major King's help with the search outside. That left Officer Gibson to talk with Carrie and the Mukherjees.

The officer greeted Ashur and Chandra warmly, as if they were old friends. "I bet we find something we can work with this time," he told them as he sat down. "Vandalism is bad enough, but shooting?" He shook his head as his eyes scanned Chandra and Ashur's troubled faces. "You know we're doing our best to stop whoever's responsible for this...we've *got* to stop it.

"Got to," he repeated.

He tried a smile then, but it didn't quite fit on his face. Carrie noticed his eyes remained worried as he said, "We'll find evidence this time. We'll have more to work with."

Then he took out a notebook and prepared to write down what each of them remembered about the evening's events.

When it was her turn, Carrie began with what she saw and heard from the fourth floor deck that afternoon. Neither one of the Mukherjees had mentioned Ashur's encounter with the blond woman. The officer nodded a couple of times while she talked about that, but he took no notes.

Probably such insults have become so common for the Mukherjees they're no longer worth noticing, she thought. *How sad.*

After she'd finished telling all she could remember about the white van on the road below the hotel and the couple in the gazebo, Kurt Gibson closed his notebook. "Time for me to have a look around in that conservatory," he said.

Ashur asked to come with him, saying, "We must begin clean-up quickly, the wedding party will be here soon."

"Sorry, Ashur, but you can't go back in yet," the officer answered. "I need to be alone. Neither of us wants any evidence compromised. Why don't you stand in the doorway until I give the okay? It won't take long since the shooter was never inside the conservatory. A bullet is the most important thing I'll be looking for."

Without comment Chandra and Carrie stood to follow the two men; when they met Melissa in the hallway, she joined them with no objection from the officer.

After inspecting the broken window, glass shards, and the window box that had crashed to the floor, as well as taking pictures of the mess, Gibson motioned to the little group huddled in the doorway, giving them permission to enter. He asked only that they stay away from the back wall, and he began an inch-by-inch search of that area.

Watching him look from the broken window to the wall, Carrie supposed he was trying to trace a possible path for the bullet. His line of fire study seemed to assume the shooter had been in the gazebo. That meant the bullet probably hit stone, since the conservatory was an addition outside the original wall of the hotel. Carrie knew if it had hit the stone wall, the bullet could be badly mangled. They might not be able to link it to the gun it came from.

As she thought about it, she realized the shooter could actually have been anywhere on the raised walkway between the conservatory and gazebo, even just outside the windows. True, the gazebo offered a degree of concealment, but when the shot came it was almost dark. Carrie shuddered and hoped Henry and the other police officer were searching carefully outside. Being here in the bright light with all those windows looking out on darkness was unnerving.

Melissa Donley had left the room only minutes after

they came in, and now she returned, bringing a maintenance man with her. While he went to work cleaning up glass pieces and spilled water, Melissa began pushing the Mukhergees' stack of empty packing boxes toward the hall, saying, "I'll store these in the office for you."

Chandra stopped her. "Thanks for wanting to help, but would you please leave the boxes where they are for now? I plan to use them as a work table."

Melissa looked at Chandra for a moment, then left the boxes where they were.

After he'd finished cleaning the floor, the maintenance man taped a clear plastic square, cut to size, over the broken window pane. Then he and Melissa began organizing tables and putting chairs in place for the reception.

It looked as if they would be ready for the wedding reception in plenty of time—assuming the missing bullet could be found.

The Mukherjees had collected the scattered flowers and were reconstructing their arrangement. Carrie watched while Ashur fastened the broken parts of the window box together with florist wire, and Chandra arranged flowers and greenery in cups she'd borrowed from a tray in the office next door. Carrie saw a stray sprig of ivy on the floor and bent to pick it up. As she did, Chandra stood back from the box stack to assess her arrangement, giving Carrie a clear line of sight toward the improvised work table. There was a small hole in the side of one box.

"Maybe I've found the bullet," she said. Activity in the room froze while she went to the boxes and pointed toward the hole. When Officer Gibson removed the box and opened it, the bullet was there, nested in green florist paper as if it were a tiny Easter egg.

"Of course we'll check again in daylight," Sergeant Trent said, kneeling to look closely at the floor of the gazebo while Henry held the flashlight for him, "but I don't think we'll find a thing. Would be nice if one of them had left a bit of cloth snagged on a nail or something easy like that."

He stood and dusted off his knees. "As you know from your own experience, most of those 'oh, look what I found' clues only show up in cop shows on television. But of course TV cops have to solve their cases in an hour, minus time for commercials. We do get a little longer to work. But our fine citizens still wonder why it can take us days, weeks, or—in some cases—what seems like forever leading to never, to solve a crime."

Henry harumphed in agreement. The sergeant was treating him like a colleague, and he felt good about that. Sometimes when he and Carrie were helping people in trouble, law officers they dealt with acted as if he were a nuisance, or worse, someone waiting to pounce on flaws in their work.

Not this man. Sergeant Lonnie Trent was probably secure enough in his position to work comfortably with any other law officer, retired or not. In fact, Trent seemed pretty laid back about everything. Henry knew that could be an important trait, especially when dealing with suspects. Got them off guard.

He also knew Trent's relaxed behavior here was an act. Even while he talked to Henry, the man's attention never wandered from his true purpose, a search for clues that, most likely, weren't going to show up.

They'd just come from the place where the van had parked on the street below, and as Henry had suspected, there were no tell-tale marks there. Now Trent was doing a second look all around the gazebo, the boardwalk, and the nearby grounds.

"Well, guess we're gonna have to give this up for now," he said. "I hope Kurt found the bullet. That poor family has endured all kinds of vandalism and harassment over the past year, ever since a couple of people with screwy ideas decided to give them a bad time. If this shooting is related, the trouble has sure escalated.

"Even though we think we know the source of what's been going on, so far there's no way to prove it. Now a shooting..." He pursed his lips, blew air. "King, I admit to you I'm really worried. I hope we learn who fired that shot before things get out of hand and someone gets hurt. Trouble is, even if we find the bullet, at the moment there's no way we'd have legal access to any gun it came from."

Taking a chance on being rebuffed, Henry asked, "What do you know about the Mukherjees' competitor—a large woman with blond hair?"

At first Trent showed no reaction, but after a pause, he said, "So you picked up on her, did you? That's Jan Owen, and we do suspect the Owen family is behind harassment of the Mukherjees. It probably stems from professional jealousy. The Owen family pretty much had the flower shop business here sewed up before the Mukherjees came to town. But shooting? If one of the Owen sisters did it, that's a big escalation, even assuming the shooter didn't mean to hit anyone." He shook his head, then leaned against a gazebo railing. "Playing with fire, Major King, playing with fire.

"Jan Owen and her sister Sonya Wells have turned out to be first class bigots, something they've successfully hidden from almost everyone but Ashur and Chandra. Things really got messy after Wells came back to town about a year ago. Sort of set Jan off, I guess. The way I see it, each brings out the worst in the other. Lots of friction there.

"Another problem. Jan is a long-time Eureka Springs City Council member. That's okay, except for a couple of things. First, it means we have to step pretty light around her. She's accumulated quite a bit of power.

"Second, she's got an idea the city needs a second visitor's hospitality center, this new one to be in the historic district downtown. I represent the police department at council meetings so I hear it all.

"Since the department would be expected to have concerns with traffic and parking, I brought that problem up when she first laid out her plan. Owen answered me by saying this new center would be for tourists on foot and those who take the trolley. Huh. You know what that would make it? Nothing but a fancy potty stop."

"Are facilities for tourists such a bad idea?" Henry asked, joining Trent at the railing.

It was the Sergeant's turn to harumph. "The site she's fixed on for this new welcome center is the building the Mukherjees own and use for their business and home. Their flower shop is on the ground floor; they live upstairs. It was vacated by the local craft guild about the time the family moved here. Ashur and Chandra did a lot of careful restoration and the place looks great now.

"The building is on a narrow, twisting street and has three parking spaces out in front reserved for customers. You know what Eureka Springs is like, horse and buggy streets, buildings crowded too close on either side. Sometimes Ashur has to meet larger delivery trucks up on the highway and transfer shipments to his van to get them to the shop. But the location is prime real estate these days.

"I think Owen's idea is certified dumb, not to mention hateful. Sure, it would be a place where a few walk-in tourists a day might come to powder their noses, change a diaper, or use a restroom. She says the center wouldn't even need to be staffed, and also says—get this—that it would be a money-maker for the city.

"You know why? Her idea is for the city to rent out the upstairs apartment the Mukherjees put so much work into. Talk about being unfair...the whole mess really frosts me."

"Do other council members want to take over their building?" Henry asked.

"No big enthusiasm yet, but you never know. Owen is pretty persuasive. I say the original tourist information center up on the highway, which has a full staff, already provides the services needed. And there are several places downtown with public restrooms, not to mention that the Owens themselves have properties in the area. Any of those would also work for what Jan wants. She could afford to donate space if this comfort station is so all-fired important.

"But, if she hollers enough and gets enough people on her side, the city could, for whatever they consider just compensation, condemn the Mukherjees' place and take it over, using the power of eminent domain. What a crock." He snorted in disgust, then stood. "Ah, well, to the business at hand. Let's go see what Kurt's found inside."

Henry had one last question. "I suppose the Mukherjees know about this, about Owen's plan?"

"Oh, yes," Trent said, "I'm sure they do. They don't say much, but they've got to know all about it."

Chapter 10

Kurt Gibson opened the conservatory's French doors just as Henry and Sergeant Trent reached them. "Hey," he said, "sheriff's dispatch just called. All quiet at the chapel, no white van, no disturbance. And we found the bullet, or," he waved his arm toward Carrie, "that woman did, and just in time. Dispatch says the wedding is over and people are heading for their cars. The restaurant is beginning to set the buffet up." Another arm wave. "I said it was okay.

"So," he turned back to them, "you two do any good?"

"Not a sign," Trent answered, "but that's good about the bullet. In decent shape?"

"Yep. Stopped inside one of those boxes Ashur and Chandra carry stuff in. Looks almost perfect. And from where it was I'd guess the shooter stood pretty close to the windows, maybe just beyond the lighted area. He—or she—was probably wearing all black, but still took some chance on being seen. Person would have to be quick."

Trent looked back along the boardwalk. "There are some bushes here, but they're not very tall above the railing." He sighed. "So now the trick is, figure out how to get the gun that bullet came from."

The two officers continued to discuss the bullet and gun while Henry slid past Gibson and into the conservatory. The room looked spotless, as if nothing unusual had happened—how long ago? He looked at his watch. An hour and a half had passed since that shot smashed the window. But now the chairs and tables were in place, flowers arranged, packing boxes gone. All was in festive readiness.

Carrie sat with Asher and Chandra in chairs at one of the round tables, and the nearest Henry could come to describing their looks was bored. He supposed everyone but the wedding consultant, who was busy directing the placement of food on the buffet table, would be free to go now. Their work here was done, at least for the present.

He suddenly felt bone tired and decided maybe it wasn't boredom but weariness that he was seeing on Carrie's face. He sure wasn't looking forward to a long drive home in the dark over those curvy roads. Once more the thought of finding a bed here surfaced, though his reasons for wanting it had now changed. Ah, well.

They all had good enough reason to be tired. He and Carrie had been on an emotional roller coaster all afternoon and evening, and as for the Mukherjees...what an ordeal they'd been through. All he wanted now was quiet and a bed, and he supposed the florists did, too.

Lonnie Trent and Kurt Gibson finished their conversation and Trent came in the room, shutting the French doors firmly and locking them. When Melissa Donley looked up, he said, "Officer Gibson will be on watch outside until the reception is over. I have the bullet, and I'm taking it to the station for safekeeping. I'll talk to you and the hotel owners tomorrow or Monday."

He turned to the little group huddled around the flower-bedecked table. "Why don't all of you go on home now. King, do you have a card? If not, give me contact information on this pad of paper. Chandra and Ashur, I'm going to follow you home, see you safely inside your building. Do you have to come back and clean up after the party tonight, or can it wait until tomorrow?

"Tomorrow," Melissa and Ashur said in unison. Ashur continued, "You don't need to accompany us, we'll be perfectly safe. We're going right home, and we can park in our garage, you know. No one will bother us." After thanking everyone for their help, Ashur and Chandra left the room. Sergeant Trent soon followed.

Henry and Carrie watched the bustle around the buffet table for a moment, then Carrie stood. "I'd better stop in the ladies' before we get on the road," she said and headed down the hall. Before he left the room, Henry had a good look at the food being laid out. He'd been right. Some of it looked exactly like what they'd been served earlier. There were even platters with boiled shrimp speared on carved toothpicks.

Carrie frowned at her reflection in the restroom mirror while she washed her hands. She was tempted to get the make-up pouch out of her purse and freshen her face but decided not to bother. Maybe she could be excused for not caring how she looked right now. It had, after all, been a very long day. Henry and anyone else would just have to take her as she was.

She smiled briefly, grateful for the certain knowledge

that Henry would not be critical of her looks. What a blessing their comfortable and close relationship was.

She took another look at her reflection and then almost wailed aloud. The enamel butterfly pin Rob had given her when he first went away to college was missing. She clearly remembered putting it on her collar just before leaving the house.

After she reported the missing pin to Henry, they scanned floors in the conservatory, office, and lobby halls, then inquired at the front desk. The pin hadn't been turned in.

"Sergeant Trent or I would probably have seen it if it dropped off outside," Henry said. "We did a thorough search there. Let's try the elevator and that room we went to upstairs."

So, once more, they took the elevator, riding in separate silence and staring at the floor.

When they were in the corridor leading to the Veranda room, Carrie turned on the small flashlight she always carried in her purse, sweeping its light back and forth across the carpet. No pin.

The Veranda Room was dark, so Carrie kept the flashlight on. She scanned the area of floor they'd crossed to get to the deck while Henry looked for a light switch.

"Here it is," he said. Carrie heard a click but nothing happened.

"Well, blast, guess that's the wrong one."

"Do you want the flashlight?"

"No, there's reflected light, I can see well enough. All I need to do is find the right switch. They've sure got a lot of them here." He continued studying the wall.

Suddenly, in her peripheral vision, Carrie sensed movement on the deck and turned toward it.

Nothing.

Then she saw it again. A red scarf? It was clearly visible in the lights on the front of the hotel. Someone's scarf must have caught on the railing. While she watched, it began flickering in and out of her vision in a nervous dance.

She took off her glasses, rubbed her eyes, looked again. It was there, flickering in the breeze. She glanced toward Henry to see if he was watching, but he still faced the back wall.

Turning toward the deck again, she saw that the scarf was gone.

The lights flashed on, temporarily blinding her. "Henry, I thought I saw..." She stopped. She couldn't just say, "I saw something red and ghostly." He'd think she was hallucinating, maybe because of being over-tired. And he'd probably be right.

"Mmm?" he said. "Saw what?"

"Uh, I mean I didn't see anything of my pin, yet. Shall we look out on the deck?"

There were flags displayed on poles fastened to the deck railing and, as they approached, the red Arkansas flag blew up, fluttered in the breeze, and dropped again. Of course, that's what she'd seen. Relief flooded over her like a cold shower.

The *porte cochere* shielded only a small part of the drive below them, and while they watched, cars began arriving from Thorncrown Chapel, pulling up to spill satin and lace and formal dress across the drive and into a rush toward the conservatory. Carrie was glad the happy crowd had no idea there'd been a shooting in their party place only a couple of hours earlier and wondered what they'd think if they found out.

Suddenly the red flashed again, this time under a tree at

the edge of the parking lot, by that...van. The Mukherjees' van? She stared. The flash of color had to be Chandra Mukherjee in her red sari, because here came Ashur, striding toward where the red had flashed. But why was their van parked at the edge of the lot? Supposedly they'd left for home more than thirty minutes ago, even before Carrie and Henry were out of the conservatory. They'd acted eager to get away and—after all that had happened earlier—you couldn't blame them. Carrie frowned. Maybe some unexpected and important business with the hotel delayed their departure. But Chandra shouldn't have been left alone in that secluded place. Foolish, after what had happened. Maybe dangerous.

If Henry saw Ashur, he didn't say anything. He was probably watching the wedding guests instead, enjoying the happiness of all those pretty people.

After they had looked down in silence for a few more moments, he started to turn back toward the brightly lit room. Then he jerked his hand away from the railing and said, "Ow. What the..." and held his hand, palm up, in front of Carrie's flashlight beam.

Her enamel butterfly lay in his palm, clasp open, the sharp pin bent in a curve. It had pricked his skin and stuck there.

She gasped as he said, "It's as if someone hooked it over the railing right where I put my hand. But—that tiny thing? Even with the pin bent like a hook, it's a miracle it didn't fall." He pulled the pin loose, and Carrie saw it had barely broken the skin and hadn't, thank goodness, drawn blood.

When they were back in the Veranda Room, Henry studied the butterfly for a moment. "I'm sure I can straighten it for you, the metal isn't heavy." He folded the piece in his handkerchief and dropped it in a pocket.

He said no more until they were waiting for the elevator. Then he asked, "Carrie, did you notice how cold that railing was? It felt much colder than the air outside. Strange."

She tried a laugh, but it came out sounding wobbly, so she stopped, waiting a moment before answering. "Well, Shirley says you can sometimes tell if ghosts are present when a room turns cold or you feel a cold draft. I'll have to ask her about iron railings. I suppose ghosts would have no problem making iron feel cold, too. Maybe some nice ghost was there and put my pin on the railing where you'd find it for me. However it happened, Henry, I'm grateful."

He turned his palm up and slowly rubbed a finger over the spot where the pin had pricked his skin. "Ghosts, huh? Well, if that's the case, then your nice ghost didn't need to stick me with it. Putting it on a table in the Veranda Room would have worked just fine."

Chapter 11

Why were the Mukherjees still at the hotel?

Once more a police officer's ingrained suspicion had kicked in, much as Henry would like to forget everything about this evening. Well...almost everything. It would be great to just forget it and head for home.

He didn't mention seeing Ashur and his van to Carrie, hoping she hadn't noticed them in the parking lot. If she decided to be concerned about why the florists were still at the Crescent when they'd said they planned to go home immediately, there would be no dropping the matter. She'd probably want to ask around, see if everything was okay, maybe even do something as dumb as drive to their flower shop and check on them. That meant Carrie McCrite and Henry King would end up spending what amounted to a night in Eureka Springs whether they ever saw a bed or not.

Bed. Now that the high drama of the evening was over, he felt drained of desire for anything but quiet and sleep.

He yawned noisily as they left the hotel, but Carrie didn't seem to notice what he considered a huge hint.

They walked around the fountain and...the space where the van had been, there under the trees, was empty!

Henry's relief almost led him to comment about it being gone, and he caught himself just in time. Whatever the reason for the delayed departure, it didn't concern them. Carrie obviously wasn't aware the Mukherjees had been here any later than expected, and now there was no van for her to see. End of problem.

He tried another yawn. Still no response from Carrie, no sympathetic, "Hey, it's late, shall we get a motel room and spend the night here?" She seemed pre-occupied and probably wasn't even noticing his yawns. Did he dare suggest a sleep-over? Normally he would, but after this afternoon's fiasco, that might not be such a good idea. Oh, well, he'd yawn again when they were in the car and see if that worked. If it didn't, he'd ask her to keep talking to him on the way home so he wouldn't doze off.

If they stayed here, they'd find a room with two beds, of course. They'd traveled together a couple of times during the past year and, at her suggestion, shared a room. She was the one who had inherited money, she was the one who paid for their trips, so he played by her rules. "Only logical," she said when he offered to go halves. "Now that I've got all this money, we might as well enjoy it. But," she'd added, "if we share a room, we'll save almost half anyway."

Eventually he'd managed to swallow any remaining bits of male pride. A policeman's retirement was adequate but didn't rise to the level of what Carrie had.

Whatever. Sleepy or not, one bed or two, there was no motel room in tonight's plans. Maybe she'd offer to drive.

Well, maybe that wouldn't be such a good idea, she wasn't used to his car yet. Having her drive would keep him on edge all the way home.

He took her hand as they approached the parking area and was surprised when she veered to the right around the raised flower bed marking the entrance. Oh, oh. Their car was on the other side of the lot. She *had* seen the van after all, and it looked like she wanted to walk by the place where it had been parked. But she still didn't comment, so he wouldn't either.

They walked in silence, holding hands.

There were security lights on poles, but the trees had enough foliage left to filter light where the van had been.

As they were passing the empty space, Henry noticed that the land fell away sharply only a few feet from the paved area, dropping into forested hillside.

They both saw it at the same time.

Flattened grass, broken stems, a piece of red ribbon lying in the grass. Without comment they stopped, then stepped over the curb and walked toward the trees.

Something was wrong here. He had that all too familiar sense of evil. When Carrie let go of his hand and reached down toward the bit of red ribbon, he stopped her. "No, don't touch it," he said as his eyes scanned the area.

There was something light-colored on the ground below them. Was it hair? Blond hair? Not that, surely. But there was a large shadow of something dark on the ground and a lighter patch next to it. He ran a hand over his head and hoped they were seeing an illusion created by a dumped bag of trash.

Carrie got out her flashlight again. The light was small, but it showed enough. What they had seen was not trash.

He swallowed an oath. If that hood had only been pulled up. Black covered the body but left a face—a face that no longer looked human—exposed. If it weren't for the face and the blond hair, they could have walked on by.

Wrong to think that. If he and Carrie hadn't found her, then who?

The Mukherjees! Why hadn't they seen...no! They couldn't have done this, not this, not such violent death.

He'd sensed something out of order here and it was obvious Carrie felt it too, so they were both doubly alert. Ashur and Chandra, on the other hand, would not have been so alert, wouldn't have sensed this, wouldn't have seen...

Then all thoughts about who and why flicked away and his training took over, guiding him into the need for immediate action. He took the flashlight from Carrie and swung it over the area below them. There seemed to be a path, or at least a cleared place, running back toward the hotel. He could get to the woman quickly that way and check for injuries, for respiration—whatever—without disturbing evidence that might be down there, or on the hillside up here, where the Mukherjees had been only a few minutes earlier.

He held out his car keys and pointed across the parking lot. "I'll watch while you walk across and get in the car. Lock the doors, wait for me. I want to check and see if she's beyond our help."

"No, Henry, I am not getting in the car. I'll go find Officer Gibson. He's on guard outside the conservatory, remember?" Before he could protest, she was gone, hurrying toward the south end of the hotel.

Henry hesitated. *Blast!* He needed to go with her, to protect her from... He took a couple of steps, then stopped.

Nope. She was an independent adult. True, in emergencies she could also be a less-than-cautious adult, but if he followed her now he'd be breaking the trust they shared. She was on her own, no matter how he might feel about that. The area in front of the hotel was brightly lit and Gibson was somewhere just beyond it. She'd be okay.

He turned away and headed around the drive toward the lower level and the path.

A quick scan with the flashlight told him the woman was most certainly dead. The body lay on its stomach, but her face was turned to the side. It looked like something irregular had been smashed into the head, a furious attack. Her wrists and ankles were bound with thin green wire wrapped at least five or six times around, then twisted tightly enough to cut flesh. He saw blood there, too, so her heart had been beating when she was bound. There was a silver-colored knife beside the body. Blood on the knife, but whether or not it had been the instrument of death was something he couldn't tell. With those blows to the head...Henry remembered the museum caretaker back in Kansas City. Looked pretty much like that.

Now it was easy to see that the blond hair was separated from the body, but not because the woman had been scalped. Close up, he could tell they had seen a wig. The natural hair on the woman was a blood-matted light brown. So, Jan Owen had worn a wig.

He was sweeping the flashlight beam around the area near the body when Kurt Gibson's voice came from above. "Oh, geez, no." It was almost a little boy's cry. A moment of frozen silence followed, then a stronger flashlight found the body just as Henry said, "She's dead."

Gibson's voice changed to all-business male as he

turned away and began speaking into his cell phone.

They were in for it now. Henry turned off the flashlight, leaned against a tree trunk, and shut his eyes.

Carrie looked at Kurt Gibson. His back was toward her as he talked into the phone.

She glanced from Gibson to the ground at her feet while her thoughts ripped back and forth between two sides of a terrible dilemma. Right now legality was winning out over what seemed morally and sensibly right—which meant she still hadn't touched the piece of cardboard lying on the ground by her left foot.

Why couldn't she just bend over, pick it up, put it in her pocket? She knew the Mukherjees wouldn't hurt a flea, let alone another human, even one who'd been as nasty to them as Jan Owen. She just knew it, and she was also pretty sure they were going to need her help now, hers and Henry's, because it had to be Jan Owen who was dead on the hillside. She'd seen the blond hair. Who else could it be? Earlier, she'd also seen a piece of red ribbon tied at the shoulder of Chandra's sari. It was probably not a coincidence that there was a red ribbon caught on a grass stem at the edge of the parking lot.

Even worse—right here, next to her foot, was a cardboard knife sheath. She'd noticed that when she first turned her flashlight on. The sheath was clearly marked with the initials "IBE" and had the International Blossom Express winged rose logo on it. The same logo was on the Mukherjees' van. There was no IBE logo on the Owen van, no advertising or identification at all.

The ribbon could have blown here from anywhere around the area, but the heavier cardboard probably was dropped where it lay. She was sure Henry hadn't noticed it, so why-oh-why couldn't she manage to just bend over, pick it up, and stick it in her pocket while Officer Gibson had his back to her? This was one of those times when principles became very, very difficult.

If only the blond hair hadn't been so noticeable on the hillside. If only she hadn't insisted they walk this way instead of going straight to the car. If only...

No! It was wrong to wish that way. Henry had said she was dead, but what if she hadn't been? What if they'd been in time to save Jan Owen's life?

Then another thought popped into her head. If she'd said yes to Henry when he wanted to go find a hotel room where they could...could, well, share their love, then they'd have been away from the Crescent long before any of this mess involving the Mukherjees came up. Goodness, if she'd said yes to Henry they'd probably have been driving home right now, or would be in bed together somewhere here in Eureka Springs, blissfully unaware of any of Chandra and Asher's problems.

But saying no had been part of principle, too. She couldn't do it because it wouldn't follow principle. Being here right now was undoubtedly where she was supposed to be. She was here because, once more, she could some-how offer help to people in need. Wishing otherwise was pointless.

Suddenly she wondered if the Mukherjees were veg-etarians and tried to remember what parts of the hotel's dinner she'd seen them eat. If she remembered her com-parative religion class correctly, vegetarianism would be one sign of belief in *ahimsa,* or "non-injury." It was what Mahatma Gandhi had taught, non-violent resistance, in-cluding respect for all forms of life.

Did the Mukherjees practice *ahimsa?* And, if so, was

there anything that could drive them to break that principle? Never mind, she was sure neither of them would ever
strike out physically at another human, no matter what.

It sounded like Gibson was finishing his phone conversation. Before he could return the phone to his belt—
when all that remained was time to act, not think—Carrie
pulled a tissue from her pocket and let it fall to the ground.
It landed perfectly, right on top of the knife sheath. Moving
like lightning, she bent, wrapped her fingers around tissue
and cardboard, and dropped them in her pocket.

She was standing motionless, head down as if in prayer,
when Officer Kurt Gibson turned toward her.

Chapter 12

It took Sergeant Lonnie Trent less than fifteen minutes, by Carrie's watch, to return to the Crescent. This time he wore black jeans and a black polo shirt. After exchanging a few words with Officer Gibson he came over to Carrie and Henry. Speaking very slowly and politely, he asked if they'd please wait for him in the back seat of his police car.

Carrie wondered what would happen if she said no, she wasn't about to sit in that smelly cage, but of course she didn't open her mouth, and she knew Henry wouldn't have objected, no matter what. She wondered how many drunks, felons, and who-knew-what had ridden in the caged back seat area of Trent's police car. Her opinion about it could be stated in one word. *Yuck.*

Henry fell asleep shortly after settling in the seat. He'd once told her that, during his years as a police officer, he'd learned to snatch short naps when and where he could. He was sure proving that now.

She couldn't sleep, at least not here. It was hideously uncomfortable, and besides, her mind was way too busy. Worse luck, Henry's ability to nap meant she had no one to discuss today's almost unbelievable sequence of events with. She watched him sleep for a while, then sighed and went back to thinking about the Mukherjees and the Owen family, as well as watching outside activity when she could see any.

A female police officer arrived shortly after Trent came and, with the men, began an inch-by-inch search of the parking lot and surrounding area. She also seemed to be the designated crime scene photographer. Carrie saw the woman carefully record the location of the red ribbon with her camera and then put it in an evidence bag. Well, that was that. One piece of supposed evidence would never be photographed. Carrie's hand closed around the wrapped knife sheath in her pocket. Maybe her impulsive action had been wrong—at the moment she was incapable of deciding. But if this piece of cardboard, no matter how it got in the parking lot, might help make the police suspicious of Asher and Chandra, she must have done the right thing. From what she'd already seen, she was sure neither Gibson nor Trent would be eager to find anything that directed suspicion toward the Hindu couple, and they already had the red ribbon.

After spending some time searching the parking lot area, all three officers disappeared over the hillside. When an ambulance arrived, Kurt Gibson came back by himself to direct it down the same drive Henry had used to reach the body.

At least there were no curious spectators around to bother anyone. Even late party-goers must be in their beds by now. The parking lot was empty and silent. Carrie shut her eyes and went back to thinking.

A sudden bounce and clunk jarred her. *What?* Another bounce. A light went on, and from somewhere far away, a male voice said, "Glad you two could catch forty winks."

Carrie opened her eyes, struggled to move from fuzzy to alert, and finally identified the bounce and clunk as Sergeant Trent getting in his car and shutting the door. She glanced at Henry. He looked wide awake, but the hair on top of his head was standing up, as if he'd run his hands through it in his sleep. She could probably use a comb too but, like Henry, didn't care enough about looks to bother getting one out of her purse.

Trent turned to look at them through the grill work and said, "Sorry about the cage, but we'll have privacy here, and this car has enough power to support leaving the light on. Okay?"

Carrie said nothing, but Henry said, "Sure," so they stayed in place.

Trent began, "Can you tell me now all you remember about what happened, all you saw here after you left the conservatory? Every little detail, please, no matter how small or seemingly insignificant. And, by the way, thanks for waiting." As he looked at each of them in turn, Carrie wondered if, really, they'd had any choice, but both she and Henry nodded.

"Okay, what do you remember that led up to discovering the body?" He took his tape recorder off the seat, held it where they could see it. "This will provide back-up to my notes." He then held up a clipboard.

"You first, King. I'll just let you talk and try not to bother you with questions, at least not until you've told me all you can think of."

Henry began smoothly, mentioning the search for the

butterfly pin first, explaining that was the reason they were still at the Crescent. Then he described noticing the presence of the Mukherjee van from the fourth floor deck, as well as seeing a flash of red he assumed to be Chandra's sari and Ashur leaving the Crescent by a door located downhill to the north of the hotel's main entrance. He told about finding the woman on the hillside with her wrists and ankles bound by green wire and added, much to Carrie's horror, that he'd seen a small silver-colored knife next to the body.

"Did you touch her?" Trent asked.

"Only enough to see if she could be alive, though I was sure it was hopeless. I did notice rigor when I touched her."

That news surprised Carrie. Wouldn't it mean Jan Owen had been dead for some time? Then the Mukherjees couldn't be involved!

"Okay, you next, Ms. McCrite."

Trent needed to prod her through the recitation after she began by saying, "I agree with what Henry said, and I saw the same things he did, except I didn't go down to the body."

After they'd both finished, the sergeant asked if either of them had any questions. Carrie thought that was probably a courtesy extended to Henry as a fellow law officer.

"I guess the dead woman was Jan Owen?" Carrie asked.

"I don't mind answering you," Trent said, "since I suppose you're both smart enough to know we aren't ready to talk publically about the identity of the corpse. No, it wasn't Jan Owen. It was her sister, Sonya Wells."

Henry and Carrie both gaped at him.

"But..." Carrie said, then fell silent as Henry's hand

touched her thigh, ever so lightly.

"We can only speculate about the wig," Trent continued, "because I know Jan's hair is real, though the blond color is fake. The only reasons I can think of for the wig off hand is either that, for some reason, Sonya was masquerading as her sister, or else," he hesitated, then went on more slowly, "someone wanted others, probably the killer, to think they were attacking Jan. And here's a warning: keep quiet about *everything* you saw. Maybe someone who shouldn't know any of the details will talk about one or more of them. You know how that works, King."

After a short silence, Henry said, "I wonder if the wig ever sat on her head. If she did wear it at any time, was it in place until she was killed? I guess you can test for the presence of fibers from the wig on the head of the corpse?"

Sergeant Trent took Henry's mild suggestion about an avenue of research without apparent resentment. "Sure, we'll check, why not? Who knows anything at this point?" He sighed. "I've already got tons of stuff to check up on.

"I can tell you for sure that, from now on, I'm gonna think attending city council meetings is a piece of cake compared to this. We hardly ever have a murder here and this one is big-time trouble all the way through." He made a sound that was probably intended as a laugh before continuing. "I wish I could just get in your car right now and go home with you."

Chapter 13

Chick-chicka-BOOM-kish-BOOM-chickity-BOOM...
r-a-s-p-"DON'T-HAVE-A-PLAN, MAN."
Kish-BOOM!

The final *BOOM* echoed inside Carrie's head and she popped her eyes open. What on earth?

Silence. The bedroom was empty of any noise but the soft "shhhsh" of her pajamas as they slid against the sheets, then a questioning yowp from FatCat.

She looked around. Her bed. Her clock, there, where it had always been. Bright sun. *Bright sun?* Goodness, 1:00? It was after noon on...on, a Sunday?

She'd slept through church!

Then it all came back, motion-picture clear. Eureka Springs, wedding research, the Mukherjees, dead woman on a hillside...

Henry had driven down her lane just before dawn. If she'd planned on attending church this morning, there would have been little point in going to bed at all.

True, she had slept most of the way home, lulled, surprisingly enough, by rhythm from the rap-rock music station Henry found on the car radio. "I'm not really sleepy now," he'd said; "that nap in the police car was enough for the present, but it never hurts to have keeping-awake noise. Do you mind?"

And right then she didn't mind. She'd merely shaken her head, closed her eyes, and let the exotic rhythm from the radio rock her to sleep. Literally—since it seemed the rock beat had stayed with her through the continuation of sleep in her own bed, going silent only when she opened her eyes to bright sunlight.

Carrie stretched her arms straight up and yawned. Ahhh. She clearly remembered Henry's good-night—or good-morning—kiss. Again she looked at the clock. She also remembered the two of them standing in her front hall and agreeing to go out for dinner at three o'clock this afternoon.

The phone on the bedside table rang.

She sat up, reached for the receiver, and, while trying to hold back another yawn, mumbled, "H'lo."

The line was silent for a heartbeat, then she heard a jagged, shivering breath.

Carrie waited, all the while thinking she should probably hang up. But curiosity took hold and she said, more clearly this time, "Hello?"

Silence, then the rasped word, "*Red.*" Heavy breathing. Silence. Then *"Red...means...warning. Red means stop."*

"Who is this? I'm going to hang up if you won't identify yourself."

It was the caller who hung up, not Carrie. Still holding the phone to her ear, she wondered if—just possibly—someone could have dialed a wrong number.

Red? Flaming hair earned her that nickname in grade school. She'd fought or yelled at anyone who used it until, by the seventh grade, the nickname disappeared. Now red remained only a color, except—she shivered—except for a bride dressed in a red gown.

What if the caller was someone who needed her help? What if that person knew her long-ago nickname and only managed to gasp a few words?

On the other hand, it could have been meant as a threat or a warning. But, why? Why?

After listening to the hum of the dial tone for several moments and wondering if she should feel fear, anger, or—what she really felt—raging curiosity dusted with unease, Carrie, too, hung up. Meanwhile FatCat bellycrawled into her lap, and the dial tone was replaced by an idling motor scooter purr. In response to this familiar sound, Carrie began absent-mindedly wiggling her fingers across the top of FatCat's head.

Should she dial *69? That would take her back to the caller's phone and make an identifying contact.

Woman? Probably. Now that Carrie thought about it, what she'd heard registered as female. At least she could be positive Henry didn't need her, but how about Eleanor or Shirley?

Oh, for good garden seed! Caller ID! She'd added it to her phone service just a few months ago. So simple. She shoved her feet into slippers, bounced a surprised cat off her lap, and headed for the handy little box on her desk.

The read-out said "Anonymous." The woman had taken some care not to be identified. Now Carrie could almost hear Henry saying, "If someone wants you, they'll call back, so drop it."

And for the time being at least, she would.

But since she was here at her desk, she'd check e-mail. As of four o'clock this morning there had been no response to the query sent to a likely-sounding Catherine King. She'd contacted her on not much more than faith. After all, Henry's Catherine could have married years ago and be a happy housewife living almost anywhere, with no connection to any organization other than the PTA and no Internet identification at all. Still, there were many possibilities on the search engines, and the one leading her to a law firm with partners named Catherine King and Sylvia Brandon had seemed especially hopeful. That Catherine King fit exactly with the few facts Carrie knew. She wondered if the woman looked at her e-mail on weekends.

While the computer was going through the familiar buzz and whistle of hook-up, Carrie headed for the bedroom to start getting dressed. It wouldn't take long to put on a sweater and slacks.

When she returned to her desk she still didn't sit down, just clicked to download e-mail and went to the bathroom to comb her hair and fix her face. She didn't want Henry to catch her mussed and still in night clothes, and he'd be here on time, if not early.

Back in the office she sat, scanning the incoming mail list. Oh! Something from "cmklegal.com." Heart thumping, she scrolled down to "cmklegal" and began to read.

Dear Carrie McCrite:

I've been thinking about how to answer you, re: your coming marriage to a half-brother I've never met.

You sound like an intelligent and sensitive woman, so, if you know any of the facts surrounding the separation between Henry and me, I imagine you can understand what a difficult situation this is—probably not unlike what faces an ad-

opted child struggling with the decision about whether or not to contact birth parents. Should I come to meet Henry and attend your wedding? My natural inclination is to say yes. Now that the three parents involved in our family's split are gone, and since I have always been curious about my brother, the opportunity seems a godsend.

There are, however, possible problems, especially if, as you said in your letter, this meeting is to be a surprise for Henry. He might not find it a pleasant surprise.

Yes, he and I had the same birth father, but, in reality, that means less than you might think. Why? From what I can tell, our father was a much different man in his second marriage—not at all like the man Henry knew. And Henry's mother and mine were probably as unlike as possible, our lives as children vastly different. I don't want to be unkind, and I never met Henry's mother, of course, but the father I knew said he didn't begin to live until he married his second wife—my mother. I won't go into all the reasons he gave except to say Henry's mother was evidently very reserved and was happiest as a solitary person.

On the other hand, our shared father was fun-loving, out-going, and tended to be what I would call devil-may-care. My mom and I loved him deeply for these qualities, and my parents were a very happy couple, in spite of the difference in their ages. (She was thirty-one and he was fifty-six when they married.) Daddy also had what I'd acknowledge as character flaws. These included his tendency to drink too much, as well as antipathy toward the "boring dailyness-mess" (his term) of the types of jobs he held. He evidently had this same antipathy toward school. He once told me he had dropped out of high school before graduating.

As I said, we loved him and were a happy family, but neither Mom nor I was blind to his problems. Almost needless to say, my mother's job helped support us. She worked on a factory assembly line making electric motors. (This was before the time when most such jobs were sent off-shore to be done by lower-paid workers.) She was a union member and made pretty good money for a woman during the twenty-five years she worked in that factory. Thank goodness, since it meant we never went hungry and always had a comfortable place to live.

Daddy died four years ago. Momma died last month, so she lived to see me well on the way to a successful career, thanks in large part to her help and wise money management.

Henry didn't come to Daddy's funeral, though I admit I watched for him. I doubt now that he even knew when Daddy died. So far as I know, Henry never saw his father after the divorce.

And yes, what Henry probably told you is true, my mom was pregnant with me when Albert King left his first wife. Daddy's disloyalty to Henry's mother had a lot to do with the breach between the two men, I'm sure, and I don't suppose I can really blame Henry for whatever he felt. But he was thirty-three (the age I am now) and a married adult when his dad left home. I guess I have always hoped he would eventually understand, if not forgive.

Ah well, that's the past.

You asked about my life. As you already know from your Internet research I'm single and a member of the Oklahoma bar, part of a two-person partnership practicing in Claremore, Oklahoma. We handle a few criminal cases, but for the most part it's wills, trusts, adoptions, incorporations, business law. It's interesting that, in mileage distance at least, I'm not far from where you and Henry live.

I went to college at the University of Kansas in Lawrence. After graduation I stayed out of school for a couple of years,

*working at various jobs until I earned enough money to begin
law school at KU. I continued part-time work while I was in
law school, and that meant it took me six years to get my law
degree. After graduation, and before I took the Kansas Bar
exam, a job search led me to this firm in Claremore. My law
partner, Sylvia Brandon, had an expanding practice and was
looking for a second lawyer in her office. It sounded promis-
ing, and it was. This has been a good association for both of
us, and I feel quite lucky to be here. In spite of the typical
problems common to many small towns today, Claremore is a
good place to live and work. I am well situated.*

*I admit to curiosity about Henry. I wonder if he's at all
like Daddy. From a photo I saw in the Kansas City newspaper a number of years ago, I do know Henry favors Daddy in
looks. Will he remind me of Daddy in a positive way? That
would be nice. And now, since Momma is gone too, I have
some twinges of renewed interest in other family members,
especially my half-brother, even though (I assume) he's rejected
me all my life.*

*He could have looked me up, just as you did. But then,
I could have found him quite easily, especially when he lived
in Kansas City. I admit I always thought it was his place, as
the elder and because the family breach began before I was
born, to initiate a contact. After all, though he may blame
my parents for what happened in his family at that time, he
can hardly blame me. If I sound harsh about this, you possibly
understand why.*

*Now, an important question. You said this would be a
surprise for Henry. If you plan to surprise him with my appearance at your wedding, you may be faced with his shock
rather than surprise. Your invitation could well end in disas-
ter—can you see this? If I am to come to your wedding (and
that is by no means certain at this point), I would insist you*

tell Henry about the invitation, and the sooner the better.

Let me know how things progress. Thank you for contacting me,

Catherine MacDonald King

Carrie looked at the time and date on the letter. It had been written at eight this morning, but surely no immediate reply would be expected, a good thing since she hadn't the slightest idea how to answer Catherine. She clicked on the print icon, then leaned back in the desk chair and shut her eyes, squeezing them tightly in a frown. What had she done? More important, what was she going to do? This had turned into another of those "act in haste, repent in leisure" things she sometimes got herself into.

Should she, as Catherine mandated, tell Henry? Or not? How on earth should she handle this? She had set something in motion that could hurt both Catherine and Henry, unless—glory be—Henry eagerly welcomed the chance to meet his sister.

And what if he didn't? Henry was proud, and it seemed obvious he'd been badly hurt by his father's adultery and disloyalty to his mother. Under the circumstances she probably would have felt hurt too, maybe even struggled with anger. She supposed Henry had a right to be angry, even now.

She just wished he'd shared more about his past with her. How was she going to tell him about contacting Catherine, explain her motives, her feeling she was doing something really good for all of them? If she did tell Henry she'd invited his half-sister to their wedding, and he was angry—or maybe not so angry, but firm about not meeting his sister—then she'd have to tell Catherine what he'd said and forget the whole thing.

Except now it could never be forgotten. Whatever happened, this would always be in the minds of at least three people...Catherine King, Henry King, and Carrie McCrite.

She looked at the clock. Henry would be here in a few minutes, so she had to quit this awful worrying and finish getting dressed. She hoped he was hungry and in the mood to eat out. She sure was.

Carrie started to push her desk chair back, then stopped, staring at the Caller ID. Should she tell Henry about her anonymous caller?

After a moment's thought, she decided to do just what he would probably advise: "Drop it."

Chapter 14

"I'm mighty glad this place is open on Monday," Shirley said as she put the final bite of barbecue sandwich in her mouth. "No wonder Bubba's is one of the best-known restaurants in Eureka Springs. I've heard of it for years—and now I'm sorry Roger and I never made it over here to eat. But you know that man, he says I'm the only living person who can cook to suit him. I almost never can pry him out to a restaurant, though I must say he's always agreeable to visit either of you two at a meal time." She winked at Carrie. "He does like your chicken pie, Carrie. Keeps saying I should give you a hint that, when you're in a mood to make chicken pie, he'll be more 'n glad to bring you a couple of our fresh chickens. Why, he said he'd even kill them for you."

While Carrie shuddered at the thought of dealing with a chicken she had to pluck and dismember, Eleanor put a hand over her mouth, trying to hold back laughter, and after she lost the battle, Shirley joined in.

Carrie didn't know whether to be embarrassed or proud that Roger liked her chicken pie—if Shirley was telling the truth, that is. Her two friends knew she made it from canned chicken. Surely Roger could tell...

Oh.

Maybe that was why he'd offered her his chickens. She sat in embarrassed silence for a moment until, finally infected by her friends' laughter, she joined them, noticing that diners all around the room were beginning to smile. A few were even laughing. Well, whatever. They couldn't know what the joke was, but at least she, Shirley, and Eleanor were helping people feel happy.

Finally Shirley took a deep breath, blew her nose, and said, "Whoee, Carrie, I'm glad you can stand a little ragging, and it's true that Roger does like your chicken pie, even if he thinks fresh chicken would improve it. But you stick your ground. We all cook different, and that's what makes visiting each other's tables so special. Now then, one of you tell me what time it is."

Carrie glanced at her watch. "Fifteen past noon."

"Good, we have time for this." She pulled a folded piece of paper from her purse and laid it on the table. "I made a drawing of a dress. This is what I've been thinking about since our wedding dress talk on Saturday."

"OOOO," Eleanor squeaked, leaning forward and stacking their messy plates at the edge of the table to give Shirley more room. "It'll be great to know what Carrie's dress is going to be like before we go to the flower shop. Let's see, Shirley."

Carrie noticed Eleanor lowered her voice before she said "flower shop." All three of them had seen the headlines shouting from the rack outside Bubba's Barbecue the minute they pulled into the parking lot. The paper pro-claimed "Local Woman Murdered." Though she'd told her friends all about Saturday's events here in Eureka Springs during their drive over, each of them bought a copy of the paper on the way in, and each of them excused the multiple purchases by saying they wanted to take copies home to Jason, Roger, and Henry. Then they had to delay ordering while they read the long article (*continued on page 2-A*) and stared at the picture of a severe-looking woman identified as "Murdered Eureka Springs Realtor, Sonya Wells."

"It's basically just like I told you," Carrie had mur-mured when the waitress went to get glasses of water, "and I'm glad to see they haven't said anything about the Mukherjees. I was so afraid..."

Eleanor and Shirley had nodded their heads in under-standing before Carrie finished her sentence, and, since the waitress was returning, that was the end of their dis-cussion for the moment.

Now Shirley brushed crumbs aside, wiped up a splotch of barbecue sauce with her napkin, and unfolded the piece of paper, turning it around so the other two women could see it from where they sat.

Carrie stared at the drawing in silence, picturing her-self wearing what Shirley had drawn. It was a simple, an-kle-length dress with a pleated lace collar edging a modest v-shaped neckline. The lace disappeared behind an ap-pliqued ribbon bow with rounded loops extending over the bosom. The bow's strings weren't fastened down, but dropped free to below the waist. The remainder of the dress front was plain, flaring slightly from just under the bosom to the hem. The sleeves were long and ended in a narrow lace cuff.

A detail drawing at the edge of Shirley's paper showed the back of the dress, where a bow copying the one on the front was fastened just above the waist. Its longer ties fell to the hem.

Amid all the noon-time restaurant chatter, the silence at their table seemed deafening. Carrie was thinking, *What a beautiful dress. And Shirley was right—this is like being girls again—it's good for all of us. How could I ever have resented their sharing the planning with me?*

Finally Shirley spoke. "Ivory, I thought. Of course, if it isn't what you had in mind, I can..."

Eleanor looked at Carrie and they both grinned. Carrie said, "Shirley, this dress is beautiful, and it's perfect. It might even manage to make me look thin!" She reached across the table and took Shirley's hand, blinking to control sudden dampness in her eyes. "How can I ever thank you? I'm so lucky to have you—both of you—as friends. Shirley, this is so..."

Eleanor interrupted, suddenly all business as she looked at her watch. "Ladies, time to pay the bill and go. I know we have thirty minutes before our appointment but I'm a bit shaky about finding the place on these curving streets, let alone locating a parking space."

Eleanor had no problem finding the flower shop after all. The building was just as Chandra described and had a window sign, which read, *Artistic Floral Designs, Weddings a Specialty.* After the car pulled into a parking space next to the shop's green van, Carrie said, "It's not one o'clock yet. Should we wait out here for a few minutes?"

Eleanor opened her door. "We don't need to," she said. "Look through the window there. I see some kind of display area in the front. It looks like they sell decorator items as well as flowers. Why don't we go in and look around until time for our appointment."

As they piled out of the car, a dark-haired young man wearing jeans with torn knees and a ripped and faded red and black sweatshirt hurried out of the shop. The three women stopped to watch him hop on a motorcycle, kick-start it, and disappear around a curve.

"Huh," Eleanor said, "I suppose, for today, he's well dressed. When I think how young people's dress has gone to rags...why, I wouldn't have let Tom..."

Shirley interrupted her with a snort. "Oh, phooey, Eleanor, maybe that's not what your son Tom wore to high school—what?—thirty years ago in a big northern city, but when did you start wearing pants and jeans yourself? I don't know as I've ever seen you in a dress, which is what used to be considered proper for ladies. Besides, where all of us live today, out in the country, kids might need to do chores as soon as they get home from school. Ours did, boys and girls both. Think about it. And that kid probably just stopped in on his school lunch break to order flowers for his girl or maybe even something for his mother. I think it's sweet."

"Well, I don't care, Shirley. If I were his mother, I'd still..."

A flash of orange flame and a mind-stopping explosive blast, followed immediately by the push of what felt like rock-solid air blowing out from the building, interrupted her. All three women were thrown toward the street and slammed into the side of the florist's van. Instinctively curious, Carrie turned toward the force of the blast and felt a sting against her cheek. Squinting, she saw the pipe-supported porch roof that stretched from the building to the curb tilt, then break in two, leaving the street-side section hanging precariously from its supporting pipes. On the building side the roof crashed down into piles of filthy, dust-clouded construction trash. She shut her eyes against the dust and smoke and, just like on Saturday evening, heard the lingering, almost musical, sounds of broken glass falling on a hard surface.

"Oh, Lord have mercy," Shirley said. "What happened? Are you two all right?"

"I'm okay," Carrie said, "just a little shaken up, and my ears are ringing. But, oh, Shirley, Eleanor's not moving. And Chandra would have been inside there. I've got to go find Chandra!

"Eleanor, Eleanor!" Torn between the need to help her friend and look for Chandra Mukherjee, Carrie finally bent over Eleanor, and, without conscious effort, began a silent prayer, not only for Eleanor, but for Chandra and Ashur. And what if the Mukherjees' son and daughter-in-law had also been working in the building? What if... Almost overwhelmed by anxiety, Carrie wailed, "Oh, Eleanor, wake *up.* "

She felt Shirley scoot through the debris to her side. "She's breathing," Shirley said, "maybe just knocked out. Do you think we should move her away from here? Could there be another explosion?"

Carrie brushed bits of what looked like wood chips off Eleanor's face. "I don't know if we should move her.

"Eleanor, can you hear me? Would you please say something to us? You've *got* to be all right, the worst part is over, and Shirley and I are here. You can wake up now, open your eyes. Are your ears okay? That was an awful noise, wasn't it?"

Amid the sound of distant sirens, Eleanor did open her eyes and said, very clearly and disapprovingly, "Carrie, for heaven's sake, move back, you're dripping blood on me."

Carrie looked down at Eleanor's jacket and saw that at least there was nothing wrong with her friend's eyesight. As she watched, another drop of blood joined the others on the jacket's front. Without thinking, she put a hand to her face, felt wetness on her cheek, looked at the blood on her hand, and then sat back on her behind so her face wouldn't be over Eleanor's clothing.

Oh, gee, she thought, as a fire truck and ambulance shrieked to a stop in front of the flower shop. *And all I wanted was a nice, quiet little wedding.*

Then, bracing her hand against the van, she struggled to her feet and, moving with zombie-like precision, headed toward where the building's front door had been. She needed to find whoever was inside when the blast came.

Chapter 15

"Clear the area, folks. Make way for emergency workers. I mean it now, MOVE!"

Carrie glanced back and was relieved to see that firefighters in yellow slickers were dispersing a rapidly gathering crowd. Satisfied that Eleanor and Shirley had plenty of helpers for whatever assistance they might need, she stepped across a stack of splintered boards and into what was left of the florist's shop.

That's when she heard, "Hey you—you, the woman in the blue jacket. Stay out of there. You! Stop!"

Carrie ignored the commanding voice and began calling, "Chandra, Ashur?" as she picked her way through what looked like a very messy cave. Except for light from the street it was certainly dark as a cave, with stalactites made of splintered wood, broken wiring, and bent pieces of pipe. She called out again and felt warm relief when she heard a faint female voice saying, "Here," from somewhere in front of her.

Stepping around wires she assumed might be live, she followed the sound and was surprised when the level of destruction became less severe as she moved farther back in the shop. Now nothing dangled from above, heavy steel pipes still supported the ceiling, and, ahead of her, a huge room-within-a-room that was probably a walk-in refrigerator seemed to be intact. The refrigerator door was partially open.

"Chandra? It's Carrie McCrite. Say something else so I can find you."

The refrigerator door opened wider and, blue sari looking spotless, hair neatly in place, Chandra stared out at her.

"Where's Ashur?" Carrie said.

"Walked to the post office," Chandra murmured. As she looked around the ruined shop her eyes went wide with horror, then closed tightly, wrinkling into slits. The thin body began to shake. She began a faint, high-pitched keening.

Now Carrie moved more quickly, ignoring the dirt and mess and forgetting the drying blood on her hands and face as she joined Chandra just inside the refrigerator door. She wrapped the tiny woman in her arms and began swaying and crooning softly, "There-there, there-there."

That was when the huge man wearing a yellow slicker and helmet appeared, blocking what daylight they had. Carrie noticed immediately he was having a hard time talking in complete sentences, though stuttered words came clearly through his face mask.

"What the...? Don't you realize...? I told you to... Why didn't you...?"

Finally he stopped, cleared his throat, and got out an understandable sentence, albeit in a voice full of tension. "Ladies, you are leaving this building with me. Right now." He put a heavily gloved hand around Carrie's arm and reached for Chandra with his other hand.

"Sir," Carrie said, trying to pull away from his hold and failing, "I am quite capable of making my own way out of this building now that I'm satisfied no one here is hurt or in danger, so—*let me go*. I will be fine walking out by myself. Carry Chandra if you want someone to take care of. I suspect her legs are feeling a bit wobbly at the moment. *Now, take your hands off me!*"

"I think Ms. McCrite will be okay, Jenkins," a familiar voice said from the front of the shop. "I can assure you she's a capable, if stubborn, lady. The power company has already shut off gas and electricity here, so that part is safe. Why don't you take Ms. Mukherjee to the front? Her husband is outside, and he's mighty anxious. He'll be glad to see you're taking good care of her."

"Hello, Sergeant Trent," Carrie said as the big fireman swung Chandra into his arms and headed toward the street. "You got here quickly. I thought maybe you were off duty."

He moved toward her, brushing through the same pipes and wires she had so carefully avoided. Without speaking, he handed her the hard hat he was carrying and pointed to her head. She got the message and put it on.

"When a small department gets emergencies like this, being off duty means nothing. And," he said, looking around the shop, "I seem to be collecting emergencies whenever you come to Eureka Springs. Is that a coincidence?" He fell silent as he turned on a flashlight and began sweeping it back and forth.

She said, "There's much less destruction back here than up front. I wonder if the apartment upstairs was badly damaged. I hope not. You said it was their home."

"I'll be looking at it next. Ashur is here and can go with me. The poor man heard the thing blow just as he left the post office but of course had no idea what it was. He came back to see this." He swept his free arm around the room. "I had to grab him and almost knock him out to keep him from coming in after Chandra. Unfortunately, I didn't get here in time to stop you, and the fire department gang was so astonished by the sheer idiocy of what you'd done, not to mention being slowed down by all their safety gear, that they didn't manage to catch you either."

He sighed, then laughed, and said, "Well, I'm glad you and Chandra are okay, but you did give us a few bad moments. You shouldn't have done such a dumb fool thing, Ms. McCrite. You've got to stop being the point dog, finding bodies, being on the scene of explosions, or I'll have to retire early. You just aged me ten years."

Carrie stared at him while crushing shame rocked through her. She hadn't thought about anything but finding Chandra. She hadn't considered the people whose duty it was to protect the public, hadn't realized that rushing into what was, after all, an unstable and possibly dangerous situation, could cause problems for anyone other than herself. Still, she wasn't about to apologize, not even to Sergeant Lonnie Trent. One did what one had to do in an emergency. He must understand that.

He was still studying the area around the walk-in refrigerator. "I don't think this is a gas explosion," he said. "You're right, most of the damage seems to be up front, and there aren't any gas outlets there. Besides, a gas accumulation near the display windows would probably disperse fairly quickly because they leak air like crazy."

Carrie said, "I'm sure it was a bomb, and I think my

friends and I saw the bomber."

He turned to look at her closely for the first time. "Well, now, that's interesting. I'd like to know why you think it was a bomb. I believe we should go outside now and have a...a...talk." His voice faltered as he surveyed her face. "Hey, you're hurt, you neglected to mention that, didn't you? We'd better find an EMT."

He took her arm and began to guide her through broken crockery, piles of dirt, and scattered plants and flowers. This time, she didn't try to pull away from the hand that helped her.

Henry looked at the clock when the phone rang. He'd been reading a novel, and the afternoon had flown by more quickly than he thought possible. The book, *Mad Dog and Englishman*, by J. M. Hayes, took him completely out of today and right back onto the Kansas prairie of his childhood. His parents had lived in Kansas during the first few years of his life while his father tried farming. This Hayes guy really knew the prairie.

The phone rang again. He should have put the hand set by his chair. He hoped it was Carrie, calling to say she was home. He'd suggest they have supper here and surprise her with broiled steak, baked potatoes, and a salad.

As he hurried toward the ringing sound, Henry wondered briefly what was going on with the Eureka Springs PD's murder investigation and how Chandra and Ashur were weathering the fall-out from Saturday night's events.

Where WAS that phone? At last he brushed aside a stack of newspapers and found it.

"Hello."

"Uh, hello, Henry. It's me. There's, uh, been sort of an unusual development here. You see, someone blew up the Mukherjees' flower shop"—she ignored his grunt of surprise—"and we, the three of us, are here in the hospital emergency room, though we're fine, really, and..." Her next words raced out. "CouldyouandJasonpleasecomerigh tawayanddriveushome?"

"Carrie! What happened? Are you...?"

Before he could get beyond that, she was talking again, still in a hurry, but no longer a tumultuous rush. "We really are fine, just messed up because there was a lot of dirt, and I know Roger is busy with the cows and besides Shirley isn't hurt, not even a scratch, just dirty like we all are, but Eleanor and I would rather not drive right now and Shirley isn't comfortable driving Eleanor's car on these mountainous roads." She took a breath. "You see?"

"Carrie, little love, are you sure you're okay? You said the emergency room?"

"Well, they wanted to be sure we really *were* okay, and I got a couple of those cute bandages they call a butterfly on my cheek, but we're mostly just dirty, really, except they cleaned my face pretty thoroughly. Eleanor's clothes are so dirty she's going to call Jason next and ask him to bring her green suit. What she has on got kind of spotted."

"How about you? Do you need anything?"

"Oh, I'll do, and besides I'd rather you didn't take time to go to my house and look for clothes. I have an extra jacket in the back of Eleanor's car and can put it on over my shirt." She paused. He could hear her breathing, and—almost—hear her mind working.

"Please come right away. I...miss you."

"I'm on my way. I'll get Jason and then call you as soon as we're out on the highway. The hospital emergency room? Didn't we pass a hospital on our way to the hotel on Saturday? Is that it?"

"Uh-huh."

"Okay. We'll be there within an hour and a half. You're sure you're okay?" He heard another "Uh-huh," and said, "Well then, hang on, we're coming. Tell Shirley I'll call Roger before we leave. Now, do you have the phone number there?"

He wrote the number down, then said, "Cara, remember how much I love you, remember you're going to be my wife, very, very soon. Remember!"

In a tiny voice, she said, "Yes, I remember."

After he'd hung up he repeated to himself, "Remember how much I love you." The words came out of his mouth without any planning.

Being in love was great, and, no matter what kids thought, it was great whether you were sixteen or sixty! If only he and Carrie could stay away from helping other people solve problems for a while, if only they could enjoy being in love, being newlyweds, until...well, at least until after their honeymoon.

He picked up the phone to call Jason and Roger.

An explosion?

He couldn't stop the thoughts. His policeman's mind began buzzing with hows and whys. And with something else. *What next?*

Chapter 16

Henry kept his eyes on the road, but he sensed that Jason had been watching him intently during his entire account of Saturday night's events at the Crescent Hotel. Now the car was silent while Jason stared out the window and studied scenery. Finally he said, "Professional jealousy, fear of terrorism, racism. Whatever this is, it's all about fear, isn't it?"

Jason Stacks's initial response to almost any new situation usually came in an outburst of opinion, not thoughtful commentary or reasoning. This philosophical question was a surprise.

Henry guided the car around another mountainous curve while thinking that something about the attacks on the Mukherjees had touched Jason deeply. He wondered what it was.

"Yes, probably based on fear," Henry agreed and waited for a response. Two more switch-back curves passed under the car wheels.

Now Jason looked straight ahead. "Maybe it's all of those things together, or even using one of them as an excuse to hide another. Who knows what's going on inside the head of anyone who commits crimes like this? But when people are afraid..."

There was another long pause before he continued. "It's not an easy thing, figuring out how people react to other people. I mean, react to those not *like* themselves. Am I right?"

Henry was carefully neutral. "Um-hm." It was beginning to sound like Jason brought baggage of his own to this conversation. Folks in their age group might well do that. Civil rights struggles versus fear of "the other," maybe a reactionary keeping to your own kind—that was personally experienced history for his generation, or at least something everyone their age had seen live on television.

Until he was almost a teenager, Henry never thought about equal rights or what others suffered because of skin color. Things were just the way they were. No questions came from a white boy growing up in Missouri and Kansas. But, when his father moved from farming to construction work, there'd been a black kid, just a few years older than Henry, on the work crew. "Fetch and Carry" was what the white guys called him instead of his name, LeRoy. At first Henry only noticed LeRoy's polished-looking chocolate skin gleaming in the sunlight and wondered what that kind of skin felt like. He'd wanted to touch it and also touch the kinky hair. They looked so...*different.*

Henry's dad got him a job on the work crew the following summer, and the two boys became cautious friends. Henry learned that LeRoy's skin felt just like his own. He never had the guts to touch Leroy's hair.

He also learned about racism in a hurry when he saw

racially-motivated cruelty for the first time in his life. Noticing that his father participated in some of the insults directed at LeRoy, he had no one to talk to about it except LeRoy himself.

Calm on the surface, LeRoy was boiling inside. "It's gonna be pay-back time someday, man," he told Henry. "Can't take much more of this. Those guys won't even call me by the name Momma gave me."

Another time, when the two boys were eating lunch together and Henry was trying to ignore scowls from the other workers, LeRoy confided, "You know, white folks killed my old man. They ain't gonna kill me."

In September Henry left the work crew to return to school, realizing that more schooling was a luxury LeRoy would probably never have. As it turned out, life itself was a luxury LeRoy didn't have. When Henry came back to the crew the following summer, he learned LeRoy had died in Korea.

Henry pretty much glossed over or ignored race problems after that, or thought he did, until his inner turmoil broke out during a race riot in Kansas City when he was new on the police force. He did his job as it was defined then, but couldn't sleep well for nights after. In the following weeks and months he overcompensated for the heartache he felt, generally treating black people he came into contact with better than he treated whites, at least until some of the guys on the force began calling him "nigger lover," and he moderated his actions.

Years later he read a magazine article that quoted an old Indian proverb. It was about not judging any man until you'd walked a mile in his moccasins. Ever since, he'd thought of that when he ran into problems with other humans, black or white, man or woman. *Try to see where they're coming from.*

It even worked on his friend, Jason Stack.

As far as the women's rights movement, well, with Carrie's help, he was struggling to understand that too. He had been shocked when he learned she'd worn white and marched for the ERA, all without the knowledge of her husband, Amos. She said doing it had been some kind of small victory for her, no matter what the ultimate result.

"It was the first tiny budding of my own independence," she'd told him only a few weeks ago.

He'd said he thought the amendment asked for an unnecessary duplication of laws already on the books. She'd replied, forcefully, that she didn't agree with him. "But," she'd added, "even if you're right and passing the Equal Rights Amendment would have been as much symbolic victory as legal necessity, that doesn't diminish its importance in my eyes. It would have meant I had Constitutional law, at last, specifically recognizing me and my rights."

The fervor of her words told him then what he'd missed before. Content mattered, but so did intent. Now, maybe, he understood.

Jason cleared his throat, bringing Henry back from his reverie.

"Some time back," Jason said, "almost thirty-five years ago, a dark fella, Muslim, applied for a job at my plant. Because the guy was so highly educated and otherwise qualified, our personnel director passed him on to me. But I was afraid. Afraid of what the other employees would do and of what customers would think. So I squirreled out of hiring him. I turned him down on some fabricated reason or other. I'll never forget the look on his face.

"I guess a lot of others turned him down too, because I found out later he gave up trying to find work in our area and went back to his home country, leaving his family here."

Jason's voice faltered, and there was a long silence before he turned toward Henry again. "About a year after that, Eleanor volunteered for an interfaith council in Cleveland. She met the man's sister. Turned out their father had gotten crosswise of the rulers in their country and, one day, both parents were taken by soldiers and never seen again. The rest of the family—two sons and the daughter, with spouses and children—escaped to the United States. They thought they could make a new life, a safe life. One brother was qualified as a physician back home and worked here as a hospital orderly until he could qualify in the United States. The sister's husband was an accountant, as was the man I turned away. The brother-in-law found a job with the government, but..."

Henry heard Jason suck in a big breath, expel it. "The sister said that the man I refused to hire disappeared shortly after he returned home, just like his parents had before him. For all I know I caused that man's death. I..."

Henry interrupted him. "You shouldn't feel guilty over what you didn't understand back then, Jason, or even over what you know now was not the best action to take. We can all learn just by living. If the man came to you today there's no question but that you'd hire him, right?"

"Yes, I would, but still...I should have then, too. You're giving me credit for more virtue than I deserve."

Silence took over the car again. For a time Henry wondered what was going through Jason's head, but that faded, and he spent the remainder of the trip thinking about Carrie, and about what they might find in the emergency room.

The tableau that greeted them at the hospital was at

least familiar, recalling the time in Hot Springs when he, not Carrie, had been the injured one and FBI and police officers questioned the two of them in a hospital waiting room.

His eyes found Carrie immediately. She did, indeed, sport a couple of butterfly bandages on her purpling cheek, and the dang things were colored to look something like real butterflies. Well, that sure added a startling touch to her face. What a bizarre town. They had toothpicks carved like miniature table legs and painted bandages that mimicked real butterflies.

And dead bodies and explosions.

He sent a brief hello toward Eleanor and Shirley, then knelt by Carrie's chair and took her hand, shutting out everyone else. "You okay...at least sort of okay?"

"More than okay, and I have these pretty decorations to show off. You already know I like butterflies, you've seen my butterfly pin. Now I'm pretending I've got butterfly tattoos." She looked pensive. "And don't think I haven't considered that—though I'd thought more in terms of one tiny butterfly on my shoulder than two on my face. What do you think, Henry? Should I get a tattoo here?" She pointed to her shoulder. "Or...maybe here, on my behind?"

He stared, unable to answer, until a grin betrayed her and both of them started laughing. "Anyway," she said when she could catch her breath, "you can quit worrying about me now. Sit down, and help us think."

Meanwhile, Jason was fussing over Eleanor, and Henry heard her say, "Oh, do hush, Jason, it's just a small bump on the head, nothing damaged permanently."

"But look at your jacket. That's blood!"

"It's Carrie's blood, Pookie, not mine, so you should go

sympathize with her while I change clothes." She took the hanging case from his hand and headed down the hall.

Henry pulled a chair up next to Carrie and sat, then noticed the female detective they'd seen in the Crescent parking lot Saturday night leaning against a wall at the edge of the seating area. Had she ever told them her name? He couldn't remember.

"Ah, hello again, Detective. I guess you've met Shirley Booth and Eleanor Stack? This is Eleanor's husband, Jason."

"Hello, Major King." She came into their circle and held her hand toward Jason. "I'm Detective Gloria Wolverton, Mr. Stack. Now that you two are here, I guess we can get started. The ladies were reluctant to say much about the bombing until you arrived."

Well, that's a new twist, Henry thought, as the detective dropped into the last vacant chair in their circle. *Surely these three aren't under suspicion for anything.*

He asked, "Then it really was a bomb?"

Everyone began talking at once, and Detective Wolverton silenced them with a raised hand. "Yes, Major King, that much we do know for sure. In fact, they've already found the remains of a crude pipe bomb in the wreckage. Sergeant Trent will be here shortly, and he'll have more information."

Henry looked at Carrie. "How are Chandra and Ashur?

"Both okay. Ashur was out of the building, Chandra was in the flower cooler. And, thank goodness, Gloria says their apartment wasn't badly damaged. It's a sturdy old building with a lot of steel pillars and bracing. The main room upstairs, which overlooks the street, is just above the shop. It has damage that Gloria says resembles what would happen in a mild earthquake. She's from California, so she knows those things."

Carrie nodded at the detective, who said, "Right. Wall cracks, a few knick-knacks broken, that's about it. Looks like there's no major structural damage up there. Downstairs, the gift shop area next to the front windows was destroyed, a lot of merchandise ruined, but the heavy pillars, tight construction, and presence of a very large and very strong walk-in refrigerator in the center of the room helped save the work area of the shop as well as the rooms upstairs. Chandra Mukherjee was inside the refrigerator, so she wasn't hurt, and Mr. Mukherjee and their son and daughter-in-law weren't on the premises. It could have been much worse. As for the three women—" she looked at Carrie—"they were on the street in front of the building, but the front overhang came down in such a way that it helped protect them. If they'd been closer, or in the building..." She shook her head.

"As it is, Ms. McCrite has only that cut on her cheek, caused by flying glass. Ms. Stack was knocked out briefly by a chunk of the overhang, and," she smiled toward Shirley, "Ms. Booth wasn't hurt at all."

Carrie spoke again. "I think the Mukherjees are with police and fire investigators at their building right now. Workers were already bringing in plywood sheets to cover the windows before we left. This is an incredible town, Henry. Help came so quickly. All kinds of people began working together to help their neighbors in need. I think the prejudice we observed in the Owen family is far from widespread here."

Henry breathed a sigh of relief. "I had imagined awful things on the way over...you hurt worse than you admitted, the Mukherjees' building nothing but a big hole, and even our wedding plans ruined."

Not, he thought, that they didn't have plenty to worry about. There had still been a bombing, and there was no way to put a bright view on the murder of Sonya Wells.

The door opened and Sergeant Lonnie Trent came in carrying a briefcase. His uniform was even dirtier than Carrie's clothing, and he looked drawn and tired. Henry wondered how much sleep he'd had since Saturday and went to pull another chair into their circle. As he did, Eleanor returned to the room looking clean, freshly made-up, and definitely out of place among her grimy friends.

The sergeant sat and, without preamble, took several sheets of photographs out of his briefcase. "These are school pictures," he said. "We've put strips of paper over the names and substituted numbers. Would each of you women look at these pages and see if any photo reminds you of the kid you saw leaving the flower shop right before the bomb went off? If you do recognize anyone, remember the number of the photo and pass the pages on. When all three of you have seen the pictures, I'll ask you about what you saw."

He handed the sheets to Shirley and said, "Look carefully, and take your time."

Henry watched Shirley and could tell when, on the third page, a photo caught her attention. She bent over, studied it, then glanced quickly through the remaining pages. When she'd seen all the photos she shuffled the pages like a stack of cards and handed them on to Eleanor.

Henry almost laughed aloud. How clever of Shirley. He hoped Lonnie Trent was impressed with this care taken to assure impartial identification.

Like Shirley, Eleanor was stopped by one of the photographs, this time on the second page she looked at. She finished going through the stack, returned to the second page, nodded, then pulled out a couple of pages, interleaved them between others, and gave the photo sheets to Carrie.

Henry watched as Carrie went through all the pages without any noticeable reaction, then did it again. Was she not seeing anyone who reminded her of the young man on the motorcycle? Maybe she hadn't gotten as good a look at him as the other two women. Finally she handed the pages back to Sergeant Trent.

Next thing the sergeant did was hand each woman a slip of paper and a pencil. "Now, write down the number of any photo you recognized," he said.

Henry was surprised when, without hesitation, Carrie wrote "Number 18" on her paper, folded it, and handed it to Trent.

Well now, maybe she didn't always give away her reactions and feelings as easily as he had imagined! He thought back to times in the past when he'd supposed he was reading her like a book. Had he been, really? He hadn't found any answer to that question when the sergeant said:

"It's definite. All three of you picked number eighteen, as did Chandra Mukherjee."

Eleanor gasped. "Of course! I think we all forgot she would have seen him."

"That's right," Trent said. "She says he came in to inquire about roses for his mother. She thought he looked familiar, though he kept his face ducked down and turned away from her as if he were interested in the displays behind him. She also got the impression he was, or had been, crying, something she thought he might want to hide from her, and therefore another reason to conceal his face. As it was, she felt sorry for him and thought the roses might be meant as an apology for a disagreement he'd had with his mother. What I think is that he knew it was possible she'd seen his photo in the newspaper, though not in connection with any of the incidents on Saturday.

"She left the boy alone in the shop while she went in the cooler to get samples of roses in various colors to show him. As it was, his interest in roses probably saved Chandra from injury. When he told her he was just getting ideas and hurried out, she went back into the cooler to put the roses she'd been showing him in their vases. That's when the bomb went off."

He pulled the strip of concealing paper off one row of pictures on a page and turned the page around to face them, pointing to a photo. Then, realizing no one could read the name from where they were sitting, he said, "You've all identified Cody Wells, honor student, and the Eureka Springs Highlander's star football player."

He looked up at them, the sadness in his eyes unmistakable. "Cody Wells. Sonya Wells's seventeen-year-old son."

After a brief silence, Shirley spoke for all of them. "No! Oh, no!"

Chapter 17

There was so much emotion in the silent room that Carrie thought the air itself must be throbbing with it. Finally she lifted her head and said, to no one in particular, "But we didn't know she had a son. The paper didn't mention..."

Sergeant Trent looked at each of them in turn before he answered, speaking so softly she almost couldn't hear him. "Yeah, we managed to keep Cody's name out of the paper. This is a small town...newspaper editor is a friend, and, well...

"See, the kid lived with his dad in St. Louis after the split. When he came to visit his mom last summer, he found out about the football program here and talked with Coach. He tried out and learned he could probably be a star player on our team. He decided to transfer, and he's old enough he has some say about who he lives with. Guess he figured that a chance to excel on a small town team beat second string in a huge city high school, so he came here."

The sergeant smiled, though his head had now dropped and it looked like he was smiling at the floor. "He made the move in time for this school year. I'm on duty at some of the games, and I see him in action. He has the potential to be a Division One player. Coach Thomas says the boy's been pretty cut up about his parents' divorce, but he's a good kid over all and a good student. Now...who knows?"

Eleanor said, "He thinks one of the Mukherjees, or both of them, killed his mother?"

Carrie glared at Lonnie Trent. "Obviously that's just exactly what he thinks," she said. "How on earth did he get that idea, Sergeant Trent?" Anger was beginning to make the cut on her cheek throb.

Trent held up both hands. "Whoa, I didn't say anything to him. But I suspect Aunt Jan has quite a bit to do with what her nephew thinks. She's been telling the police about her belief—no, her *conviction*—that one of the Mukherjees killed her sister, and I suspect she's not keeping that idea to herself when it comes to talking with Cody."

"What are you going to do about him?" Shirley asked.

The sergeant picked at a spot of dirt on the knee of his uniform trousers for a couple of moments before he answered. "Oh, we'll probably end up charging him with the bombing. There aren't a whole lot of choices here. I now have four reliable witnesses putting him on the scene. I suspect, with a little nosing around, we can find evidence proving he made that bomb, and there are enough pieces left to allow for fingerprinting. He isn't exactly a sophisticated criminal, and I doubt he did a good job covering his tracks. Still, I'm not ready to put him in jail yet. His dad arrives today for the mother's memorial service. I hope he can take some time off work and be with his son during the most difficult part of this mess. The kid sure needs a caring parent right now.

"Making and placing a bomb is a serious crime. It could lead to severe injuries or even death. This one certainly did cause property damage. If Cody's convicted, the Mukherjees' insurance company will probably see to it that the Wells family or their insurers end up paying for that damage.

"Assuming Cody made and placed the bomb, of course he has to take responsibility for what he did. I'm afraid he's gonna grow up fast during the next few weeks. But it's sure too bad," he said, shaking his head. "I think putting a kid in jail can sometimes send him down a path toward more criminal activity."

The sergeant's voice faded into silence and Carrie thought how difficult, even how agonizing, some part of every law officer's job is. She knew enough about Henry's career in the Kansas City Police Department to understand what Lonnie Trent was going through. She looked at Henry, noticed that the shadows of sadness on his face mirrored what she saw on Trent's. She reached over, took Henry's hand, and was rewarded with a gentle half-smile.

"Ah, well, we'll see," Trent said. "And as for Aunt Jan? I have no clue what to do about her, other than try and get her to keep her yap shut and her suspicions to herself. It's obvious she's poisoning the kid. Wouldn't be surprised if she put him up to the bombing, but that's off the record."

He glanced up at Detective Wolverton as he said that, and Carrie thought he looked nervous. Maybe the detective was a stickler for by-the-book policing, and Trent believed she wouldn't approve of any off-the-record conversation.

Henry said, "Is there any evidence at all that indicates the Mukherjees are responsible for Sonya Wells's death? I assumed, since I noticed the rigor, that she was killed earlier in the day, possibly at a time when witnesses could vouch for their whereabouts."

Carrie stared at Henry and wondered if he had consciously revealed what they both knew was confidential information. Whatever. She wanted to hug him. A glance at Sergeant Trent told her his expression was bland, unreadable.

Detective Wolverton said, "That's privileged information, Major King, but correct. It will be some time before we have an autopsy, but what we observe indicates early afternoon as the time of death." She looked around the room, her eyes resting briefly on each of their faces: Shirley, Eleanor, Jason, Henry, and Carrie herself. "None of you is to reveal this to anyone else yet. Do you understand me?"

Everyone nodded.

After a pause, Henry stood. "Well, we'd best leave you to your more-than-difficult task. If you're through with these ladies for now, I suggest we get out of your way and head home."

Carrie couldn't believe she'd heard him correctly. He wanted to *leave?* No way!

"We can't leave Eureka Springs now," she said. "I, for one, want to talk more with Chandra, give her our support, and see when we can have a new appointment for wedding planning."

"But..." Henry began.

She rushed ahead. "I'm sure she and Ashur will be glad

to know we have no plan to change florists. If they're willing, I still want to use them for our wedding. I suspect you guys would like to see the flower shop site anyway, just for curiosity if no other reason. Am I right?"

"Whoa," the sergeant said. "That place is off limits. It may not be dangerous now unless bits of stuff fall from the ceiling, but it's still a crime scene. I don't want any of you messing around inside the shop."

"Carrie, I don't think this is wise," Henry said.

"I have no intention of going back inside the shop," Carrie answered, "and you men are forgetting that Eleanor's car is there. We need to pick it up.

"Besides," she said, warming to her cause, "I came to Eureka Springs for a business appointment with Artistic Floral Designs. I intend to keep that appointment—in the street, if necessary. I should think it would be doubly difficult for the Mukherjees to think they're losing business because a bomb messed up their shop. And, if they need my help cleaning up the mess, well, I can even do that."

She stood, and Shirley and Eleanor came to stand beside her, each of them looking determined.

Sergeant Trent said, "No way are you cleaning up yet. I repeat—it's a crime scene."

"I didn't mean clean up right this minute," Carrie said in her stiffest voice. "But we can at least go there to offer moral support."

Henry and the sergeant both shrugged and Henry said, "Then Jason and I will come along, help keep these women out of trouble. All right with you, Sergeant?"

Carrie bristled instantly at Henry's implication he was needed to keep *these women* out of trouble, but the pique shut down just as quickly when he winked in her direction. So, it had—probably—been a joke. She might have known he'd realize how such a comment would, as he sometimes said, "rattle her chains." And that, too, was supposed to be a joke.

Trent said, "Oh, go on, all of you." He waved his hand in a sweeping motion. "But don't you dare cross any yellow tape!"

Carrie marched out of the room, followed closely by Shirley and Eleanor. When she got to the parking lot she turned, saw that Jason had grabbed Eleanor's discarded clothing, and he and Henry were hurrying to catch up with them.

The Mukherjees were easy to find. They stood on the sidewalk at the front corner of their building talking to a man who held a clipboard. The third parking space in front of the shop was now occupied by a van boasting "Expert Remodeling" on its side panels. Carrie was amazed to see repairs were already being planned. Henry slowed as they drove past the building, and everyone gawked.

"Well, that sidewalk cover sure is a wreck," Jason said, his voice sounding quivery. "Looks like it's very heavy. A good thing none of you were under it. Shop itself is boarded up, can't tell much about that. Our car's covered with dust but I don't see any damage." His words ran out into silence.

Carrie waved at Officer Gibson who was standing guard, keeping traffic and sight-seeing pedestrians moving. A pick-up truck pulled out of a parking space down the street and Henry took its place. "Now what?" he asked.

"Now we get out," Eleanor said, "and walk back to the shop. We talk to the Mukherjees about the wedding, then we ask if there is anything we can do to help them today. We look at our car, check up close for dents. Okay?"

From her place beside Henry in the front seat of the car Carrie turned and gave Eleanor a thumbs-up sign.

Jason said, "Now, sweetheart, maybe we should just leave those poor folks alone."

"No, Jason, we should not. We should be good neighbors to people in need of help. Seems to me this family needs us right now. We're here, we can at least offer friendship and support."

"But, but, you've never even *met* these people before today," Jason said. "How can...?" He sputtered to a stop and, suddenly and surprisingly, looked pensive.

At that moment he and Eleanor might have been the only occupants of the car. In the front seat, Carrie and Henry remained quiet while their friends worked through what seemed to be more than just a decision about the Mukherjees. Shirley, sitting next to Eleanor in the back seat, gazed out the side window at buildings across the street from where they were parked.

Eleanor released her seat belt and squiggled around to face her husband. "No, Jason, I hadn't met them before today. Does that really matter?"

After a reflective silence, he said, "You're absolutely right, my dear, it doesn't matter."

He opened the car door, got out, and bent down to offer a hand to his wife.

When the five of them were within a few yards of the Mukherjees, their steps slowed, then stopped. Chandra and Ashur were so intent on their conversation with the contractor they didn't look around.

Kurt Gibson glanced toward their group but merely nodded and didn't tell them to move away. Carrie suspected Sergeant Trent had warned him they were coming to see the Mukherjees.

After they'd stood in a huddle on the sidewalk for a few moments she wondered if she should say something to get Ashur and Chandra's attention. She didn't want to interrupt and began to feel uncertain about the rightness of their presence here. Maybe they should simply get Eleanor's car and drive away.

That's when Ashur turned and saw her. He hurried over, hands extended. "Chandra has told me how you ignored danger to come find her in the wreckage," he said, "and now, I see that you were hurt when she wasn't even touched. How can we ever thank you sufficiently? Once more, you have come to our rescue in a time of crisis. I think you are what is called a guardian angel."

Carrie wasn't sure what to say in the face of this commentary, so she said nothing.

Henry wasn't so tongue-tied. "We're here to assure you we still want Artistic Floral Designs to plan our wedding, provided you're willing and it isn't too much of a burden at this time."

Ashur smiled ruefully and waved his arm toward the boarded-up shop. "As you can see, everything is on hold right now. But of course we have the greenhouses with a selection of flowers and plants, and if we get the shop put back together by the time of your wedding, there will be other flowers to choose from as well. We are fortunate the damage wasn't worse."

All of them looked toward the stairs at the side of the building as a door slammed and a young man, taller and more athletic than his father, stormed down, feet banging on the wooden steps. He appeared to be possessed by some strong emotion, and when he got close enough to speak, his voice betrayed him. It was shaking with fury.

"Dad, Sergeant Trent just called. They're about ready to charge Cody Wells with the bombing, but aren't jailing him yet. The boy's father is supposed to be here soon, but in the meantime Trent is leaving him in the custody of his aunt. That viper! She probably put him up to this in the first place. You just wait, she'll find some way to get him off without any punishment. After all, he isn't a *foreigner.* *He belongs!*"

By now the young man had joined their group and was glaring malevolently around the circle of white faces. "So, what do *you* want?" he asked.

"This is my son, Purdy," Ashur said calmly. "Purdy, please say hello to Carrie McCrite, the woman who risked her life to help your mother after the bomb went off. We will be doing the flowers for her wedding. Here is her friend, Henry King. He's the groom in that wedding. The other people came to Eureka Springs with them to take part in wedding planning and arrived just as the bomb went off. Ms. McCrite and Mr. King were also with us Saturday night when someone shot into the Crescent Conservatory. Then too, they acted to save us from harm."

Purdy Mukherjee's stormy face began to relax, its cherry-tinged color returning to light mahogany. Carrie could tell he was making a strong effort to control his emotions as he said, "My apologies for my attitude, it's just that..."

They all sensed new movement by the apartment's side door and glanced back toward the stairs.

Purdy's face softened into a gentleness that matched his parents' customary bearing as a pale, ethereal-looking brunette appeared on the landing. With an exclamation, "Rebecca!" he hurried toward the stairs and raced up them to the woman's side. While the little group watched in silence he put his arm around his wife and they started down the stairs, one careful step at a time.

Carrie thought she might ordinarily have said this sprite of a girl floated down the stairs, except right now she looked very pregnant and wasn't floating anywhere—unless you made an unfortunate comparison to a floating whale.

Purdy led the young woman to them and said, "My wife, Rebecca. As you can see, she is to present us with a son next month. This is one reason I'm easily agitated. You must forgive my behavior, we haven't had a baby before. Besides, with Saturday's events and now this," he swept his arm toward the shop, "there has been so much..."

He shook his head as if to dispel demons and continued. "I want to remain calm—for Rebecca and for our baby." He looked at his wife with such love in his eyes that Carrie glanced away, embarrassed to be a spectator at what she considered a very private moment.

When Purdy spoke again, his animosity toward Cody Wells had either been shoved aside or forgotten. "We have decided," he said proudly, "that this baby will be named Ashur Charles, after our fathers."

Rebecca smiled at them absent-mindedly before she turned to her husband. "Purdy, I came to tell you that... I've called the doctor...Charlie has decided to come early. We need to go to the hospital now."

Carrie looked at the young woman more closely and thought, *Wow, presentation time.*

Ashur said in an almost-squeak, "Oh, my," and hurried away toward Chandra. Purdy seemed dumbstruck and stared at his wife without moving.

Eleanor spoke up, her voice firm with the authority of a woman who has had three children and watched the birth of two grandchildren, "My car is right here. Purdy, help your wife into the back seat. Jason can drive. I'll ride with him and the two of you. Henry, you, Shirley and Carrie bring Purdy's parents as soon as they're ready to come."

She smiled over her shoulder as she unlocked her car. "Fortunately, we already know exactly where the hospital is."

Chapter 18

After quick consultation with his wife, Ashur drove away in the green van, heading for Rebecca and Purdy's home next to the family greenhouses at the edge of town. He would pick up Rebecca's hospital bag and be sure the greenhouses were secure for the night. Chandra rode directly to the hospital with Carrie, Henry, and Shirley.

When they joined Eleanor and Jason in the waiting room, Eleanor reported the doctor had arrived and said everything was progressing normally, though the baby was early. Purdy would stay with Rebecca during labor and delivery. Chandra left the room at once to find the doctor and her children.

As soon as she'd gone, Eleanor said, "Jason, Shirley, and I might as well go home. There really isn't anything more we can do for the Mukherjees tonight, and there's no need for us to sit here and wait for the baby. Carrie, you and Henry can report to us later."

Shirley nodded. "Fine with me. I'd just as soon get on

home. Milking time will get me up early enough in the morning. I'm ready, except I'd like to stop off in the ladies' before I leave. Do you mind waiting for me?"

"Nope, we'll be in the car," Jason said.

Chandra was down the hall speaking with the doctor, and Henry had picked up a magazine. Ignoring them both, Shirley took Carrie's arm as soon as Eleanor and Jason left, pulling her toward the restroom. When they were inside, she said, "Maybe you and Henry will stay here a while and you can spend time with Chandra alone? She needs help. The two of us had a few words in the back seat of the car on the way over while you and Henry were talking.

"It's easy to tell she's mighty worried that the police suspect her and Ashur of murdering the Wells woman. What with that, plus being scared someone is going to shoot them at any moment, their shop being bombed, and this new grandbaby—well, it's a heavy load to carry. I don't reckon she has real cause to worry about being accused of murder, but she doesn't know that, and we all got sworn to silence about the time of death. Give the poor woman your ear, I'm sure you can help her. She's honestly afraid she'll be in jail or shot to death before her grandchild knows her.

"I was also thinking, because of how we all are—older folk who have a reason to be here doing wedding planning—that the three of us, you, me, and Eleanor, could come back later this week to help the Mukherjee family. For one thing, it's possible we can find out things the police can't. We might visit the Owens' flower shop, maybe catch Ms. Owen there, and besides talking to her about wedding flowers, we'd be real nice, get on her good side. Could be we might hear something important. What do you think?"

"Good ideas," Carrie said. "If anyone ever needed our friendship, seems to me Chandra does. I'll do what I can."

When the two women came back into the waiting room, Henry put down his magazine and stood. As he walked toward them, Shirley asked, "How about FatCat? Is she okay? Should I go by your place and feed her?"

Henry was now close enough to hear and he said, "I stopped by Carrie's on the way to pick up Jason so I could feed FatCat and give her fresh water. I also got Carrie's overnight bag and found an extra outfit for her since I had no idea if she was badly enough hurt she'd have to spend the night here. I brought my travel things too and a change of clothes. I didn't know if we'd need to stay over, you know..."

Shirley was facing away from him, and she winked at Carrie. "That's good, Henry. Well, call and give us baby news tomorrow morning, and don't you stay up too late. It's been a wearying day." She hugged Carrie and was out the door.

Henry said, "I guess we are planning to spend the night here? How about I go to the Crescent now, find out if they have a room with two beds? Maybe they aren't so busy on Mondays."

Carrie could see down the hall behind Henry's back and it looked like Chandra was finishing her conversation with the doctor. Eager to get Henry out of the way, she said, "Why don't you do that? If they have a room, you can go ahead and put our things in it if you like. And...thanks for thinking to bring my stuff. I was really in a mental fuzz when I told you not to bother with bringing me clean clothes. All I wanted then was to see you as quickly as possible. Besides, who'd have known we'd get a baby coming tonight?"

She opened her purse and located a charge card. "Here, use this at the hotel."

After a short hesitation, he took the card and said, "There's a fast-food place up on the highway. You want me to bring us burgers?"

She said, "That would be great, but call me before you leave the hotel. Chandra may want something too, and I don't know if she eats meat. I'm pretty sure she wouldn't eat beef at least. She'll be back soon, I'll find out."

Henry gave her a quick hug and a forehead kiss. He was gone by the time Chandra walked back into the room and dropped on the couch. Carrie sat next to her and took her hand. "Everything going okay?" she asked.

"Yes. Even though Charlie's a month early the doctor says things look good, and, because of the circumstances, he may come quickly. I'm sure Rebecca hopes so. But, poor Purdy. He faithfully practiced the breathing and those other preparations with Rebecca. He was so calm, big-man cool, was all ready to be her labor coach. But now he's gone funny on us. Can't seem to say a coherent word except, 'Oh, Rebecca, oh, oh,' over and over. I wouldn't be surprised if he faints when the baby comes. I could tell he was embarrassed to have his mother see this, so I stepped out for a while."

Silence fell as Chandra retreated into her own thoughts. From the look on her face, Carrie guessed she wasn't as happy as a new grandmother should be when the grandchild's birth is going well. Carrie agreed with Shirley that the concern went beyond a new baby or even Wells's murder. Being shot at? Repeated vandalism? Harassment? How much was a person supposed to take?

If only she could explain to Chandra that Sonya Wells

probably died in the afternoon, that would ease a big chunk of her worries. *If only!*

"You okay, Chandra? You've had a lot of trouble the past few days."

More silence. Carrie decided to prod.

"What information do the police have about the murder of Sonya Wells?"

For a minute Carrie thought even that direct question wasn't going to get a response, but then Chandra began to cry. Evidently Sergeant Trent had not shared any hopeful information with the Mukherjees. Inwardly she cursed him for not telling them about the probable time of death. It was sure too bad that detective had sworn the rest of them to silence. She understood the reasons, but a little comforting knowledge would mean a lot to Chandra right now.

Carrie pulled tissues from a box on the nearby table and put them in Chandra's hand. "Everything will be okay, you'll see. The police can't really suspect you or your family."

The crying became quieter as Chandra lifted her shoulders in a shrug.

Carrie decided talking about Saturday might help the poor woman, and maybe she could manage, off-hand, to inject a positive fact or two.

"Saturday night Henry and I saw you in the hotel parking lot about thirty minutes after we thought you'd left. Did the police ask you why you were late leaving that night?"

Chandra blew her nose and, speaking to her lap, said, "Yes."

Carrie tried to think of a question that would require more than a simple yes or no answer. "Okay. So what was your reason for being delayed?"

"There was a note..."

Working to encourage conversation, Carrie said, "A note? What kind of note? Where was it?"

A sniff. More nose blowing. "After we left you, we went straight to the van, and there was a business card under the windshield wiper. It was Melissa Donley's card and had a note printed on the back saying she wanted to talk with Ashur in the hotel right away about a last-minute change in wedding plans. We assumed she meant the wedding we're decorating for clients of hers this weekend..."

The words were cut off by a choking sound. Chandra said, "Oh, all our beautiful things are ruined. How can we be ready for the weekend? Purdy and Rebecca won't be able to help because of the baby. I planned to clear my schedule at the end of the month so I could stay with Rebecca after Charlie came. Now Purdy will have to do that."

"Never mind," Carrie said, "Eleanor, Shirley, and I will come over later this week to help both you and Rebecca. We're not flower artists like you, but maybe there's plain stuff we can manage. And if you need workers to climb ladders and help Ashur build and carry things, Henry will come, too. Besides, I'm sure you have friends here who can help."

Chandra shook her head but said nothing.

"So, back to the note. What did you do about it?"

"Ashur pulled the van out of the area near the front of the hotel so the incoming wedding party could have our space. He parked in the first empty slot we came to, then went to find Melissa."

"She only wanted to talk with your husband? The note said 'Ashur'? It didn't mention you?"

"That's right, and at first we wondered why. But then

we decided Melissa might have gotten a last-minute phone call from the bride, or another person connected with the wedding, asking about financial arrangements. They do get jittery and often ask more and more questions the closer the time comes. We thought they must want quick clarification on a financial matter. Since Ashur is the one who takes care of the technical and financial part of the business and Melissa knows that, it was logical he would go to clear up questions like this by himself.

"At first I was afraid to wait alone after what had happened in the conservatory, but I was very tired, and I remembered Kurt Gibson was on guard nearby. When Ashur left, I locked the doors of the van and waited."

"You didn't see or hear anyone in the parking lot or the woods next to the van during that time?"

"No, but I had my eyes closed. I may have dozed off."

"You know something, Chandra, it's possible Ms. Wells was put on that hillside long before you came out of the hotel to go home. Have you thought of that? Maybe that's why you didn't see or hear anything—she was already dead."

Chandra stared at her, and Carrie changed the subject, not wanting to let what she'd just revealed stand out.

"How long was Ashur gone?"

"A long time. Finally I began to worry. I was just getting out to go in the hotel and see what was wrong when I saw him coming from the worker's door by the hotel laundry. After he got in the van, he said he couldn't find Melissa.

"When he didn't see her on the first floor, he asked the desk clerk where she was, and the man said Melissa had gone home. Ashur told him she'd left us a note requesting a meeting that night. The man then said she could have clocked out and gone to the New Moon Spa on the lower level. Evidently she sometimes goes to the spa after work to relax and drink herbal tea with a friend who's a masseuse there.

"So Ashur went to the spa. Melissa wasn't anywhere around, and they told him the masseuse had left for the day. He walked down the hall past the massage and water therapy rooms but saw no one. That hall has an exit leading to the maintenance shop and laundry and then to the outside. He came through, let himself out the employee entrance, got in the van, and we went home. We didn't see anything really unusual in all this, though we were puzzled about Melissa leaving a message and not staying to meet with Ashur."

"Did you keep the card with the note?"

"The police asked us the same thing. Ashur told them he dropped it in a trash can near the hotel entrance. He'd read it, after all. He knew what it said."

"Did they find it?"

"I don't know if they even looked."

"I'm sure they looked, so they probably have it. Do you know if the handwriting appeared to be Melissa's?"

"It was printed. Just a few words on the back of her business card. I didn't think about handwriting. I'm sure Ashur didn't, either."

"Did she sign it?" Carrie was sure she already knew the answer to that question.

"No, she didn't. I do remember that."

"Did the police comment on any of this?"

"No."

"And after Ashur got back in the van, you went home?"

"Straight home. Then, on Sunday morning that woman detective, Gloria Wolverton, came to our apartment. She told us about the murder and asked us to describe our actions on Saturday beginning at noon. That was how she put it, 'describe your actions.' We told her all four of us were in our shop making last-minute preparations for the evening wedding. Then we loaded both vans, Purdy and Rebecca left for the chapel, and we came to the Crescent."

"Did customers come into the shop while you were working there?"

"Yes, several. Saturday is often especially busy because people pick up flowers they've ordered earlier for Saturday evening events."

"Well, then, you all have alibis."

"So what good is that? Look at what happened today. Obviously the police told Jan Owen, and maybe Cody, they suspected us."

"Chandra, I can assure you no one told Jan Owen or her nephew they suspect you of anything. She thought that up by herself. But it sounds as if you know it was most likely Sonya Wells's son who came to your shop and left the bomb?"

"Yes. I thought the boy who came in about the roses looked familiar, and I then remembered seeing his picture in the paper. He's one of the best players on our high school football team. When Lonnie—Sergeant Trent—showed me photographs, I identified his picture.

"The poor boy, what he must be suffering. I think about when Purdy was seventeen and what he might have done if someone hurt either of us, or if he even *thought* someone did. It amounts to the same thing in the mind of a seventeen-year-old boy. To have his mother killed..."

Carrie wasn't at all surprised this woman had compassion for the person who was supposed to have bombed her shop.

Now Chandra lifted her head and stared at Carrie. "Saturday night you and Mr. King knew exactly what to do about that shooting. He acts like he has experience with these things, and I heard you tell Kurt Gibson you two worked as detectives, to help people. If this is so, can we hire you?"

Carrie's cell phone interrupted them, and when she answered, Henry said, "They had a room, so we're fixed up for the night. Any thoughts about supper yet?"

Carrie explained the possibility of supper to Chandra who said she liked the bean-veggie burritos from the drive-in, and would Henry bring enough for Ashur and Purdy, too? Carrie gave their order and turned toward Chandra again.

"No, you can't hire us. We don't help people for money. We just help people."

"Can you find out who shot at us and who killed Sonya Wells?"

"That's a job for the police. I'm sure they'll accomplish more than we could."

Chandra was holding Carrie's hand so tightly it had begun to hurt. "But they suspect us and don't seem to understand Ashur and I would never think of doing something like that."

"Chandra, I'm sure they couldn't really suspect you. If it seems that way, don't forget we humans sometimes judge others in the light of what we ourselves might do under similar circumstances. It may be that Kurt Gibson and Lonnie Trent would have wanted to strike out at the Owen family, to retaliate, if they were in your place. I don't mean they'd actually do it, or that they think you would, but they still could believe they understand how someone under stress might, especially if they'd been shot at like you were on Saturday night."

Chandra protested, "They are officers of the law. They should not judge."

"They're human," Carrie said. "But I'm only making guesses now, since we can't get inside their heads. In the same way, they can't get inside your thinking. They don't know anything for sure, but I don't agree with you that they believe you or Ashur could ever be killers."

Chandra relaxed, if only slightly, and the two women sat together in silence, holding hands. Then Carrie said, very softly, "What those men really know about you will take over. What's true governs them as it does you."

Dear God, she thought, *that has to be right.*

From somewhere behind them a woman's voice said, "Mrs. Mukherjee? Your grandson is going to make an appearance soon. Would you like to come with me?"

Chapter 19

"I didn't have to lie about it," Carrie said as Henry drove out of the hospital parking lot. "He really is a beautiful baby, month early or not. All that dark hair... And his skin is such a pretty color, not even red—honey tan I'd call it. Hmmm? Didn't you think he was beautiful?"

"I've never been around new babies," Henry admitted, "so I have nothing to compare him with. He's sure little. Did you see his fingers? Amazing things. Are just-born babies always that tiny?"

"He's a bit small by today's full-term averages. What did the nurse say, five pounds, ten ounces? But we humans do start out small...compared with what we grow to later."

Henry was still full of wonder at the evening's baby event—his first, as he'd just admitted—but he wasn't sure he wanted to admit how naive he'd been about newborns. His only previous experience came from stories shared by fellow officers who had new babies, or the depiction of a baby's arrival on some television series.

Carrie, however, was obviously glad to talk about the baby. Probably all women were.

Well, he could tell her what Purdy Mukherjee said. After all, Purdy had been there to assist his wife through the whole thing.

"Purdy told me how fathers take part in a baby's birth today. He said his role was to be strong for Rebecca, especially at the worst times, encourage her, remind her when to pant in breaths like this." Henry demonstrated. "He wiped her face with a cold cloth and gave her crushed ice to suck on if she wanted it. He described what happened when it was time for Rebecca to push the baby out, and he was right there, of course, to welcome his son the minute his head appeared. Amazing!" He glanced at Carrie, felt a sudden melting tenderness for her, and for all those who had given birth. He reached over to touch her hand, but quickly turned his attention back to the road, negotiating a sharp curve and barely missing a parked car.

At the same moment Carrie swallowed a giggle and decided not to burst Henry's bubble about how strong the new father had been. Chandra's version of Purdy's part in his son's birth was sure different, and undoubtedly more accurate. Carrie would have been willing to bet Purdy loved having the awed Henry as an audience while they bonded over bean burritos and hamburgers and the young man related his role during labor and delivery to a totally ignorant listener. That would provide a needed boost to the ego of a man who fainted at the sight of what, admittedly, could be a messy and painful process.

Nope, best not to tell Henry that big daddy had welcomed his son by babbling through most of the birth and passing out the minute the baby appeared.

"Of course," Henry continued, "you know all about this unless things have changed since Rob was born."

"Hmmm, babies still come pretty much the same way," Carrie said, "but the procedure for dads has changed. Back when Rob was born, prospective fathers were usually stuck in an institutional waiting room until after their baby arrived. Not that it would have mattered with Amos. He was in the middle of a big embezzlement trial he couldn't get away from and didn't arrive at the hospital until two hours after his son did. His first view of Rob was through the nursery window. I was asleep by then and wasn't aware Amos had finally come."

"He missed a lot," Henry mumbled, and that was the end of the conversation. They had arrived at the Crescent Hotel.

An hour later they were each seated in an elegant double bed, leaning on pillows propped against carved Victorian headboards.

"If this is an ordinary room, I can't wait to see the fancy ones," Carrie said as she bounced her hand up and down against the puffy quilt. When she pushed against it, the soft comforter flattened. As soon as she lifted her hand, returning air puffed the indentation under where her hand had been.

Henry watched her play with the comforter for a moment, then shrugged. "It is fancy. All I asked for was a regular room with two beds. This one sounded okay and, for a place like this, seemed reasonable. I could almost afford it by myself." He laughed, and Carrie heard irony instead of humor.

"Henry, my love," she said, "we've had this discussion before. You and I both know quite well that your daughter's job at the brokerage firm made it possible for her to trace the investments Evan stole from me and from Amos. I wouldn't have this extra money if I hadn't met you and gotten to know Susan. So, even if you're old-fashioned enough to think that the fella always has to pay for the lady, you've got to admit you have as much right to enjoy what she recouped for us as Rob and I do."

He lifted his hands, palms up and smiled over at her. "I don't see it that way."

"Well, I do, especially since we're getting married."

"Which reminds me, Carrie, we need to go to a lawyer and make out a pre-nuptial agreement."

"Not right now, I hope. Right now I'm trying to get you to see that the extra money I have is all Susan's doing. So, accept sharing and hush. Didn't your mother tell you it was good to share?"

He gave up. "Okay, okay. Old habits die hard. But, I guess it can't be much of a habit with me because, of course, Irena was the one with money in my first marriage. I'm doomed to be a kept man."

"Come to think of it, my father was a kept man too... more or less. Mom often had to work to keep us in food and pay the rent. You'd think letting the woman pay would come easier for me now."

"Kept man, hm? That ought to add to your ego, Henry King. Two women have considered you well worth any price, or at least I know this one does. And phooey, money is just something we're given to use in doing good for ourselves and others. Who cares what the source is?"

When he started to open his mouth, she added, "Legal source, of course."

There was a moment of silence before she said, "You

mentioned that your mother often had to work to keep the family in food. I'm sure Catherine's mother had to do the same thing."

"*Catherine?* What's *she* got to do with this? Huh! I suspect her mother was a working woman all right...in the oldest profession, if you get my meaning."

"Henry! What an awful thing to say. Besides, it isn't true. That woman worked hard on a factory assembly line making electric motors. She got good wages for a woman because she was a union memb..."

Carrie swallowed the rest of her sentence as she noticed the look on Henry's face and realized what she'd just revealed. She'd done it again. Blabber mouth!

Well, Catherine said she wouldn't come to their wedding if Henry didn't want her. That meant she had to ask him about it some time. It might as well be now.

Very slowly he threw back his comforter and came to sit on the edge of her bed. Carrie noticed he was careful to keep plenty of air space between them and made no effort to touch her. For an unguarded moment, she was sorry.

"It sounds like we have something to discuss."

So she told him—about wanting to surprise him by inviting his sister to their wedding, about the Internet search, about Catherine's reply to her inquiry.

He was quiet for a long time, then went back to his own bed, settled himself, and remained quiet for an even longer time. Finally, he spoke. "I don't know what to say, I really don't."

"Because you're mad at me?"

"Noooo, not that. And I was already suspicious you might have tried to contact her. When we were having dinner on Sunday you were deep in thought about something. I tried to figure out what it was and she came to mind. After all, you'd asked what family members I had left when we were discussing wedding plans, and I told you about her. You love a mystery, Catherine is obviously a big mystery. It was possible she was the subject of your deep thought. Right?"

She grinned at him. "I hate it when you're psychic. No, take that back. Actually, I'm relieved. Yes, I did contact your sister and…"

"Half-sister."

"I contacted Catherine King. She's thirty-three years old now and a partner in a law firm in Claremore, Oklahoma."

Henry's exclamation told her he realized how close his sister was when talking about miles.

"Henry, she's eager to meet you. I won't go into the reasons she hasn't tried to before; you probably can guess most of them anyway. She hasn't had an easy life, but she did love her father—and yours—and isn't sorry her parents married. I can let you read her e-mail if you want, she didn't say I couldn't show it to you. But she won't come to our wedding unless you know I invited her and you want her to come too. So there. End of story. Up to you."

"Carrie, I can't even begin to talk about this now. Give me some time to think."

"Okay. Let's talk about something else: Sonya Wells's murder. At the hospital, Chandra asked me if we'd help find the killer. She believes the police suspect her or Ashur or both of them and is more than a little concerned they'll be arrested. That, together with the shooting, the bombing, and the baby…well, she's very disturbed.

"I wish the police would tell the Mukherjees about time of death, and I'm glad you mentioned rigor in the waiting room, though I'm not sure Eleanor and Shirley know what that implies. I couldn't say much to Chandra, of course, but did manage to hint that Wells might have been killed in the afternoon, not at night. Anyone could speculate about that.

"She told me why she and Ashur were at the hotel late on Saturday night and what all of them were doing in the afternoon." She repeated the story of the afternoon wedding preparations, the business card under the windshield wiper, and what Ashur and Chandra had done after finding it. "Henry, surely we can help them?"

He thought for a minute, then said, "There really isn't much we can do that the police can't do better. It sounds like they're conducting a proper investigation."

"But there may be things they won't think to ask, or facts we can discover more easily than they can."

Carrie pictured the knife sheath that was still wrapped in a tissue in her jacket pocket. She knew she should tell Henry about the stupid thing she'd done in the parking lot on Saturday night, but just couldn't seem to manage it.

The fact she'd removed the piece of cardboard from the scene certainly reduced its value as possible evidence, for better or worse. That realization had flashed into her thoughts within minutes of when she concealed it in the tissue and picked it up. She was then, as now, horrified by what she'd done on impulse, thinking she was acting only to protect the Mukherjees from accusation based on false evidence. By the time she'd realized the further implications, Kurt Gibson had joined her and she didn't have the courage to take the knife sheath out of her pocket and admit her stupidity.

Did the cardboard have important fingerprints on it? The killer's fingerprints? The Mukherjees'? That question, too, had been rocketing back and forth in her mind for two days.

"Henry, tell me the truth. Do you think there's a possibility Chandra or Ashur killed that woman?"

He thought about it and realized reluctantly that he enjoyed going back to recall helpful ideas from his police training and experience. "No, not really," he said finally. "They don't fit the profile. And, if their alibis hold..."

Without willing it, his mind returned to the woman at the museum in Kansas City. She'd seemed so unlikely a killer, and her harmless appearance was probably what had cost the caretaker his life. She certainly didn't fit any pre-determined profile, especially a visual one.

He shifted uneasily under his comforter, still bothered by the museum murder.

"Well, then," Carrie said, "*that's* something we can do. We are coming at the investigation with fresh minds that don't believe it's possible the Mukherjees could have done this killing. We start by knowing they don't fit the profile you're talking about. On the other hand, Trent can't help suspecting them, at least until witnesses prove where they were when she was killed. Right?"

"Yes-s-s."

"Okay. First question. What about that knife by the body? I suppose they're going to test it for fingerprints? Can we find out the results?"

"Not quickly enough to do any good in the near future. All that has to go to Little Rock. Besides, the knife had a fancy handle. It was decorated with a rose that had wings and the initials IBE. Might not show clean fingerprints."

"I'm not talking about matching prints with just anyone. Can't they compare local prints right here?"

"Possible. But even if they find prints, they aren't likely to share that information with us."

She blew a raspberry of frustration. "What *can* we do? There has to be something. I guess I could ask Chandra about the knife."

"I wouldn't. Remember, we aren't to talk about that. Trent rightly believes someone might mention details only the few of us, plus the killer, would be aware of."

"Hmmmm. Then we need to learn who might have had access to a knife like that. Maybe we can think of some way to find out if there were knife cuts or stabs on the body. Or—was it put there only to throw suspicion on the Mukherjees?"

Henry had already thought of that possibility. He considered it again while Carrie reached for the phone book in the bedside table and opened it to "Florists." She skimmed down the page. "Artistic Floral Designs seems to be the only firm here with the IBE logo by its name. Otherwise, no flying roses. Not everyone may brag about their affiliations in ads, but several shops do list other national delivery services."

Carrie's voice faded into the background as Henry sat in his bed, thinking now about his wedding, and his wedding night...

If only we could have been just us for this short while, just a simple bride and groom, only for a few weeks, no crimes hitting us in the face, no people in need, no...

"Henry?"

If only... "Um, yes, little love?"

"There's probably something we can do to help."

"You're right, of course. There are things we might do to help find the truth. But, for now, I'm beat. I guess that baby wore me out." He reached for the light switch. "I'd just as soon get a fresh start on all this in the morning. How about you?"

"Probably right. We'll get a better start in the morning." She turned out her light, too.

"Henry?"

"Umhm."

"This is what we're meant to do. Help out, I mean."

"Probably right, little love," he said, "probably right."

Chapter 20

Tat-tat.

Henry turned on his side and tucked the comforter over his exposed ear, pushing the sound away.

Minimum consciousness assured him that he and Carrie were safely asleep in a quiet hotel room. There was no need to awaken, no pending crisis to face. The night was peaceful. He prepared to drop back into sleep.

Swish-shh, swish-shh.

Huh? Carrie must be moving between her sheets, turning over. Was she awake? His mind pictured her moving next to him in the same bed. A few more weeks and...

Thinking about Carrie in the second bed brought back images of their recent vacation trip to Hot Springs, where he'd asked her to marry him, getting on his knees while she sat on one of the beds in their hotel room. He'd wondered then if men still knelt to propose, but though Carrie smiled at him, she didn't laugh, so it had been okay. She said it was romantic. *And...she said yes.*

Carrie had explained rooming together in Hot Springs was cheaper and more convenient than phoning back and forth between rooms. ("It's only fair. If women can room together as friends, why can't we?")

Henry thought the experience was kind of like a try-out for being married.

Remembering Hot Springs, his lips curved in a smile until, unbidden, another image from that trip flashed into his head. He saw death approaching at the hands of a homicidal lunatic. He'd probably been in more danger then than at any time during his long police career, and Carrie was the one who saved his life. She'd come just in time, swinging an iron pipe, putting her own life in terrible peril. So they'd survived, and partly because of what the experience taught them about their feelings for each other, they were getting ready to be married.

A shiver chilled his spine and he forced the near-death memory away, directing his body to take deep, even breaths. His thoughts moved on, but they still weren't quiet.

Why? Because now Carrie had promised to help the Mukherjees. That meant the two of them were involved in detective work again. But that was his Carrie.

In Hot Springs it had been her curiosity about a hidden treasure that drew them into mystery and murder. More often, though, people seemed to sense that Carrie could somehow help them in times of deep trouble. Then, without willing it, the two of them would be at work together, using her warm heart and quick mind, his reasoning, law-enforcement knowledge, and detective skills. Ah, well. Maybe he should accept this as destiny, his and hers. He was certainly aware she thought of it that way.

And now it was Chandra and Ashur. Well, they'd do

what they could, but their wedding must remain the most important thing on the agenda. He was sure Carrie felt that as strongly as he did.

He turned back to his other side, pulled the comforter up, and, once more, imagined Carrie snuggled warmly against him. Mmm, soon. He was a lucky man, lucky—coming late to love.

Coming late to love. Sounded like a song title.

Maybe he'd just write a song for Carrie. He'd played the guitar when he was in college and even wrote a few songs back then. People said, even now, that his voice wasn't half bad. Since he was no longer Police Major Henry King, he had more time for music. But he'd have to buy a new guitar, do a lot of practicing, maybe even take lessons. It had been a long time...

He moved his legs, felt the smoothness of the sheets and, imagining music, began the pleasant drop into slumber.

Tat-tat. Tat-tat. Swish-shh.

This time the sounds jerked him into full awareness and he pushed the covers back, listening. A knock?

Tat-tat.

More like something rattling. He sat up, scooted to the edge of the bed, eyes searching the darkness for movement. Carrie? Had she gotten up to go to the bathroom?

No, not Carrie. He could hear the soft wiffle of her even breathing coming from the next bed.

Tat-tat. Swish-shh, swish-shh.

He pushed his feet into flip-flops, stood, and slid quietly toward the hall door. Ear against wood, he waited.

Once more the silence teased him into confused annoyance, and he stepped back from the door, wondering if he should open it and check the hall outside. He hesitated, not wanting to disturb Carrie.

The next sound made the decision for him. The "Tat-tat" was so loud that she mumbled, "Henry?" and he heard her sit up. The bedside lamp went on, and she asked, "What was that noise?"

He didn't look back, simply shook his head as he opened the door, very slowly.

Their room was in the north wing of the hotel, at the intersection of two corridors. It faced an elaborately outfitted stairway coming down from the floors above them and stopping, for no reason he could understand, on their floor. Getting down one more floor to the lobby level meant a walk to the main stairs and elevator at the opposite end of the north-south corridor, or using the much smaller back staircase around the corner from their room. He'd investigated all of that before they settled in for the night. Richly carpeted and neweled stairs that ended suddenly outside their hotel room on the second floor seemed odd, if not unnerving. He'd wanted to figure out why they stopped instead of continuing to the lobby level. The "why" hadn't been answered...some historical oddity of construction, he supposed, but at least he'd learned there was an easy way to get to the ground floor from this end of the building.

Now Henry pushed the door wider so he could survey the entire area and jerked to attention as a bit of floating red fabric disappeared through the back stairway door. He started to run in that direction, looked down at his plaid night shirt, and froze where he was. His gaze went past the nightshirt, past bare toes in travel flip-flops, and found two red roses lying at his feet. Their blossoms looked perfect, but the stems were twisted, as if someone had attempted to break them and hadn't succeeded. He stared down and his brain tried to process what the roses meant.

Suddenly feeling vulnerable, he pulled back into the room. If anyone came into the hall, they might think seeing a man dressed in a nightshirt was startling, even funny. Well, maybe they wouldn't. Nightshirts suited the atmosphere of this place.

Carrie, in her blue pajamas and white socks, joined him near the open door. "What is it? Oh, look there, how pretty! But, poor things, their stems are broken." She bent and picked the roses up, then jerked one hand away. "Ouch! I thought they took the thorns off gift roses."

Henry stuck his head out the door again. The hall was empty. No flowers at room doors, no nothing. He decided not to say anything about seeing—or thinking he had seen—something red.

He slid backwards into the room, shut the door, and turned to see that Carrie had the thumb of her right hand in her mouth. She held the roses, stems flopping, in the other hand.

Without a second thought he yanked her thumb out of her mouth and knocked the roses to the floor. "Go spit out the blood, rinse your mouth, and wash your hands," he commanded, then softened his tone as she looked up at him, eyes wide with surprise. "Uh...you don't know if they have pesticide on them, or...well, you can't be too careful."

Without a word, she did as he'd said, returning to stand with him and stare at the flowers lying on the floor.

"Henry, what's happening?" she asked. "You didn't order roses, did you." It was a statement, not a question. "Then why are they here?" She gave a little laugh. "A mistake? The wrong room? Left by one of the resident ghosts?"

He shrugged and, making sure the door was locked

and bolted, returned to bed, leaving the flowers on the carpet inside the door. In a minute she, too, climbed into bed, but instead of turning out the light, she picked up the phone.

"Hello. Front desk? I'm calling from room number... oh, you know where we are? Good. We were awakened a couple of minutes ago when someone knocked on our door. We opened it to find no one there, just two red roses lying on the carpet. Did anyone carrying roses come in the hotel just now?

"No one? Outside doors are locked?

"Oh. Someone could probably get up here from inside the hotel without your noticing them? Roses from the dining room? Uh-huh, I see.

"No, no harm done, we were just a little surprised to have roses delivered at two a.m., that's all. It's odd...

"Well, yes. The same to you."

She hung up and looked over at Henry. "I guess you got the gist of that? Supposedly no one can get in from outside at night unless the desk clerk admits them, but a person already inside can use either stairway without being seen or heard, assuming they're quiet. And, guess what—the hotel has red roses on tables in the dining room this week. He thinks our roses must have come from there."

She sighed, then changed that to a grin as she reached for the lamp switch. "He told me to have a nice night."

Henry was rarely aware of dreaming, but when he next looked at the clock, it was 4:30 and his mind hummed with "The Case of the Roses in the Night." In his dream he'd been a Sherlock Holmes-type character, with Carrie as his Watson. Their concern? Solving the presence of a long trail of blood-red roses left outside their bedroom door.

He stretched and turned over, thinking about the two roses. Why were the stems broken? Why had he thought of poison on the thorns? And what were the sounds he'd heard before he opened the hall door? True, this was a very old building, odd noises were to be expected. But the sounds had been organized; periodic *tat-tats*, and then the soft swishing that made him think of long skirts, or maybe Chandra's sari.

No, not Chandra. She moved in almost total silence.

Had he really seen that flash of red?

The next thing Henry knew it was seven o'clock. Carrie was sitting upright in her bed, reading by a small book light. The smell of coffee told him she'd already brewed their morning cup.

"Well, hello there," she said. "I didn't know how much you were awake during the night so I tried to be quiet. Did the smell of coffee wake you?"

"Nope, hunger did. If it's okay with you, I'm going to shave and dress right away, then, as soon as you're presentable, let's go to the dining room for breakfast."

She smiled, nodded, and went back to her reading while he headed for the bathroom. On the way he picked up the wilted flowers and, lifting them close to his nose, sniffed, detecting nothing but a faint rose scent. In the light of day it seemed ridiculous to assume two roses could be harmful. The flowers were undoubtedly intended for someone else and the room numbers simply got mixed. In hindsight, he and Carrie should have left them on the carpet outside their door.

Well, too late now.

He dropped the roses into the bathroom trash basket.

As they left the dining room, Carrie said, "Before we check out I'd like to go downstairs, look at the spa, and see if we can't find the basement exit Chandra said Ashur used. I'm curious to know if events could have happened as she described. It isn't that I don't believe her, it's...well, I want to see for myself. What do you think?"

He nodded agreement and they headed toward the south stairway.

The spa was open, but there were no employees at the front desk. Puzzled about which door to go through, Carrie looked around the foyer, seeing a display case featuring a wedding gown and accessories, and information about the services offered to bridal parties in the hotel's beauty salon and spa.

Henry had just asked, "What now?" when several women dressed in housekeeper's uniforms came through a door marked *Private* and Carrie caught a glimpse down a long hall luxuriously outfitted with subdued lighting and soft colors. As soon as the women were out of sight, she went to the door and tugged on the handle, but it wouldn't open.

Henry said, "Guess it's an automatic lock, the kind that has to be set to allow access. Maybe we can find a way in from the parking lot and follow Ashur's path in reverse." They turned to go back up the stairs, but just then two more uniformed women absorbed in a conversation in Spanish came from the hallway. Carrie quickly slid around the wall and leaned against the door to keep it from closing. The women paid no attention to her. As soon as they disappeared from sight, Carrie pushed the door open and she and Henry slipped through.

He took a minute to look at the lock mechanism on the back side of the door before they started down the hallway. Neither of them said anything as they moved past doors opening into empty rooms containing whirlpool tubs and massage tables. It was exactly like Chandra's description.

They came to the end without incident, and, hesitating only briefly, Henry pulled on a door like the one that had brought them into the hall. It wasn't locked. They stepped out of luxury into a concrete and corrugated metal room full of tools, an odd assortment of broken furniture, and parts for various pieces of machinery.

Just then another uniformed housekeeper carrying a stack of towels came through from their left. "¿Qué...what you want?"

"Making a building inspection," Henry said quickly. "This is the maintenance shop? For repairs?"

"Si. Repair things. Used to be dead place long ago. Muertos, still many ghosts." Her tone was matter-of-fact, as if she'd seen those many ghosts and they didn't impress her at all. Then she turned and pointed to a door on the wall next to them. "Cold place, keep bodies. Locked. No use now."

"I see," Henry said. "Thank you...gracias."

The woman nodded vigorously, signifying, Carrie imagined, that she'd done her duty for the inspectors.

As she turned to leave, Carrie asked, "Pardon, can you tell us more about the ghosts?"

"Uhnn, si," the woman said, nodding again as she shifted the towels to one hip and raised fingers to count. "Uno. Tall man in high hat, black suit. Medico, long time ago. Dos. Child. Girl." She shook her head from side to side as if unwilling to say anything about the child, and went on. "Tres. Carpintero. Man here to build. Fall from..." She pointed up.

"Is there a bride?" Carrie asked.

Once more the woman nodded and held up a fourth finger. "Bride. She kill...she kill propia marido...man she marry...she love other man...not love man she kill."

The ghost bride! And a story like Lucia di Lammermoor.

"Does the bride wear a red dress?"

"Si, rojo," the woman said, still nodding as she slipped through the door to the spa hallway, ending the conversation.

"Whew," Carrie said. "All kinds of ghosts. I remember reading that the Crescent Hotel building was used as a hospital in the late '30's. If she meant this room was once a mortuary, that would fit with a hospital. And the door over there, which is *not* locked, by the way—the padlock is just hanging there—once led to a refrigerator for *bodies?*"

"Uh-huh," Henry said. "Not exactly what I expected to find, nor a ghost bride like Lucia."

"Oh, you know Lucia? Somehow I didn't expect you be familiar with opera."

"I did make it to a few of them with Irena over the years we were married."

"Ah," Carrie said and walked to the refrigerator. She lifted the lock and opened the door. Cold air blew against her face as she looked inside, then gasped. The small room was full of greenery...and red roses. "Well, now we know where the hotel's stock of roses is kept," she said. "But who brought two of them to our room? Surely it was a mistake."

She and Henry stared in silence at the refrigerator's contents, then she shut the door quickly as voices echoed into the repair shop from somewhere beyond them. Hooking the padlock back on the latch loop she said, "We'd better go. I'm sure this is where Ashur came through, aren't you?

It's exactly as Chandra described."

They turned a corner, went past a row of busy commercial washers and dryers, and were looked at curiously, but otherwise ignored, by two laundry workers folding sheets and chatting in Spanish. They passed through what appeared to be a break room and came out the exit door onto a driveway leading down from the hotel parking lot. They could see where Ashur parked the flower shop van when he returned to the hotel on Saturday night. The spot where Sonya Wells's body had been found lay directly in front of them, its location still marked by disturbed underbrush.

"Well, we've verified at least part of Chandra and Ashur's story," Henry said. "So how about settling up with the hotel and driving down to their flower shop? Maybe we'll have access to the bombed-out area now. Don't know what we'll find that the police haven't, but I'd still like to take a look around. I can't think of anything else to accomplish here for the present, can you?"

"Before we go to Artistic Floral," Carrie said, "why don't we find Jan Owen's shop? I'm curious about that place, not to mention its owner. I suppose they're closed because of Wells's death, but let's gamble on it. After the story you told me about Owen wanting the city to make the Mukherjee shop into a public *toilet,* I'd like to get a better sense of what she's really like, beyond the ugliness we saw on Saturday. I'll bet she treats customers politely and might even want to chat with us about her sister's death. If she's there and recognizes us from Saturday, she shouldn't think it peculiar if we say we've come to ask about flowers for our wedding."

"Red roses?" Henry asked.

She looked up at him. "Why, Henry, what a clever idea. Yes, we'll say we'd like red roses."

Chapter 21

"Oh, my goodness," Carrie said as Henry pulled into the parking lot, "it looks like a monster cuckoo clock."

She gawked at the dark wood building, trying to take in everything from the lace-cut, scalloped gables and balcony railings to mullioned windows with mum-filled flower boxes under them.

"I've seen one of those clocks," Henry said. "A Black Forest Cuckoo. An aunt of Irena's sent us one as a wedding present. It didn't fit with Irena's decorating ideas; she hated it, and eventually gave it to her maid. I found out later the thing cost several hundred dollars. It had all kinds of moving and jiggling parts and a pair of center doors just like this building has. Little people marched in and out of the doors as the clock struck." He laughed. "I thought it was fascinating and wanted to keep it, but Irena overruled me."

For a couple of minutes they sat together in comfortable silence as Henry remembered the cuckoo clock and

Carrie looked around at a mini-forest of tall pine trees surrounding the chalet-style business building. It was obvious
that Owen control over a large amount of Eureka Springs
real estate had allowed them to remain aloof from neighbors, and there were none near by. Carrie assumed that
two houses, barely visible through the woods behind the
chalet, belonged to family members.

"Well, shall we approach?" Henry said finally, opening
the car door. "Looks like someone's in the flower shop at
least."

One of the doors ahead of them was labeled *Owen Real
Estate Investment Company*. The second announced *Owen's
Flowers*. Windows on the real-estate side of the building
were dark, but an *Open* sign showed in one of the lighted
shop windows.

Carrie almost expected to see someone in either dirndl
or lederhosen behind the counter, but a girl in jeans and
a sweater greeted them. "May I help you? This is the time
of year for mums, you know, and we're having a special on
potted mums this week. Would you like to see the colors
available?"

"No mums today, thank you," Carrie said. "Um,
Henry and I are here to talk about our wedding flowers.
We're getting married in the Crescent Conservatory the
day after Thanksgiving." She smiled brightly, then realized
the girl was staring at her face. "These?" She touched one
of the butterfly bandages. "I had an accident with a...glass
door. I love the bandages, don't you? I, ah, I assume I'm
speaking to one of the Owens?"

"Oh, no, I'm Cindy Sturdevant, Ms. Owen's assistant.
Jan isn't here. A tragic thing has happened; her sister Sonya
was killed on Saturday. Jan has been busy with arrangements for the memorial service and all, but I'll be so glad

to help you. We have a photo album showing some of our wedding and reception designs, or we can follow your own ideas. Tell me what you're thinking of. Any plans yet?"

"Well, yes, sort of," Carrie said, ducking her chin and smiling shyly at the girl. "And I am sorry to hear about the death. But life, and plans for flowers, whether funeral or wedding, must go on, mustn't they?"

Cindy nodded, and Carrie thought it looked like she was struggling to put a sad look on her face.

"I really appreciate your willingness to help us now. Henry and I have driven quite a long way to get here, and it would be disappointing not to accomplish what we came for. When it comes to flowers, I'm not up on the latest ideas, and of course I want everything to be special, so..." Carrie looked down and fiddled with a button on her jacket. She seemed unable to meet the girl's steady gaze as she continued, "I need someone young like you to guide me and tell me what's done today. I want the latest thing."

And then, God forgive her, she giggled.

Henry watched, fascinated. He wondered if this amazing woman of his had ever been on the stage. All of a sudden she seemed to be struggling with shyness and acted as if she hadn't a clue what to do about wedding flowers. But the girl behind the counter was sure responding. *Probably thinks she's got a live one on the hook,* Henry thought. *I'd better keep my mouth shut and smile a lot.*

Cindy leaned toward Carrie encouragingly. "What kind of flowers do you like?"

"Well...I...what do you think of red roses? Wouldn't they be festive, near Christmas and all, and so pretty in that white room?" Carrie hesitated, then stuttered slightly as she continued. "B-but maybe not. I want something really special for us." She turned her head up and beamed an adoring look at Henry, batting her eyelashes at him.

The laugh he cut off just in time turned into a coughing fit.

After Cindy brought him a glass of water and things had settled down, the two women went back to flower talk. Within five minutes Cindy had Carrie agreeing that roses by themselves "simply wouldn't be special enough."

Finally Cindy reached out, patted Carrie's arm, and said, "You can trust me and Owen's Flowers completely. I'm going to be planning this as if you were my own grand...uh, mother. And, don't forget, our wedding designs are famous all around this area. I promise you'll have a wedding to remember."

In another few minutes they had progressed from roses to white orchid table bouquets tied with red ribbons, and Cindy was busy selling his more-than-willing bride on full orchid swags around windows, doors, and the buffet table. The swags would be centered with red rose nosegays and streamers "draping gracefully," as Cindy explained it, pointing to the album with excitement rising in her voice. "I know you don't want anything ordinary, and you just look like an orchid woman to me. See this?" Her finger tapped the album page. "We'll substitute white orchids for the white roses showing here, and we'll also be able to incorporate the red roses you said you liked."

Henry felt sure the girl's rising excitement was due to the fact she'd found such a willing and pliable customer who seemed to have no budget limitations.

He continued in the role of bystander whose only part in all this was to smile and nod whenever the girl looked his way. He couldn't have commented anyway; he'd gotten lost a long time ago among all the talk of swags and ribbons and various types of flowers. The only thing he did understand was the money. It was amazing such ridiculous-sounding concoctions could be so expensive when anything Owen made would end up in a trash bag minutes after the reception was over. But of course he was sure Carrie had no thought of going along with such outlandish over-flowering, whether Owen or the Mukherjees did it.

Pretty sure, at least.

Now Carrie purred, "You are very kind to help us in what I know must be a difficult time for you. I'll bet the sister's death is doubling your work load." She looked at the girl in sudden alarm as a thought seemed to strike her. "The shop won't close, will it? Obviously you're perfect for this creative work, but will you lose your job...if the shop closes, I mean?"

"Oh, no," the girl said, "it's actually the opposite. You see, Sonya Wells—that's the dead sister—did want to close the flower shop. I'd have been out of a job if she'd had her way, but now Jan can carry on.

"You saw the office next door? Well, Ms. Wells said Jan Owen should get out of the flower business and help with the real estate investment business over there," she pointed in the direction of the office next door, "because that's where all the money is. The two of them own an awful lot of buildings and land jointly. They inherited it all from their dad. The land sales and lease agreements bring in huge amounts, but they're certainly not creative like this shop is. Jan is a *creative* person. She shouldn't be stuck in an office. I know I wouldn't want to be!"

"So," Carrie said, "things are working out for the best after all. I'm so glad Ms. Owen plans to continue in the flower business."

"It's her whole life. She grew up in the flower shop and helped her father run it for years. She took over after he died. But, worse luck, he left it to both sisters. I think he shouldn't of done that, he should of left it just to Jan, not her sister."

"Oh, my." Carrie clucked sympathetically.

Henry and Carrie were now seated on stools next to the counter and Cindy pulled up a third stool before she continued, leaning toward them confidentially. "Jan had this fantastic building created for our new location a year ago." She waved her arm around, indicating, Henry supposed, the entire structure. "It was finished about the time her sister Sonya came to town after her divorce.

"Jan simply lives for this place, kinda like she's married to it, you know. The sisters had awful fights about keeping it open. You can imagine they'd fight since Sonya cares— oops, cared—nothing about creative work. She was all computers, calculators, and money counting. Don't you think that's just terrible? She even called this shop an albatross, and of course her saying that really hurt Jan."

"Oh, I do understand," Carrie said, and now she patted the girl's hand.

A whole lot of baloney going on here, Henry thought.

Cindy continued, "I'm afraid Sonya was winning, simply because of where all the family money came from, you know. Money always makes the decisions, doesn't it!"

Carrie clucked again and shook her head. "I can see how it would in this case. My, but it's been difficult for you."

"You better believe it," the girl said. "I've had to walk a fine line between those two women, both of them my bosses. But Jan will be fine now. Everything will be fine.

You know, she's been so mopey and sad part of the time, angry the rest—what with her worrying about the future of this shop. Now she can keep it open forever if she wants to."

"And you'll keep your job."

"Yes, you bet I'll keep my job.

"Well, back to business," Cindy said, reaching under the counter for a pad of forms. "Shall we fill out a contract for your wedding flowers?"

"Oh, of course, that's a good idea," Carrie said, then paused, frowning as if a thought had suddenly struck her. "Oh, dear, come to think of it, I can't. My two friends who live where we do, on the other side of Spavinaw County, are helping me plan the wedding. They couldn't come today, and they'd never forgive me if we designed all the flowers without them. I'll bring them here later this week and you can go over these ideas with the three of us as if you were just creating them. We'll do a contract after that. Okay?"

"What day will you be coming back?" the girl asked.

"Umm, not sure yet."

"I'll be off Thursday and Friday," Cindy said. "I've been working overtime alone since Sonya Wells's death, so I get compensatory time off and Jan will take over in the shop until the end of the week. Her nephew is out of school right now, of course—he's Sonya's son—and he'll be here too in case she needs to go to the lawyer's or something. Otherwise things are pretty much winding down. The memorial service was this morning.

"Are you sure you don't want to sign a contract now? It would mean a lot to me."

"No, I just can't hurt my friends, you know how that is." Carrie leaned toward Cindy and spoke conspiratorially. "But I'll be sure and tell Ms. Owen privately that you helped us make all the plans today. Just leave her a note about what we discussed. You'll get credit, I'll be sure of it."

Considerably cheered, the girl was all smiles again as Carrie and Henry thanked her and headed for the parking lot.

"Eeuuu," Carrie said as soon as they got in the car, "can you imagine all those orchids? That lovely room would simply disappear under them. I think orchids should only be used singly or in graceful sprays, don't you?"

Henry—who hadn't a clue—nodded, then said what was on his mind. "Carrie, do you think your play-acting, really lying to that girl, was right? You sure got her hopes up."

For a minute she was thoughtful, then said, "I did bend the truth, but any sales clerk is used to customers like me. A friend of mine who owned a gift shop even had a name for people who took her time for ages and ages, then left without buying anything. 'Playing customer,' she called it. Besides, I can't believe Cindy honestly thinks all the thousands of dollars worth of guck she was dreaming up for us is attractive, so she was bending the truth too."

She looked up at him. "And we sure found out a lot of interesting stuff, didn't we?"

He nodded, thinking about what they had heard and moving ideas around in his head.

"Did you see any knives like you found next to Ms. Wells's body?"

"No. It looked like their main work area is way in the back and I didn't see any knives at all."

"Me neither."

Silence filled the car until, finally, Carrie spoke his

thoughts aloud. "During your time in law enforcement, how often did you see cases where one sibling killed another?"

"Over all those years, too many."

"Well, then, do you think Jan Owen might..."

"And there's a very long history of that. You'll know about Cain and Abel, of course, and many other instances when brothers—and sisters, too—had serious or even dangerous disagreements, though in most cases they didn't go as far as murder. Jacob and Esau, Rachel and Leah, probably; Joseph and his brothers."

"*Henry*, those are people whose stories are in the Bible!"

"I am quite aware of that, my love."

"But you told me you didn't even *own* a Bible."

"Still true, though I'd like you to pick one out for me as a wedding present."

"Then, how...?"

"Simple. I used my head and went to the University of Arkansas Bookstore. Bought *Cliffs Notes*."

"*Cliffs Notes? On the Bible?*"

"Exactly. Pretty neat stuff. It's arranged chronologically, more or less, and..."

The rest of his words were drowned by her laughter. When it began to subside, he said, "Well, you don't need to laugh at me, I had to start somewhere."

"Oh, I'm not laughing at you, Henry, I'm laughing with delight. In fact, I think I'll order a copy of those *Cliffs Notes*, now that I know such a thing exists. I'd enjoy reading it, too."

"Oh. Okay," Henry said as he started the car. "Well, next stop, Artistic Floral. I'm thinking that's where we'll find the source of the knife I saw next to Sonya Wells's

body. But the big question still is, was it a red herring...
or what?"

Chapter 22

Yellow crime scene tape no longer barred access to Artistic Floral Designs, and as Carrie and Henry walked toward the building, they heard scrapes and clunks coming from behind the boarded windows. When they reached the entry opening, they saw Ashur and a boy in a knit cap at work near the rear of the shop. A battery lantern stood next to the work area, and a bare bulb on a long extension cord gave additional light. New bracing boards on four by six inch wooden posts stood guard across the front of the building, but otherwise it looked like the same dark cave Carrie had walked into the day before.

"Appears we'll have a free hand at whatever's left to see," Henry said, "but doing that shouldn't take us too long. So, what would you think about stopping by the hospital after we finish here? I'd like to—if you think it's okay, of course—I'd like to see the baby again and try to imagine Susan and my grandson being so small. Since I wasn't around when either of them was born, well, I thought maybe I could look at Charlie and picture how they looked."

"Good idea," Carrie said softly, thinking back to when she'd discovered Henry had a daughter he'd never seen, born after a one-night-stand and adopted by the sister and brother-in-law of the woman he'd spent the night with. He not only missed Susan's birth, he missed events like her high school and college graduation, wedding, and the birth of his grandson. My goodness, it was no wonder he wanted to see Charlie again.

"I have no idea what kind of visiting rules the hospital here has, but I'd like to go see Rebecca and the baby too. Usually maternity ward visits aren't strictly regulated."

"Good," Henry said, and Carrie smiled at him, touched by his interest in babies. If only she'd met Henry thirty or forty years ago, they could have... Oh, well. He had Susan and she had Rob. Now they'd share those children, and maybe there would be more grandchildren some day.

The two of them stepped inside the shop, pausing near the front to announce their presence. "Hello there, can we offer help?" Carrie hollered, not wanting to cause another surprise for a man who'd already had too many surprises over the past few days.

Both Ashur and his helper turned toward them, and Chandra's voice said, "We're trying to see what's worth saving before reconstruction begins." The jeans and sweatshirt she wore on her slight form had fooled Carrie completely. But then a silk sari could be ruined in this mess.

Henry turned on the flashlight he carried, and they followed a cleared path toward the area where the Mukherjees were picking flower containers, gift items, and tools from the wreckage.

About midway back Carrie stopped walking. Without

saying anything she reached for Henry's hand, pushing against it to force his flashlight beam toward the floor near the damaged work table. Silver-colored streaks turned into scattered metal knives, a dozen or more, with most of the blades still covered by smudged cardboard protectors. Carrie bent, picked up one of the knives, and held it toward Henry. "The same?" she asked quietly.

He nodded.

She kept the knife, and when they reached Chandra and Ashur, showed it to them. "You want us to get these off the floor for you? There sure are a lot of them back there, and, except for dirty cardboard blade covers, they don't seem to be damaged."

"Oh, thanks; two or three will be plenty," Chandra said. "There'll undoubtedly be more coming from where those did. They're florist's knives the IBE reps leave when they call on us—used for cutting stems without crushing them. Ve-ry sharp. I rarely use one. I have some Japanese shears I favor, so after the representative leaves, I toss the new knives in a box under the work counter. That's why there are so many." She laughed as she turned a molded plastic flower pot in her hands, inspecting it. "I never met a knife I couldn't slice my finger with. If you need such a thing, feel free to help yourself, but don't say I didn't warn you. You might as well take several. Lonnie Trent took one when he was here." She picked up a cloth, dusted the pot off, and stacked it in a box holding similar pieces.

Carrie wondered how on earth she was going to get either Ashur or Chandra to say enough about the knives to reveal whether or not someone outside the shop could have had one. Had Sergeant Trent asked them questions about knives, too?

"I don't like sharp knives either," she said. "Do all florists use these?"

"Something similar, probably," Chandra answered as she reached for another pot.

"Looks like you're accumulating quite a bit of undamaged merchandise," Henry said. "When is reconstruction beginning?"

"Should be in a week or two," Ashur told him, "assuming our insurance company gives the okay. Their adjustor has already come here twice with contractors, and they're supposed to turn in bids before the end of the week. I know one of the companies, in fact we talked to the owner yesterday. He showed up on his own not long after news of the bombing got around and boarded the windows for us. We'll probably choose him if we can, since he's the one who did the work when we originally remodeled the building.

"But we'll have to wait and see. This morning I heard from someone whose information I trust that a council member here is trying to get the city to condemn our building. She's proposing they rebuild it as a tourist rest station." He shook his head and appeared to be surveying the floor.

Chandra put down the pot she was holding and stared at her husband. After a moment she said, "You didn't tell me that, Ashur. We'll fight it, of course. That is, we will if we're not in jail."

Carrie tsk-tsk'd and handed the knife to Henry, facing toward him to lift her eyes in what she hoped was a questioning look.

Henry's head ducked almost imperceptibly before he removed the knife cover to test the sharpness of the blade, then said to Ashur, "I should think this would be handy for a florist, though it looks more like a steak knife to me.

I'll bet you use them, but of course anyone"—he glanced at Carrie and Chandra—"should be wary of the blade..." He let his voice trail off while his thumb continued to rub lightly across the sharp edge.

Ashur shrugged, eyeing the knife. "No, I don't use them. Chandra does most of the work with flowers, but I agree, they can be handy. We all keep one in our on-site kit, just in case. And we have several at the greenhouses. Purdy often uses an IBE knife to cut stems when he's bringing flowers or greenery to the shop."

He put a roll of ribbon, still plastic-wrapped, in the box beside him, then rested a hand against his back and rocked back and forth. *Straightening out kinks from bending over so long,* Carrie thought.

Henry looked toward Chandra. "Do you ever use a knife out on jobs?"

If the Mukherjees wondered why Carrie and Henry were so interested in knives they were too polite to say so, and Chandra answered easily enough. "No, I always carry my shears with me. In fact, I haven't seen my knife for some time and hadn't thought of it until now." She looked around the wrecked shop. "I wonder where my on-site kit is? I don't remember seeing it since Saturday evening."

"It's still in the van," Ashur told her. "I noticed it this morning."

Since Carrie couldn't figure out how to ask more about knives without sounding like an idiot with a knife fixation, she said, "We have a little free time before we go back home. Is there something we can do to help you here?"

"No, but thank you," Ashur said. "We need to keep track of what's usable and what has to be replaced, so it's better if we search through the wreckage ourselves, even though it's a slow process." He grinned. "Of course we took time off to visit Rebecca and Charlie this morning."

"How are they doing?" Carrie asked. "We thought we might drop by and see them before we leave town."

Chandra nodded her head. "That would be good. You might see if you can do something to cheer Rebecca up. She's so worried about everything, how to care for Charlie, taking time away from the business, and, of course, the bombing and the death of Ms. Wells. It's a lot for a new mother to handle."

"Or any of you," Carrie said.

Chandra smiled vaguely and studied a wilted vine she'd pulled from a pile of broken pots and dirt. "I suppose these plants are beyond saving," she said to no one in particular. "I should have done something about them before now."

"You probably couldn't have," Henry told her, "because of the crime scene tape. They're a legitimate loss for insurance purposes."

"Do you want us to scoop up some of this dirt and try re-potting the better-looking plants?" Carrie asked. "Maybe if we water them they'll come back."

Chandra studied her for a moment. "You really *do* want to help, don't you? Okay, give it a try. We've already found our trowels, they're right here. You can use some of these unbroken pots, then gather the filled ones in those flat trays stacked in the corner. Please though, do not forget that what we need most is help learning who shot at us and who killed Sonya Wells."

"We're not forgetting," Carrie said. "We're working on that, and I know the police are too."

Chandra looked at them with eyes that betrayed both sadness and fear, and as Henry began scooping dirt into pots, Carrie changed the subject. "My friends and I will

be back here toward the end of the week to help you however we can. Baby-tending, helping with decorations for
your next wedding job, hauling things, whatever. We also
plan to spend some time investigating the bad things that
have been happening to you. How about Thursday and
Friday?"

After a pause, Chandra replied. "I don't know what
to say except thank you. Yes, we can use the help. When
you came here to see about your wedding, you certainly
got more than you bargained for. There is no reason you
should be involved further in our problems, I know that,
especially after our shop blew up in your faces. But I am
also hopeful that many people in the United States—the
real United States—are like you and your friends. I'm glad
this quality hasn't been lost.

"Thursday and Friday will be good. The entire
Mukherjee family is grateful, and probably our daughter,
Rohanna Jayne, will be the most grateful. She's away at college and, since learning what happened, feels she should
quit her classes and come home to help us. I'll tell her
we have good friends who will help in her place, and she
should stay in school. It's been hard for her, hearing about
all this from such a distance."

"Oh, my, yes, it would be," Carrie said. "Where's she
going to school?"

"New Haven, Connecticut, so far away. This is her
third year."

"Yale?"

Ashur entered the conversation. "That's right. She has
a generous scholarship and hopes to become an architect.
We are quite proud of her."

"Of course she should stay in school," Carrie said as
she watered the last re-potted plant. Impulsively, she add-

ed, "Some of us can probably come back to help you next week, too.

"Now, where shall we put these trays of plants? Will you be taking them to your greenhouse?"

"Yes," Ashur said, handing her a set of keys. "There is room in the back of the van right now. I'd just returned from taking a load to the greenhouse workroom a few minutes before you came. You'll see the space when you open the rear doors."

Carrie and Henry nodded as they each picked up a flat of plants and headed toward the entrance.

Henry boosted Carrie over the bumper and into the back of the van as soon as the doors were open. She knelt and surveyed the interior while Henry looked on from the sidewalk. "Here are a couple of tool trays with all kinds of things in them," she said quietly, pushing one of the trays toward the back where Henry could see it. "I wonder which is Chandra's." She began poking about in the first tray and after a moment said, "No knife in this one." A search of the second tray got the same observation. "No knife here, either."

"Well, then, it appears they've misplaced more than one," Henry said. "And it looks to me as if it would have been very easy for a person who wanted one of those knives to make off with it—as simple as just picking it up if Ashur, Chandra, or the young couple turned their back on a tray at a preparation site or left a knife they'd been using lying around somewhere.

"You could also steal a knife from inside the shop without too much difficulty. If the person tending the shop went in the cooler like Chandra did for Cody Wells, a so-called customer could have come around behind the counter to take one or more knives out of the box without much chance of being caught—assuming the timing was right. Doing that would take planning though, whereas picking one up at a work site could just be a finders keepers sort of thing.

"And we can't forget that the Mukherjee family has the easiest access to them."

Carrie frowned but didn't say anything because, of course, Henry was right.

He leaned through the door again to look more closely at the tool tray nearest him, then picked up one of the rolls of wire it held. "Is there a wire cutter in that other tray? Good. Can you get me a couple of feet of this without Chandra or Ashur seeing you?"

Carrie glanced toward the shop, then, shielded from view by Henry's body, she unrolled wire and clipped it off. "Does this look like what you saw wrapped around Sonya Wells's wrists and ankles?"

"I think so," he said. "I thought I'd like to keep a piece just in case, though it's probably ordinary stuff that any florist, and maybe others, could have."

She handed him the wire and, after curling it and twisting the end, he put it in his jacket pocket. Then he began lifting flats of plants onto the van floor. Carrie shoved each one toward the front of the van, crawling along the floor behind it, fitting the trays together like puzzle pieces so they wouldn't slide around while the vehicle was in motion.

"Well," Carrie said finally, "no matter what we might think about Jan Owen, we haven't exactly narrowed the field of suspects, have we? We haven't proved anything."

"Nope, we haven't," Henry said as he lifted another flat of plants, "at least not yet."

Chapter 23

When Carrie and Henry got to the hospital a little after 1:30, a receptionist gave directions for finding Rebecca without making any comment about visiting hours. They passed the nursery on their way down the hall and looked in the window. There was one baby, wearing a pink cap. "Not Charlie," Carrie said, "must be feeding time."

When they found Rebecca's room, Carrie raised her hand to knock just as a familiar voice said, "You think about it, Rebecca. I'll get in touch later," and the door jerked open. Melissa Donley's wide-eyed surprise was followed by a look of wariness that seemed totally out of place for a visit to a new mother.

Think about what? Carrie wondered, as a vibrating tingle of unease wiggled from her neck to her tail bone. Nevertheless she managed a cheery-sounding, "Hi, there, Melissa," as the woman brushed past her, side-stepped around Henry, and hurried down the hall, sending a quick hello over her shoulder.

"Guess she's late for something," Henry murmured as the two of them turned to look in the room and saw Rebecca seated in a rocking chair, nursing Charlie. Her head was bent over the baby, but when she lifted it to look at the new visitors, Carrie thought it looked like she'd been crying. What was wrong? Did it have something to do with Melissa's visit? If she had come to see Rebecca and the baby, the two young women were probably friends, so why would there be a reason for distress? Carrie hoped they could talk with Rebecca long enough to get some clue to the undercurrents pulsing in the air here.

Henry interrupted her thoughts as he jerked back, bumping into the door and sending it closed with a thump. "We should come back later, we...I'll, uh, wait outside."

"Oh, don't be silly," Rebecca said. "Your being here doesn't bother me. Everyone knows how babies eat, the basics at least. I'm just learning the finer details of feeding him myself—and now, I'm supposed to get rid of accumulated gas." She let the piece of flannel that was folded across one shoulder fall over her exposed breast and sat Charlie in her lap, nestling him securely against her stomach. Supporting his head with her thumb and forefinger, she began gently patting him on the back.

After a pause, Henry said, "Wow, that boy produces a good one, doesn't he?" and Carrie stifled a snicker, realizing Henry had probably never heard a baby burp in his life.

At least his comment brought the hint of a smile to Rebecca's face. "I guess I'll let him do it in public for a while without saying anything," she said, "but it doesn't sound exactly polite, does it? Please, won't both of you sit down? I'm glad you came, because I've wanted to thank you for helping Chandra and Ashur. They told us what happened

Saturday night...and then the bomb on Monday... They've sure had a pot full of ugliness lately." She looked down at her son, but not before Carrie saw renewed distress in her eyes.

Chandra had been right, this young woman was deeply troubled. Was it all because of the baby's early arrival and the terrible events in Purdy's family? Of course those would be enough to distress anyone, but what about Melissa Donley's remark? Once more Carrie wondered what Rebecca was supposed to think about. It might be her imagination, but the way the wedding planner had spoken the words made them sound almost like a threat.

Charlie went back to nursing, this time with the flannel still in place so that it covered Rebecca's exposed flesh and part of the baby's head. Henry seemed to have gotten over his discomfort and was totally absorbed in baby-watching.

After a short silence, Carrie said, "I see you have a vase of red roses. I thought I smelled roses the minute I came in the room." She stood, walked to the flowers, and sniffed. "These don't seem to have much fragrance, though. They're like the ones in the Crescent Hotel dining room. I suppose dining room roses can't have a strong scent because, after all, who wants to smell roses while eating steak and onions?"

Rebecca said, "Melissa brought me the roses, but the scent comes from her perfume, *Glory of Roses*. She wears it all the time."

"Oh, perfume! I do remember smelling roses Saturday evening when we were with her. *Glory of Roses*. Well, it's nice and light."

Rebecca didn't comment so Carrie said, "My friends Shirley Booth, Eleanor Stack, and I plan to come back here later in the week and stay a couple of days so we can help you and your family. One thing we could do easily is take care of Charlie while you rest, go out to lunch with Purdy, or whatever you want. I'm sure you'll be settled at home by then and might welcome a change of scenery or a nap, or even another woman to talk with."

"Why would you do that for us?" Rebecca asked, her voice suddenly chilly and suspicious.

Carrie ignored the chill. "Well, seemed to us that you and your family could use some friendly support. We can manage the time, so, why not? Besides, Artistic Floral Designs will be doing the flowers for Henry's and my wedding at Thanksgiving, which gives us a personal interest in seeing the business get back on its feet."

After a long, studied glance at Carrie, Rebecca nodded and went back to watching Charlie. She reached out to touch one of his hands with a cautious finger and, once more, almost smiled.

For a while the only sound in the room was the creak of the rocker, the slushy sounds of a baby sucking and, occasionally, soft grunts from the same source. Carrie was trying to figure out how to get the conversation around to Melissa again when Henry spoke. "I guess you and Melissa Donley are good friends?"

Hurray for you, Carrie thought.

"Not good friends. We know each other."

"It was nice of her to come see you and the baby and bring the flowers."

"Yes."

"Do you two often work on weddings together?"

"No. She works for the Crescent and Basin Park Hotels. Owen does most all the flowers for her unless people contract with us privately."

"Owen has a contract with those hotels?" Henry sounded surprised and Carrie certainly was.

Rebecca hesitated a minute, studying their faces and obviously trying to decide something before she answered. Then she said, "No, but Melissa can easily influence people's decisions. I'm sure you're able to figure out how that works. Please, don't quote me though. I'm telling you this in confidence. I doubt Ashur and Chandra have a clue to what's going on or even wonder why they get fewer wedding jobs for Eureka Springs' premier hotels than they do from all the other places. And if the hotels' management ever caught on, I'm sure Melissa would be fired."

"Pay-off?" Henry asked.

Rebecca shrugged. "Jan must be paying Melissa. Why else would Melissa do it? And it would have to be quite a bit of money to make it worth her while. But I just can't understand Jan's reasoning. It isn't as if Owen's Flowers has no business or she needs the jobs to support herself. There's that land company... It all seems so dumb to me."

Alarmed, Carrie asked, "How about the other consultant, Tiffany Albright? Is she in on it?"

"I've never heard anything indicating she was. I doubt it, since I'm sure the hotel people don't know what Melissa is doing, and if both wedding planners were making extra money on the side by directing flower jobs to Owen, it would be harder to conceal. To keep things real-looking we'd always have to get some of the jobs, and we get at least half of Tiffany's. The weddings aren't scheduled with a planner's name so there's not much chance anyone who isn't in on the scheme can trace Owen weddings back to Melissa's sign-up. Besides, the two women don't always follow their weddings through from sign-up to clean-up. They help each other." She looked thoughtful. "But I guess, for that reason, if any other outsider understands what's going on it would have to be Tiffany."

"How did you figure this out?" Henry asked, sounding, Carrie thought, just a bit skeptical.

If Rebecca heard the scepticism in his voice, she didn't react to it. "I've overheard parts of conversations Melissa was having with clients, and sometimes—when quick turn-around between events means Jan Owen and I are working in the same area and Melissa is there as well—the two of them say more than is wise. Once, without even trying, I heard a whole conversation about influencing arrangements for an upcoming event. They're more careful now. I think they saw me that time and realized I might have heard what they said."

Henry asked, "Did you ever report this to anyone?"

"No, of course not. How could I prove it? I haven't even told Purdy. I'm afraid he might do something stupid."

"Maybe some of the clients Melissa has influenced would be willing to testify."

"I doubt it, she's smart. Being in the business, I understood what was going on when I overheard her, but I don't think clients would. Besides, poking into it would just cause more trouble for us—for Artistic Floral Designs. We already have plenty of that, don't you think?" Her brow wrinkled in obvious distress and her fingers began twisting the border of Charlie's gown.

She's frightened, Carrie thought. *I wonder if Melissa threatened her? If so, this young woman is carrying a heavy burden. I wonder why she's telling us about it, though? Sympathy? Or what? Are she and the rest of the family still in danger? Certainly Cody Wells is no threat now. But, what about that shot into the conservatory and the murder of Cody's mother? Are they connected to this client influence scheme?*

When Rebecca had been silent for a few moments, Henry said, "I suppose you and Melissa are about the same age. Did you both grow up here?

"No."

"No? So, where are you from?"

"She's from Dallas. I grew up in Jonesboro."

"Ah, yes, I forgot, the Mukherjees lived in Jonesboro while their children were growing up."

"Yes."

"You met Purdy there, I'll bet."

"We were friends in grade school, but not after we got older. I didn't date Purdy until we were both students at the University of Arkansas in Little Rock."

"You still have family in Jonesboro, then?"

"Mom and Dad."

Carrie broke in. "Will your mother be able to come and help you with the baby? I'll bet she can't wait to see him."

"No, my mother will *not* be coming here. In fact, I haven't seen her since I told my folks I planned to marry Purdy."

"Oh, my, that's too bad. They're missing a lot. Do they know about Charlie?"

"No. They wouldn't be interested."

"I can't believe that."

Rebecca gave her a disgusted look as if to say, *How little you know about the world,* but she didn't speak.

"Objections to Purdy's religion?"

"Yes, and his ethnic background. My parents are ignorant bigots, but that's nothing you need to be concerned with."

Wooo, there was sure bitterness in that reply, Carrie

thought, *and she's letting me know it's none of my business. Maybe it isn't, but...*

"We humans don't always manage to rise to the best of our many choices concerning how we think, talk, and act, do we?" Carrie said. "I know the Mukherjee family has become too used to prejudice."

"Oh, yes, especially recently, and yet they remain so naive! I wish...I just wish they'd wake up. All of us should leave this city, this state, as soon as we can."

"Where would you go, Rebecca?"

"West Coast. California. Melissa says there are lots of Hindus there, mixed marriages, too. Charlie could find friends like himself, live a normal life."

"I've always thought of Eureka Springs as a town that accepted all types of people. What happened to that?" Carrie asked the question, though she was sure she knew the answer.

"9/11 happened. All the buried prejudices boiled out and new ones popped up like weeds. After a year or so passed, things did quiet down and we thought it was over, but in the last few months...well, you see what's happened just this week." Tears began streaking down Rebecca's cheeks. "We *must* leave here. If Ashur and Chandra won't leave, Purdy and I will have to go without them. I don't want Charlie or any other children we may have growing up as outsiders, suffering things like Chandra and Ashur are suffering. And now it's becoming dangerous for all of us. People are suspicious. Melissa says, because of the knife, they think..."

"I'm sure no one suspects any of the Mukherjees of causing harm to a single living thing."

"She says there's ugly talk all over town. Terrible things. They're calling Purdy and his folks the dumbest names, like 'sand niggers,' and calling me a 'sand nigger slave.' People don't know or care that we aren't Arab or Muslim, or even that I'm Christian, though of course they should never, ever use that awful term about anyone, anywhere in the world. It's hideous...stupid and ignorant and ugly." Now she was crying in earnest. "Why do people have to be that way? Even my own folks..."

Not surprisingly, Charlie began to wail, and Rebecca, now crying as openly as her son, just stared at him hopelessly.

Carrie went to the rocker and gently lifted Charlie into her arms, took a blanket that was draped over the edge of the rolling crib, and, putting it around and in front of the baby, held him against her shoulder. She began humming tunelessly and patting his back. Slowly the sobs of both mother and son faded. Charlie hiccuped, then burped.

She shifted the baby so he was cradled in her arms and looked at Henry. For some reason he was staring into the distance. It looked like his thoughts were miles away. She walked over to him and asked, "Would you like to hold Charlie? That is, if it's okay with his mom?"

She glanced toward Rebecca, who nodded as she wiped her eyes. After giving Henry a few simple instructions and positioning his arms to receive the baby, Carrie laid Charlie in Henry's lap.

Henry figured he must have stopped breathing when Carrie handed the baby to him. He looked so delicate, was probably fragile as heck. Everything about him was miniature. *Careful, careful.* Carrie had warned him about protecting a baby's neck and head.

He'd been thinking about Rebecca's parents when Charlie arrived in his lap. There were so many people in the world who couldn't open up to change. They couldn't—or wouldn't—put themselves in another's shoes or even think about anything that wasn't like what they were used to. People could be totally without understanding. That was exactly what he and Jason talked about on Monday.

Nuts. Some folks were just plain dumb, robbing themselves of all the good they'd experience if they chose to be open. Rebecca's parents had robbed themselves of a daughter, and now, a grandson.

People robbed themselves...

That's when he remembered Catherine, and his thoughts began jumping back and forth between this baby and other babies he might have known, if...

Charlie had fuzzy, dark hair. What had Susan's hair been like? How about his grandson, Johnny? And, Catherine as a baby? He could at least have seen her. He'd had a choice. He didn't go.

Henry could feel the soft pliability of the tiny body and tried to soften his own arms, mold them to the baby. Suddenly Charlie tensed, raised a fist, and made a noise that sounded almost like a sneeze.

"Why did he do that? Is he okay?"

"He's fine," Carrie said, smiling at him, "and I wish I had a camera."

Henry rubbed the tip of his forefinger against Charlie's hand, marveling at the exquisiteness of everything to do with this baby. That's when Charlie gazed up, opened his fist, and grabbed the caressing finger. And that's when Henry felt dampness in the corners of his eyes.

Carrie decided Charlie and Henry were getting along fine, so she turned toward Rebecca, who was leaning back in the rocker, looking very tired.

"Why don't you crawl into bed? We'll leave so you can nap. Is a nurse going to come get Charlie, or does he stay here? I bet he'll go to sleep easily, and I don't think he needs a diaper change yet."

"Don't go, I want to ask you about something. And a nurse won't come now because Charlie stays here with me. I feed him every couple of hours, and I changed his diaper just before you came."

Carrie helped the young woman slip out of her robe and get into bed. There was a pillow propped against the headboard and she leaned on it while Carrie took her place in the rocker.

"I wanted to ask you something, too, Rebecca. Have you actually heard anyone say these ugly things Melissa is talking about?"

"No, but I saw the writing on the flower shop window, and...there's the shot, and the bombing..." She sighed. "Carrie, you're a Christian, I suppose?"

"Yes."

"Well, I'm a bit rusty, but I wanted to ask you—didn't Jesus say those who follow him should love each other— love the ones considered different from themselves? I know he loved both his mother and a woman who was a sinner. He loved Peter *and* Judas; a tax collector and Lazarus.

"I remember from Sunday School that Saint Paul wrote about all being part of one body, whether Jews or Gentiles, bond or free—or at least something like that. *What are those words supposed to mean? What do they mean to my folks?* The Mukherjees' religion teaches them to love every living thing, and they sure turn the other cheek. Aren't we Christians taught that, too? It's got to be more than pretty words. It *is* more than pretty words, isn't it, Carrie? Loving your neighbor as yourself and all that?"

"Yes, they're words to live by, not just pretty words. Remember that now, as you go to sleep."

Carrie helped Rebecca slide down under the covers. Then she lifted the sleeping baby out of Henry's arms and laid him gently in his crib.

After one last look at mother and child, Carrie and Henry tip-toed toward the door. Before they reached it, Rebecca murmured, "You can't talk about what Melissa's doing. Please..."

"I understand," Carrie said. "Don't worry." She turned off the light and pulled the door closed with a soft *click*.

Chapter 24

Neither of them spoke until they were in the car. Key in hand, Henry stared out the front window and said, "They named Charlie after her father and that dumb fool doesn't even know it. The very fact they wanted to call the baby Ashur Charles amazes me, though. Says something pretty great about those two kids."

"Uh-huh. I could get really, really angry at Rebecca's parents, and about my own helplessness in the face of such hurtful idiocy. Useless, though. I just pray...ah, well, Rebecca's dad will find out about little Charlie some day. And when he does..."

Carrie reached for his hand and the two of them sat in silence, holding hands, while the dashboard clock moved past 2:39 to 2:40, and then 2:41. Finally Henry said, "When he finds out, I know just how he'll feel. Lower than dirt. And he deserves it."

Carrie turned her head to study Henry's profile and wondered what he meant to convey with that remark. She didn't wonder long.

"Time to head for home," he said, putting the car key in its slot. "When we get there, let's call Catherine and invite her to our wedding."

Carrie didn't answer. She couldn't think of anything that wouldn't sound trite, and trite simply wasn't good enough for this moment.

They'd traveled several miles in silence before Henry spoke again. "Carrie, what do you think about the ugly comments Melissa repeated to Rebecca? I'm beginning to be suspicious of some of the information we're collecting. We do know there are evil things going on here, but how many people are really involved? Is it one person...two...a whole bunch? First it seemed to be the Owen family. Now add Melissa Donley and what she said. Is antipathy toward the Mukherjees that widespread?"

Carrie said, "For a start, I'd like to find out who might be saying the ugly stuff Melissa's talking about. Why on earth would she come to the hospital just to share something like that? It's cruel to Rebecca and, right now, pointless. A new mother can hardly pick up and leave town right away. I've been trying to figure out how we'll learn who's saying what. Could we go to the police station, find Trent or Gibson or maybe Detective Wolverton, and ask them what they've heard? Would they tell us anything, or are they as much in the dark as we are? If threats have been made, that's sure relevant to the cases they're working on, assuming what Melissa repeated is even partly true."

Henry ran a hand over his head and said, "I don't think the police—even the three officers we've met—would respond to questions like that from us. In Kansas City, I wouldn't have talked with a civilian about it; not yet, at least."

"I was afraid you were going to say that, and I doubt we could pull off any kind of man-and-woman-on-the-street survey, asking something like 'What do you think of Hindu florists?' Come to think of it, most of the people on the street here are tourists anyway. We'd have to go to shop clerks, workers in motels and restaurants, city employees, and start conversations. It could take us days to learn anything."

Henry said, "I have another thought. You told me several months ago you met people from all over northwest Arkansas at that church event you went to in Fayetteville. Were any of them from the church here? What do you think about coming back to Eureka Springs tomorrow evening and attending their Wednesday service? Maybe you'd find someone you recognize and, after church, could start a conversation."

"Brilliant, Henry. What you suggest is sure worth a try. Since Eleanor, Shirley, and I are coming back here on Thursday anyway, you and I can just come a day early. I'm sure I met several people from here, though I can't remember faces right now."

She hesitated. "What we were planning to do on Thursday and Friday is girls-only stuff, though."

"Okay. I'm sure there's something I can do to help the Mukherjees while you three are busy being girls only."

"Settled then, we'll come back tomorrow evening. I'll call the Crescent in the morning and make the proper reservations for all of us."

As soon as they walked in Carrie's house they went to the room she used as an office. While he waited for her to find Catherine's number, Henry thought about those times on

the force when he'd had to tell people their loved one was
hurt or dead, the victim of some violent crime. Hardest
thing the job required. This wasn't the same, of course—
couldn't compare—but it was still difficult enough to remind him of those old times. His chest felt tight and he
took a huge, noisy breath as he watched Carrie pick up the
phone and begin to dial.

They'd agreed to use the speaker phone. Carrie would
open the conversation, then he could speak. The idea of
being alone with Catherine, even on a phone, terrified
him. He simply couldn't talk to her one-on-one yet.

"Brandon-King."

"Carrie McCrite calling from Guilford, Arkansas. Is
Ms. King available?"

"Ms. King is in court this afternoon. May I have her
return your call tomorrow?"

Henry shook his head violently, though he didn't really understand why he was doing it. Watching him, Carrie
said, "No, I'll call her back, thank you," and hung up.

"So?" she said.

"Uh, yes. So, we'll try again tomorrow."

"That's right, we will. Why don't you come for breakfast? I'll fix some of those caramel pecan rolls."

She leaned back in her desk chair and looked at him.
"Right now it's getting close to suppertime and my tummy
is reminding me we skipped lunch, except for ice cream. I
have stuff here to make two of my special chicken pot pies,
and there's strawberry gelatin, too, with real strawberries
in it."

"Sounds good. Thanks, Cara."

But he was thinking about his half-sister, not food, as
they got up and headed for Carrie's kitchen. He couldn't
begin to picture a young woman named Catherine

MacDonald King. Heck, he was so blank about her it had been easy to imagine she didn't exist for over thirty years. And now? Still not a clue.

But her e-mail to Carrie had sounded...nice.

"Brandon-King."

"Is Catherine King available, please? Carrie McCrite calling."

"Just one moment, please."

"Catherine King speaking."

"Catherine, it's Carrie McCrite, I have your e-mail, and I..."

"Carrie! Did Henry...what did he say?"

"...have Henry with me and we're on my speaker phone. Okay?"

"Oh. Well, hi, Henry." Catherine's laugh sounded way too school-girl nervous to have come from a woman used to appearing in a courtroom.

"Hi," Henry said.

Carrie, hoping to push things beyond the level of single-syllable greetings, said, "I told Henry about your e-mail, in fact I let him read it. Hope that's okay."

"It's okay. I thought you might."

"We both want you to come to our wedding. We're eager to meet you."

"You said *both* of you want me to come?"

"I did. In fact, it was Henry's idea to call. Are you with a client or terribly busy right now?"

"Just doing research. I don't have any appointments until ten."

"Then why don't I let the two of you talk? Here's Henry. You and I can make wedding plans later."

Carrie turned off the speaker and held the receiver toward Henry, who looked as if he'd frozen in his chair. He certainly wasn't smiling.

"Better to jump in a cold swimming pool right off than freeze one toe at a time," she said. "You might start by asking her safe stuff, like about her law practice and how she likes Claremore. You don't have to talk about your family right off the bat."

Henry cleared his throat, and as Carrie left the room she heard him say, "Did Dad ever give you a bat? He and I used to spend hours practicing, throwing a ball back and forth, or him pitching, me trying to hit. Did you ever do that with him?"

Carrie barely made it to the kitchen before she started laughing. Baseball? Well, she just hoped Catherine was ready for whatever conversation pitch Henry threw her way. In any case, they *were* talking to each other.

Chapter 25

Carrie and Henry had made no further fact-finding plans when they walked into church in Eureka Springs on Wednesday evening. An usher greeted them warmly, obviously assuming they were tourists when he asked if they were enjoying their visit to the area. Strangers stood out here.

Carrie led the way into a back pew and began looking around to see if she recognized anyone. More people trickled in as the organ began a prelude, and many of the newcomers sat near them. It was the same in her church at home: everyone wanted to sit in the back. At least it was easy for her to find a few faces she recognized.

The service started and Carrie's mind slid off into a very un-churchy contemplation of the Mukherjees' problems until Henry pushed his arm against her side. She came to attention and heard the final words of a Bible reference: "...*stranger that dwelleth with you shall be unto you as one born among you, and thou shalt love him as thyself; for ye were strangers in the land of Egypt:"*

Wow. Where was that from?

As soon as the service ended, people came to say hello. She'd counted on this natural friendliness: it offered an easy opportunity to ask questions about feelings toward the Mukherjees.

After introducing herself and Henry, Carrie said, "We're here in Eureka Springs hoping to help Ashur and Chandra Mukherjee and their children. Do you know them? They own a flower shop and greenhouse business here and have recently been the target of hateful and violent attacks. I'm sure all of you've heard about their shop being bombed on Monday. What you may not know is that someone also shot at them when they were decorating for a wedding reception at the Crescent on Saturday evening.

"These people aren't exactly strangers, they've lived in Arkansas for thirty years, but I was struck by that Bible passage about love for strangers and tonight's message on brotherhood. They relate to our reasons for being in your town."

Carrie looked around the group. She certainly had their attention.

"The Mukherjees' daughter-in-law, who's Christian, had a baby boy on Monday. Yesterday someone visited her in the hospital here and told her people are calling the family terrible names and threatening to hurt them if they don't get out of town. Can that be true? Henry and I need to know if there really are bad feelings generally toward the Mukherjees or if the hospital visitor perhaps created the story for her own reasons."

A tiny woman with a fluffed halo of white hair spoke up first. "Oh, my. I know the folks you mean, and we've all heard about that young boy leaving a bomb in their shop. I think it's the reason for our lesson on brotherhood tonight. My name is Annie McKenzie, by the way, and I remember seeing you...wasn't it in Fayetteville?"

Carrie smiled at her and nodded.

"Anyway, about that flower shop. I've often sent flowers or gifts from there since it's just a block from my house and I don't drive anymore. I'm usually waited on by a woman who wears beautiful silk saris and has a red dot on her face." She touched a spot above the bridge of her nose to illustrate. "The woman explained it shows she's been praying, or something like that. Occasionally a young woman wearing jeans is there instead, and she has light skin, so I bet that's the daughter-in-law you're talking about. I could tell she was expecting.

"Those women are always friendly and helpful, and I haven't heard anyone say bad things about them. I don't get around town much now, but I can't believe people in general would be so ugly, and to tell it to that girl..."

There was a general murmur of agreement from the group.

"So," Carrie said, "you haven't heard ugly words or gossip about this family? No racist terms or threats?"

Heads all around began to shake, and several people said, "No."

A woman in a bright green polyester pantsuit spoke up. "I'm grateful to say I haven't heard a single thing like that. I think the hospital visitor must have an overactive imagination, but...repeating it? How cruel. It tells me I should increase my prayers for this community."

Now there were nods of agreement, followed by a contemplative silence. In another moment people began to say goodnight and move away. Conversation about the

Mukherjees was obviously over. Carrie and Henry echoed the goodnights and headed for the front steps.

They'd walked to church from the hotel and had gone only a short way along their return route when the usher caught up with them.

"I didn't want to say anything in front of the others," he said, "but I've heard there is ugly talk about the Hindu family at the high school. I'm Tom Russell, and my wife Lisa teaches there. Cody Wells is in one of her classes. If you know about the bombing, I'm sure you know who Cody is?"

"Yes," Carrie and Henry said in unison.

"Well, kids are gonna support their football star, and though Cody is new here this year, he's very popular. Bright boy, Lisa says. She likes him."

"Then there is talk at the school?" Henry asked.

"Yes. The kids are using some ugly terms, but according to my wife, it's just talk; so far, at least. They bluster, copy each other, mostly don't know what they're saying, and certainly don't think about the consequences. Anyway, I bet that's where your source of gossip is. I'm a letter carrier here so I do get around, and I haven't heard anything but sadness and sympathy from adults over what happened to the Mukherjees on Monday. I'm sure a few resent them for various reasons—misguided though they may be—but they'll generally keep such things to themselves and not talk about it outside a small circle.

"As for the bombing, no one wants to believe Cody is responsible, but everyone has also heard about the murder of his mother. Most think he acted out of grief and igno-rance. It was emotion, not reasoning.

"People here like the Mukherjee family, at least those who know them or have had personal dealings with them.

I think most of us agree they don't seem the type to hurt anyone, let alone kill. And why would they have any reason to hurt Mrs. Wells anyway?"

Carrie realized that the vandalism and threats directed toward Chandra and Ashur over the last few months weren't general knowledge, which was probably a good thing. She wasn't about to get any more gossip started, so she merely said, "I'm sure they would have no reason. But this whole situation is deeply disturbing and frightening for the family. Henry and I are trying to get it stopped."

"That's commendable—but I'm curious," Tom said. "Just how did you two get involved since you don't live in Eureka Springs?"

"We're getting married here over the Thanksgiving holiday, and Artistic Floral Designs is decorating for our wedding," Carrie told him.

"For gosh sake, I assumed you'd been married for years. I think I heard your last names were different, but these days that doesn't signify much, especially to a mail carrier." His voice faded away and he cleared his throat.

"Well, this is where I turn off. Hope to see you at church again whenever you're in the area. If you need anything more while you're in town, here's my card."

"Thanks for your help," Henry said, putting the card in his pocket as Tom headed down a side street.

When they'd gone another half-block, Henry spoke again. "That Bible verse about the stranger being as one born among you sure was a good one. How do you think the Mukherjees would react to being given a copy of that?"

"If someone quoted a wise passage from Hindu sacred writing—like one of the Vedas—for your benefit, how would you react?"

"I see what you mean. So we can quote away."

"Yes. I could probably find the passage in my Bible and copy it when we get back home. I didn't hear where it came from, and I don't have a concordance with me."

"Leviticus. I asked specifics. Chapter 19, Verse 34."

"Oh, you!"

Henry ignored her dig. "How about the school being the source of gossip?"

"Plausible, don't you think? If that's the case, I'd like to tone it down before it spreads out into the community at large. But, here's a question, Henry. How did Melissa hear it? It sounds like she exaggerated what was being said, but I think she knows about the school gossip."

"She could have gotten it from Cody or his aunt Jan."

"And that could confirm a connection between Melissa and Jan Owen."

"Yes, it could."

"So, what next?"

"Why don't I see if I can get an appointment with the school superintendent tomorrow while you three do your girl stuff?"

"Oh..."

"What?"

"Nothing, and here we are at the hotel." Carrie cut off what she'd been about to say, '*Can't you wait until later? I'd like to go to the school with you.*' She didn't want Henry to think she didn't trust him to stop talk at the school on his own. She did trust him, of course. She was...quite sure about that.

It took a moment for Henry's eyes to adjust to the lobby lighting after they walked in from the dark street, so he almost missed seeing Melissa Donley jerk away from a computer behind the registration desk. He realized she'd seen the two of them first, and her quick movement probably meant she didn't want them to know she was looking at hotel registration information. But why would she care about that?

Ahh, because she'd probably been looking up Henry King and Carrie McCrite. Otherwise, why the appearance of guilt? Why turn her back on them? Everything about her demeanor shouted subterfuge.

Okay, Miss, he thought, *it's time we gave you a little shove.*

He wasn't sure Carrie would agree with what he felt he had to do now, but there was no chance for discussion, so he merely took hold of her hand and walked to the counter.

"Hello, Melissa, got a minute? The three of us need to talk."

"I'm busy...checking on wedding scheduling," she said, lowering her voice in mid-statement as a reservations clerk came out of the office area. "I'll be busy for quite a while."

"That's okay, we'll wait," Henry said. He led the way to the tufted Victorian couch across from the counter and sat, pulling Carrie down beside him, then turned to watch Melissa.

"What's going on?" Carrie asked. "What do we need to talk with her about?"

"I think she was at that computer checking to see if we were registered or were coming here soon. Otherwise why the intensely guilty actions as soon as she saw us? Did you catch that? It was as if we'd caught her with her hands in the cash drawer. I think our appearance unnerved her only because she was looking for information about us at the moment we walked in the door and she wasn't sharp enough to conceal her reaction. That's why I felt we should—while she was at a disadvantage, off-balance so to speak—offer a challenge and let her know we overheard her conversation with Rebecca at the hospital."

"But we didn't overhear anything. Rebecca told..."

"Rather than risk getting Rebecca in trouble for talking to us, I thought we'd put the blame on our shoulders. It's a small, but important, lie, just in case."

"You already know I'm willing to adjust how facts are reported for what I consider justifiable reasons. Interesting to learn you can do it too. But—hey, hadn't we better look away lest she wonder why we're staring at her and whispering."

"I want to make her nervous. Keep staring."

Melissa pretended to ignore them as she poked at computer keys for a few minutes, glancing at the reservations clerk frequently and then lifting her eyes toward the area where they were sitting. Finally she turned away and walked through an opening into the lobby hall, disappearing in the direction of the dining room.

"Shouldn't we follow her?" Carrie asked.

"I have a feeling she'll be back," Henry said. "Under the circumstances, she can't really ignore us."

"What do you plan to do, confront her about the stories supposedly going around town?"

"That's exactly what I'm going to do," Henry said.

"But..." She subsided as Melissa came into view and headed toward them.

"How may I help you?" she asked, her words dripping sugared mush.

"Just wondered if you have any advice about a way to

stop the slanderous gossip you report hearing about the Mukherjee family. You know the town better than we do, but we know slander when we hear it."

"I have no idea what you're talking about."

"Really? Yesterday we overheard you telling Rebecca Mukherjee about name-calling and threats. Or is that something you made up? We've checked around and can find no basis for what you told her."

"But you can't have..." She stopped, and though she appeared cool, the shake in her voice said it all.

Without glancing down, Henry knew Carrie was watching Melissa's face as intently as he was.

Finally Melissa said, "This is none of your business, you know. I understand from Tiffany you plan to be married here, and we're of course delighted you chose us for your wedding. But you needn't concern yourselves with anything else going on in town. You can't possibly understand local problems. No matter what you think you heard, none of it involves you or your wedding plans."

"Oh, but it does," Carrie said. "It involves the florists we've chosen."

"Then I suggest you change florists," Melissa said, "and stick with making wedding plans, or..."

"Or, what?" Henry asked, his voice sounding just as melodramatic as the words themselves did.

But Carrie was the only one who heard him. After giving them an acid smile, Melissa turned away and hurried toward the hall leading to the main staircase.

"Well," Carrie murmured, "as they say, that may have put the cat among the pigeons."

"Yes, and I'm sorry about that," Henry said, "but we needed to shake something loose, and seeing her tonight gave us an opportunity. So far we've heard a lot of interesting talk and we've heard ugly things, but the more we learn, the less we have that points specifically to Sonya Wells's killer. There's nothing concrete. So, cat among the pigeons it is.

"As a result, little love, from now on you're staying close to me or with Eleanor and Shirley. No going off alone, not even to the public restrooms. That means all three of you."

He frowned. "I wish I knew what progress the police are making, but we have no legitimate way of finding that out. We don't even know if they do or really ever did suspect the Mukherjees of Sonya Wells's murder. Maybe I'll eventually have to see how much I learn by going to the station and asking questions. Who knows—might hear some answers."

He got to his feet. "Well, shall we head for bed? We have a lot to accomplish tomorrow and Friday. I just hope that red rose ghost leaves us alone tonight."

Carrie shivered. "That's why I picked two rooms next to each other at the south end of the hotel this time," she said. "Shirley and Eleanor will have the room next to ours starting tomorrow night. I didn't want any of us to be near the spooky stairway that goes nowhere. And, by the way, don't say anything to Eleanor or Shirley about our experiences Monday night. Shirley is a pretty serious believer in ghosts."

"We aren't," Henry said.

"No, of course we aren't."

Chapter 26

When Henry came out of the bathroom, Carrie looked up from her magazine. *"Pajamas?"* she said. "Now that's a change."

"Hmumm. Since we're living celibate lives, I decided to be more discreet in my dress. But, never fear, as a married man I plan on returning to my comfortable night shirts."

She laughed. "Oh, your night shirts are modest enough. But they're kinda like kilts. I've wondered what men wear under them."

He lifted his eyebrows. "Marry me and find out. And, what do you usually wear under nightgowns? Anything?"

"Henry King, shame on you. Cotton underpants, if you must know. Can't account for other women."

"You're the only one I'm interested in."

She smiled up at him and realized a conversation about what one wore under nightclothes was treading on quicksand.

"So," he continued, "let's say tonight I'm matching pajamas with pajamas. That's what you have on, my dear, and fetching they are, with those little flower bouquets all over."

He sat on the edge of her bed and touched a bouquet on the front of her pajama top. "I like that one, it sorta stands out."

"Henry..."

His arms went around her. As she shut her eyes, a warm mouth touched hers, and she realized the magazine was going to be a mass of crumpled pages.

His hand brushed the skin under her pajama top. She felt so incredibly soft there. Henry decided he preferred Carrie's softness and round curves to whatever those perky calendar girls must feel like. He had no personal knowledge of course, but the picture pin-ups looked slick, smooth, and...frightening.

This soft woman was—would soon be—all his.

He hoped his hands didn't feel too rough against her delicate skin.

Henry's touch awakened absolutely amazing feelings. *Why hadn't she ever felt like this with Amos? What had been wrong between them? He'd never made her feel this...warm. Henry made it so lovely to be close. With just one light touch of a finger, he could...*

She shivered involuntarily.

"I, uh, think you'd better go over there now." She freed an arm and pointed to the bed on the other side of the night stand.

Thank goodness he went.

She rubbed her hand across the magazine to smooth it

out and stared down at a page. She was still staring when Henry said, "Well, well, listen to this!"

Startled, she awakened from her reverie and looked over at him. He held up the book he'd been reading and she recognized it as one she'd seen on sale in the lobby downstairs: *The Crescent—Crown Jewel of Eureka Springs*. Henry rested the book against his bent legs and read aloud:

"'My experiments show that when loving married couples share a bed in the hotel, the red bride does not appear to them. Couples on honeymoon prove an exception to this general rule. It's as if she wants to spy on the type of love denied to her over a hundred years ago. Her appearance then is generally quiet. There is none of the regular tapping or moaning, only the soft swish of a bridal gown and puffs of chilled air. When individuals are sensitive, they may also glimpse a wisp of red fabric.'"

"Does it say why she wears red?" Carrie asked, already imagining the answer.

"Red for the blood of the man she was forced to marry—and killed."

"Like Lucia."

"Yes."

"Nonsense," Carrie said, suddenly feeling cranky because he'd reminded her of the red bride. "Nonsense," she repeated. "Besides, with my white curls and your grey hair, we certainly wouldn't look like a honeymoon couple to any ghost—imaginary ghost."

Henry cocked his head to one side and his wide-set dark eyes studied her. "Well, my dear, love is love at any age, no matter who observes it. Besides, the guy who wrote this book seems to have done a lot of research. Makes me wonder, though, where does our ghost get information about the marital status of couples staying in the hotel?

I'll bet she's psychic!" He laughed, which made Carrie feel even more vexed.

"I have no idea and I don't care." She put her glasses and magazine on the night stand and slid under the covers, turning her back to him and pulling the sheet over her head.

She heard his startled, "Huh?" and then the soft *thup* of the book being put down. In another minute he turned the lamp off, and except for a tiny night light, the room went very quiet and dark.

She usually made a trip to the bathroom before going to sleep at night. A couple of hours later she was reminded that her crankiness had caused a break in normal routine.

Something moaned when the toilet flushed. Then she heard *tat-tat, tat-tat*. The noise seemed to be coming from the hallway.

She scurried past the hall door and bounced into bed, once more pulling the covers over her head.

The tapping stopped. Carrie knew, because it took her a long time to go back to sleep. She was imagining Henry, strong and warm, lying beside her.

The mood that swamped her at bedtime had disappeared when she awakened the next morning.

Henry was in the bathroom, so she had time to lie in bed and think. She'd overreacted again and it was silly. She wasn't some teenager, she was a mature woman, getting ready to marry a man she truly, deeply loved.

She slapped at the pillows, then pushed both of them behind her and sat up. At times she felt overwhelmed by love for Henry. And when his kisses and touches came, it was like drowning in a strange and unfamiliar ocean of new sensations. That part was a little frightening.

The bathroom door opened, filling the air around her with clean, soapy smells floating on damp heat. "Well, good morning, Cara," Henry said. "You were still asleep so I went ahead. Now it's all yours."

Neither of them said anything about the previous night's events, and she chose not to tell him what she'd heard when she was in the bathroom after he'd gone to sleep. Probably her imagination anyway. Old buildings could be creaky.

Carrie and Henry were finishing breakfast when Eleanor and Shirley walked in the dining room. Carrie noticed that her friends looked excited and happy. Watching them as they came toward the table, she marveled at how kind they both were. They seemed truly eager to join her in helping the Mukherjee family.

The four sat over coffee while Henry shared information about what they'd learned at church and told them about the confrontation with Melissa Donley. "Partly because of that," he said, "none of you should be alone from now on. Always stay in the company of at least one other person. Don't forget for a moment that we're dealing with a killer."

After they had all nodded solemnly enough to satisfy him, Carrie said, "Guess we should check in with Asher and Chandra first and see how and when we can best help them."

"I hope I'll learn about making bouquets and corsages and wedding decorations," Eleanor said. "I've always wanted to do that, and I really enjoy flower arranging. I wonder..." She paused, then ducked her head and fiddled with her coffee spoon. "Maybe I could apprentice here. You know, come over a few times after all this is over and learn more about the business. I've often thought I'd like to open a little flower shop in Guilford. What do you think?"

Both Shirley and Carrie stared at her. Carrie was trying to picture Eleanor as a business owner and couldn't, but Shirley was either kinder or had a better imagination. "Well," she said slowly, "you'd be good at it—with the public, I mean—and Jason could do the bookkeeping and business stuff." After a pause she began to smile broadly. "It sounds like fun. Maybe, after Junior comes back home to work on the farm, you'd let me help out in your shop, off and on. You might need a hand sometimes. I wouldn't ask you to pay me," she added hastily.

"That *would* be fun," Eleanor said, "but, so far, it's just a dream." Carrie stared at them in amazement and couldn't think of a thing to say.

Henry broke in. "Okay, plans for today. This morning I'm visiting the school, then I'll stop by the police station. I've decided to ask if they'll share new information they might have with us. We haven't seen anyone from there since Monday, and I think I'd better explain we're trying to uncover whatever we can about the murder of Sonya Wells at the request of the Mukherjees. I'd like Trent and the others to know, because working together can be a good deal for all of us, provided they're flexible enough to agree. I'll assure them we're being discreet, will stay out of their way, and report all findings to them at once. I'm sure they realize civilians sometimes talk with other civilians more freely than they do with uniformed officers—like the people at church did with us last night. The police department would probably be concerned about liability so won't be able to give us an official okay, but I don't think there'll be any open objection to a little extra detective work on the side.

"You three go on with your plans now, and let's meet back here for lunch at one o'clock. Just remember, no going off alone." He got to his feet, pulled Carrie's chair back for her, then turned to Eleanor and Shirley. "May I help you ladies bring your luggage in from the car?"

The three friends found Asher, Chandra, and Purdy at work inside the wrecked shop, filling boxes with the last few items that could be salvaged. After the boxes were loaded in the trunk of Eleanor's car, Chandra joined the women and they drove to Rebecca and Purdy's home, located next door to the family's two greenhouses.

First, Chandra knocked gently at the house and a tired-looking Rebecca welcomed them in for a brief admiration scene with baby Charlie. Then Eleanor, Shirley, and Chandra headed for a workroom in one of the greenhouses to begin creating flower baskets for a weekend wedding, and Carrie stayed behind to watch the baby while Rebecca napped.

Using the time alone, Carrie put a load of laundry in the washing machine, then began dusting furniture. She'd just moved a second load to Rebecca's dryer when Charlie let his hunger be known. On cue, his mother awakened.

While the baby was nursing, Carrie settled in a chair nearby, leaned her head back, and shut her eyes, listening for ideas about how to direct their conversation. The silence was broken only by baby noises and she relaxed, letting her mind wander.

Then Rebecca said, "I like your hair, sort of silver and white. Hope when I'm your age, my hair looks like that."

Startled, Carrie replied without thinking, "You'll always be beautiful. It won't matter what color your hair is, brunette or grey."

She's making conversation, Carrie thought. *Wants to ask me something and doesn't know how to do it.*

Silence returned. Finally Rebecca spoke again. "Anything new about the murder of Sonya Wells?" There was timidity in her voice, and Carrie wondered if Rebecca might be afraid of the answer she'd hear.

Carrie explained how she and Henry learned that the slanderous talk Melissa reported wasn't happening anywhere but between a few teenagers at school. "I believe Melissa invented that story," she said.

The young woman looked startled. "Why would she make up such awful things? I don't understand."

Carrie thought back to what Rebecca told them about Melissa's conversation in the hospital and suddenly sat upright in her chair.

The knife! Hadn't she said Melissa mentioned a knife?

"When Henry and I visited you in the hospital, did you tell us Melissa said people suspected the Mukherjee family of killing Sonya Wells because of a knife?"

Tears began streaming down Rebecca's cheeks. "It's my fault," she whispered. "The knife that killed Ms. Wells was mine. I gave it to Melissa a couple of weeks ago. I'd been cutting stems to arrange flowers in a vase at the wedding chapel downtown when she saw me and came in. She admired the knife, and since we have so many of them, I gave it to her. She told me Tuesday that she never used it because it disappeared at the Crescent a short time later. Can they tell if it was mine? My fingerprints..."

"Henry saw the knife that was next to Sonya Wells's body. He said it had a lot of decoration on the handle and probably wouldn't show clear fingerprints. Besides, Melissa's fingerprints would be there with yours, and possibly others."

"Not Melissa's. I couldn't find the cardboard cover for the knife so I wrapped it in green florist paper when I handed it to her. She said on Tuesday that she'd never unwrapped it, so my fingerprints would still be there and the police would think, you know, that I..."

Carrie jumped to her feet and went to take Charlie as his mother began crying. She laid the baby against her own chest with his head resting on her shoulder and patted his back gently while Rebecca's loud sobs continued. Carrie looked out the window and hoped the three women in the greenhouse next door couldn't hear the noise.

After a couple of bubbling sounds Charlie fell asleep against Carrie's soft front, and, assured that he wasn't going to begin crying too, she turned back to Rebecca and said, "Hush now, and listen to me. I know that knife couldn't be yours."

She had Rebecca's attention. "But, how?"

"Because I have something to confess, too. As you know, Henry and I found the body. I saw a knife sheath in the parking lot just above where Ms. Wells was lying, and, since it had the IBE logo on it, I thought I'd be protecting your in-laws if I picked it up and put it in my pocket. What I did was wrong and stupid. There may well be a killer's fingerprints on it, and picking it up made possible evidence worthless. The police would only have my word now that the cardboard cover was ever in that parking lot.

"But, I think the knife Henry found must have had the sheath on it before it was put next to the body. I don't think a knife was what killed Ms. Wells anyway, or at least it wasn't the only weapon used, since her head was smashed with a rock. Therefore, I'm convinced the knife was left there to direct suspicion toward one of you. If so, the cover must have been dropped in the parking lot for the same reason, to direct suspicion at the Mukherjees."

Carrie's brow wrinkled as she tried to focus her thoughts. *That darn cardboard cover, why...*

"Oh, wait a minute...that means...that means if the cover was intentionally left where the police would find it, then I'm wrong about fingerprints. There wouldn't be any belonging to the killer. If he or she didn't wear gloves, it would have been wiped off."

She took in a huge breath, and Charlie, sensing the movement under his little body, snuggled closer to her.

"I do hope I'm right. I've been feeling a truck load of remorse ever since understanding I'd tampered with evidence that could have told us who really killed Wells."

She looked at Rebecca and her mouth twitched with the wisp of a smile. "I still regret picking up that cardboard, but maybe it did no harm after all.

"Here's something else. Since the police aren't saying anything about finding the knife, and Henry and I haven't told anyone, how did Melissa know about it?"

She and Rebecca stared at each other, and Carrie was sure they were both thinking the same thing.

She handed Charlie back to his mother, who settled him in to continue nursing. Then she looked up at Carrie, who was still standing. "But why on earth would she do such a terrible thing? I can't believe someone could just... kill..."

"Ummm, we've discovered several things that might help us figure that out. You said Jan and Melissa are probably close friends, and you believe Jan is paying Melissa a percentage fee to direct business her way, right?"

Rebecca nodded her head.

"Henry and I learned when we visited the Owen Shop on Tuesday that, though Jan is totally devoted to her floral business, her sister Sonya wasn't. She wanted Jan to close it down and join her in the land investment office. I suspect the shop hasn't been doing all that well recently, and, rightly or wrongly, Jan blames your in-laws for her diminished income.

"If sales were decreasing and Sonya wanted Jan to close the shop, well, it would give Jan plenty of reason to try and get all of you out of town. Didn't the ugly stuff start a short time after Sonya Wells moved here?"

Rebecca was staring up at her, wide-eyed.

"Then what if—motivated by friendship with Jan as well as the extra income gained by directing business toward Owen's Flowers—Melissa decided to get rid of the person threatening to close Jan down?"

"But," Rebecca said, "*murder*? That's a terrible response to what was really a business dispute."

"It seems so to us. But how do we know what's been going on inside Melissa Donley's head?"

Carrie noticed that Charlie had fallen asleep again. "Do you want to hold him, or shall I put him in his crib?"

"I think I'll hold him for a while," Rebecca said. "He's so normal, so real." She kissed her son's head, then continued. "On the other hand, what you're talking about doesn't seem real; it's an ugly nightmare. And what are we going to do about it?"

"Well, for one thing, protect ourselves, because you could be in danger too. If Melissa realizes she mentioned that knife to you and the presence of a knife by the body isn't general knowledge, she'll be afraid of what you might say. Henry has already warned Eleanor, Shirley, and me that we must be extra careful simply because we're investigating the murder, and also because Melissa knows we discovered there is no bad talk about the Mukherjees around town generally. He said we shouldn't spend any time alone while we're here in Eureka Springs, and he hasn't heard what you and I know yet, which makes Melissa look even worse.

"I think we should tell the police about this as soon as we can. If we tell them and make sure Melissa finds out we did, we won't be in danger. It would be out of our hands. So, shall we talk to them right away? I bet they'd even come here. Okay?"

Slowly, Rebecca nodded.

"Henry was going to the police station this morning. Maybe I can catch him there. Ideally he'll tell the police and bring an officer here. We'll face this together and feel better for it, won't we?" Carrie smiled, and Rebecca managed a small grin in return.

"The phone is over there," she said. "And would you see if you can get Purdy on his cell phone? I'd like him to be here, too."

Chapter 27

Sergeant Lonnie Trent had been barking at them for several minutes. Barking was the only word Carrie could think of that fit the sergeant's sharp, jerky delivery.

Now he paused to look from face to face around Rebecca and Purdy's living room.

Carrie shut her eyes while in the background Trent's voice began again.

Was he angry because she'd concealed the knife cover? Well, that was understandable.

Angry at those who hadn't called him the very minute something that might have bearing on his case occurred? Again, understandable.

Angry at all of them for, as he said—rather too theatrically in Carrie's opinion—"putting themselves in harm's way"?

That part, at least, was not their fault.

Mostly, she guessed, Trent was angry at himself because he felt stumped and frustrated by this case and had an audience here who not only, as politicians often said, "felt his pain," but shared it. He also knew that most of them were counting on him to remove the pain as well as the danger facing every one of them, right down to baby Charlie.

She lifted her chin a notch higher. As far as she was concerned, the sergeant had every right to feel frustration. She felt it too, plus a significant amount of fear.

And the most frustrating thing of all was happening right inside her own thinking. A door there seemed to be stuck shut, closing out logical insight and the ideas her detective work thrived on.

The sergeant slapped a hand against his thigh—*snap*—which brought her back to his words.

"Our department doesn't have the personnel to guard all you women. But three of you can sure help me by getting out of town. Go home. King, take your female friends back to Guilford—get 'em away from my jurisdiction."

Ah well, Carrie thought, tuning him out again, *angry or not, he isn't actually yelling and his face isn't red.*

Poor man, this is quite a bit of serious crime for him to deal with. He said they're not used to murders here in Eureka Springs. Now he has murder, bombing, people being shot at. No wonder he feels frustrated. Proves he can use our help, even if he doesn't want to admit it.

She realized the room had gone quiet.

Carrie came to attention and claimed the silence quickly. "But Sergeant, you wouldn't know as much as you do about Melissa Donley's possible role in all this if it hadn't been for Rebecca and the rest of us." She pointed to Rebecca, to Henry, and then swept her hand to indicate the women seated on the couch. "We have been of some help to you, and we haven't really gotten in your

way, have we? Besides, Henry already told the three of us
we must stay together, never be alone, and we'd be safe. As
for Rebecca and Charlie, a little caution and guarding by
your department will take care of their safety.

"Henry, Shirley, Eleanor, and I are here in Eureka
Springs today for three reasons." She held up fingers.
"First, to help the Mukherjee family get their business up
and running. Second, to assist Rebecca Mukherjee as a
new mother. Third, to see if we can help clear the family
of any suspicion in the murder of Sonya Wells and learn
who shot at them Saturday night.

"As I understand it, the probable time of death and
an investigation of where Mukherjee family members
were during the day on Saturday have pretty much elimi-
nated them as suspects in this killing. You have witnesses
who saw Ashur, Chandra, and their children in the places
they said they were. You have said Wells was probably not
killed where we found her and where evidence was set up
to make the Mukherjees look guilty. Therefore our wish
to prove this family innocent of any part in the death of
Sonya Wells has been fulfilled.

"The shooting? Well, we'll leave out the shooting for
now." Again, she came up against that door taped shut inside her head but, ignoring it, continued. "As for our work
in the flower shop and to help a new mother, that's totally
out of your jurisdiction, isn't it?

"Now—when are you going to talk with Melissa
Donley? As soon as she realizes every one of us knows she
slipped up by mentioning the knife, and also realizes we
figured out the only gossip about the Mukherjees is at the
high school, we'll all be safe, won't we?"

Trent eyed her sourly. "Someone from the department
will talk with Ms. Donley as soon as possible. Until we do

that, Rebecca will keep her doors locked and stay away from windows, especially at night." He looked toward Rebecca. "And young lady, be sure that cell phone with our number in it is by you at all times, you hear? Call if you need to go out for any reason. We'll find someone to drive you, we can manage that much."

He got to his feet and held out his hand, palm up. "Fingerprints or not, I'll take the knife cover now, Ms. McCrite."

She went to her jacket, removed the tissue-wrapped cardboard, and handed it to him. "I know I was a fool," she said as she sat down again, "if it's any comfort to you."

He didn't comment, just stuck the cover in his pocket and spoke to Henry. "I give up on these three." He pointed toward the couch. "They're all yours, Major King."

Humpf, Trent was treating them like chattel. She was glad to see that Henry did not look pleased.

When he reached the front door, Sergeant Trent stopped and turned back. "Okay, now I'm gonna tell you something for your own good...not to shock you. I think you already know most of it anyway. The attack on Sonya Wells was vicious. Bashing someone's head in by repeated blows with a rock is ugly. The killer must have been driven by fury or desperation or both. He or she wouldn't even have had to be especially strong, because we think an autopsy will show Ms. Wells was comatose at the time of the attack. There were no signs she resisted her killer.

"Detective Wolverton found the wrapper from a sleep medication prescription bottle caught in the waste pipe of her toilet. The prescription was in Wells's name. There were two empty glasses in the dishwasher. No fingerprints. Somebody washed those glasses before they were put in there. Unusual, don't you think?"

Eleanor said, speaking as slowly and thoughtfully as if the solution of this whole crime depended on her opinion, "Well, no, I don't think that's unusual at all. If I were a killer tidying up and had used a glass for poison or something, I'd wash it, of course. Any of us would." She looked around the room, then at Trent's stoic face. "I mean... wouldn't you, Sergeant Trent?"

Trent stared at Eleanor for a moment before he went on. "Anyway, there was no sign of a prescription bottle in or around the house. With the label gone, the container could have been tossed in the trash anywhere. Needle in a haystack. Too bad, because it may have had something we could identify—residue or fingerprints, maybe.

"What I'm saying this for is so you'll all take the danger seriously and be very careful. Someone out there is desperate."

Carrie saw his lips pinch together in a straight line before he turned to the door, yanked it open, and hurried out. In another minute they heard his car start.

"I hope we can settle this soon," Carrie said while the four friends ate schnitzel, cabbage, potato pancakes, and applesauce at the Bavarian restaurant that night. "I'd like to begin enjoying wedding preparations."

"Well, yes," Eleanor said, pausing to sign the charge ticket the server handed her, "but first things first. Carrie, we'll get to you in plenty of time, but we still have a job here. So, what's on for tomorrow? I know what the three of us plan, but how about you, Henry?"

"Since you're working on flower arrangements with Chandra, and Purdy's staying with Rebecca and Charlie all day, I told Ashur I'd help re-build latticework arches for tomorrow night's wedding and go with him to install them at the hotel."

"We're all accounted for then." Eleanor picked up her purse and started to stand.

"Wait a minute," Henry said. "I want to be sure you really are spending the day with Chandra. Together."

"That's what we plan," Carrie assured him.

The next morning the three women had just spread out their work materials under Chandra's watchful eye when Eleanor said, "Chandra, would you excuse the three of us for about an hour? We have a bit of work to do before we start here. If Henry comes back from taking measurements at the hotel and looks for us, would you tell him we're doing flower research and are definitely staying together?"

"I don't feel comfortable lying," Chandra said.

"Oh, you won't be," Eleanor assured her. "We truly are doing flower research—at Owen's shop."

Shirley and Eleanor were chattering away, telling Carrie what they'd learned about decorating and filling flower baskets the previous day, when Eleanor turned her car into the Owen parking lot. An immediate silence swallowed their conversation until Shirley said, "Land-a-mercy, look at that thing. It's like a..."

"Huge cuckoo clock," Eleanor finished for her. "Carrie, I'm amazed you haven't mentioned this, er, structure."

"To see is to believe," Carrie said as they opened car doors. "Oh, there's the white van. Owen must be in the shop. Now, Eleanor, are you comfortable with what you're going to say? Henry and I learned a lot here, maybe the three of us will, too."

"Yes, I'm ready. Let's go do it," Eleanor said, still staring at the building.

Jan Owen had her back to the entrance when Carrie opened the door for her friends and followed them inside the shop. The florist—whose bulk and big blond hair looked even more impressive in the ornate building—continued fitting purple foil around a pot of lavender mums, and, for a minute, she didn't acknowledge the arrival of customers. The three women lined up at the counter, waiting. Eventually Owen, still not looking in their direction, said, "Help you?"

"We're here about a wedding," Eleanor said, "to plan flowers."

The businesslike tone got the woman's attention. She wiped her hands on her green coverall and turned around. When she saw them, Carrie thought she looked suspicious for just a few seconds before she caught herself and smiled, then glanced quickly toward the rear of the shop.

Following her gaze, Carrie saw Cody Wells through a wide opening into the shop's work room. Good, he was here too, as Cindy Sturdevant had promised. It looked like he'd been unpacking glass vases and lining them up on a shelf. The boy sensed his aunt's sudden attention and looked toward the front room. When he saw the three newcomers, he froze, and the cardboard box he held teetered dangerously over the edge of his work table. He steadied the box and, like his aunt, quickly returned his face and actions to normal.

Sensitive kid, Carrie thought. *He recognizes us from the day of the bombing.* She'd wondered if the boy saw them as he rushed out of Artistic Floral on Monday and was glad there was still a bandage on her cheek. He probably realized why it was there.

She watched him go back to lining up vases. It didn't hurt at all to remind Cody Wells of what he did that day and that people were injured. She had a feeling it would matter to him.

Eleanor continued, "I'm a wedding planner from Guilford, and this woman," she waved a hand toward Carrie without introducing her, "is to be married here later this year. My assistant and I," another hand wave, indicating Shirley, "would like to inquire about your ability to help us."

Jan drew herself up to her full height which must be, Carrie decided, at least six feet tall plus hair. "We are the top floral designers in this area."

Eleanor took a date book from her purse, opened it, and pretended to study a page. "Yes, you are recommended, along with a firm called Artistic Floral. We have not spoken to them about this wedding yet. We had planned to go there on Monday, but there was an...interruption. Perhaps we won't have to interview them, depending..."

"We can fill your needs to greatest satisfaction," Owen said, "and I am sure you'll prefer doing business with an American-owned firm. Most do."

"American-owned?" Eleanor let the words hang in the air.

"Artistic Floral is foreign." The big blond made the word *foreign* sound like a curse. "People from India."

This couldn't be going better, Carrie thought.

"My goodness, there must be a lot of people from India here in Eureka Springs." Now Eleanor's voice oozed smugness. "I happen to have an acquaintance who's with the Eureka Springs Police. He told me when I talked with him just this morning that a Hindu couple here was first suspected, then cleared of involvement in a murder case the police are investigating. Murder! Isn't that simply terrible?"

Owen sneered, revealing a row of too-perfect white teeth. "Oh, those are the people I spoke of, and I doubt they've been cleared." She glanced toward her nephew again and lowered her voice. "It was my own sister they killed last Saturday night. One or both of them murdered her in the woods right next to the Crescent Hotel parking lot."

Eleanor shuddered. "Tsk, tsk, how tragic for you." Shirley and Carrie produced sad faces and shook their heads in unison.

"That's why I doubt they have an alibi. I, for one, saw the husband there by himself that night, though he didn't see me, thank goodness. The tragedy is, those Hindus meant to kill me instead of poor Sonya—get rid of the business competition, you know. They killed her by mistake!"

Owen was warming to her story in response to three listeners with sympathetic expressions. "You'll understand that I must look my best at our customer's weddings, and I have several wigs to use in case my hair gets mussed and I haven't time to go to the salon. Sonya was taking my oldest wig to a friend whose daughter has the role of Martha Washington in a school play. I'm sure, in fun, my sister just popped that wig on her head and those foreigners mistook her for me and..." She made a slicing motion across her throat.

"Oh, no, you poor dear," Eleanor said. She raised her voice as if for emphasis. "But my friend *did* say most definitely that the Hindu couple is in the clear. They've accounted for where they were during the period of time involved, and a number of people confirm it."

"But, I saw him..."

Whatever Jan Owen planned to say was cut off by a

crash from the work room. Everyone turned to look toward Cody Wells as he stared at them, one hand clutching an empty cardboard box.

Carrie didn't need to guess what had happened. She was becoming very familiar with the sound of breaking glass.

Jan Owen's agitation and the resulting tirade directed at her nephew ended any need for continuing their wedding flower charade. Eleanor told the back of Owen's green coverall that they'd return at a better time, and the three women all but ran out of the shop.

After Eleanor's car began moving, Shirley said, "Whoee...she did unload just like you said she might, Carrie. Looks like she's another one who doesn't see granny ladies as anything beyond wrinkles and addlepated curiosity."

Carrie leaned forward from the back seat. "I've found age and grey hair often give us a huge advantage over younger people. Many folks, women especially, are willing or even eager to dump their problems on a sympathetic, non-judgmental granny."

Shirley laughed. "We're the 'Granny Detectives.' I like that." She glanced back at Carrie and reminded her to fasten her seat belt before she said, "I'm more than glad that boy was in the shop. Now he's heard the truth about Chandra and Ashur. Tell me, though, how are we gonna let the police or Henry know what happened back there without giving up we didn't exactly follow today's plan?"

Carrie could still picture the look on Cody Wells's young face after he heard the Mukherjees weren't suspects in the killing of his mother. "He was starting to cry," she said. "Did you see that? A teenaged boy, and he was crying, and his stupid aunt just kept yelling and yelling as if she had no sense of how he felt. Or," she said more slowly, thinking it through, "maybe she did."

Shirley turned to stare at Carrie. "His mother is dead. Is it so surprising he would cry?"

"Well, no, but why right now, when he found out the Mukherjees had nothing to do with his mother's death? Crying isn't unexpected under the circumstances, but I wonder..."

"I wonder," Eleanor stuck in, "if Cody Wells just learned his aunt lied to him and if he might not talk to the police on his own. Is that what you were going to say, Carrie? Maybe we won't have to tell anyone what we've done, at least not right away."

Shirley asked, "But, wouldn't his aunt try to stop him from doing that? Talk to the police, I mean?"

"She might," Carrie said, speaking slowly as she thought of something else. "Girls, help me here. Jan Owen said she saw Ashur at the Crescent on Saturday night. What was she doing there—if she really was there?"

The three women fell into an uneasy silence until the car turned onto the greenhouse road. Then all of them started to speak at once.

"It means..."

"That could mean she..."

And Eleanor's voice, emotional and ragged, spiking above the rest, "Do you think it's possible she killed her own sister? Just banged her to death with a rock?"

Silence returned until Eleanor's car pulled up by the workroom door. Then Shirley said, her voice almost a whisper, "I'm more than glad we're getting back to our flower baskets."

Chapter 28

At last Carrie felt like a bride-to-be.

Water swirled, steam drifted, a masseuse awaited. She leaned back, shut her eyes, and spent a moment lamenting the modesty that kept her from trying something like this years ago.

Eleanor and Shirley had stopped off to look at local artwork in the lobby gift shop, but they would soon be enjoying similar pampering in rooms next door. She couldn't wait to find out what Shirley might say about such luxurious treatment. Or Eleanor, for that matter, though she was used to *the spa experience*, as she put it.

Carrie let her thoughts float free. Out of the blissful ether a picture formed. Two bridesmaids, Eleanor and Shirley, standing with matron-of-honor Susan. Perfect, even if that meant every woman at her wedding would be in the wedding party.

Except Catherine? She started a giggle but ended up sputtering instead when water sloshed into her mouth.

Catherine could be her flower girl.

Hmmmm, what should her attendants wear? They probably wouldn't want dresses alike. Carrie lifted the toes of her right foot above the water and stared at them for a minute as they wiggle-waved at her. Oh, never mind dresses. Shirley and Eleanor could figure all that out for themselves.

She pulled her toes back under the swirling water and reminded her shoulders and forehead to relax. Ahhhh, bliss.

This spa trip was a really good idea.

Earlier, after Chandra gave final approval to their table full of flower baskets, all that remained was for Henry and the Mukherjees to deliver a van load of completed wedding frou-frou to the hotel and set everything up as Chandra dictated. Wanting to see their handiwork, the three women followed the van in Eleanor's car and peeked in the Veranda Room to observe decorating progress. Chandra was busy arranging some of their flower baskets on white pillars along a newly-created center aisle. Henry, on a ladder, helped Ashur weave garlands of flowers through lattice arches set up to frame the bride and groom.

And, anticlimactically, Chandra's three volunteer flower basket designers were out of work. That left them at loose ends, free to do whatever they pleased while waiting for Henry. Suddenly, brilliantly, Carrie thought of the Crescent Hotel's New Moon Spa.

The spa could fit them in. She, Eleanor, and Shirley had the time. They certainly deserved a relaxing treat after two days of murder anxiety contrasted with very fulfilling work as florist assistants.

Her offer to treat her friends to a whirlpool bath and massage was accepted—enthusiastically by Eleanor, timidly by Shirley.

Now, alone and naked in the tub, Carrie realized she'd felt timid too. Thank goodness Shirley and Eleanor were lingering in the gift shop and she'd had the dressing room to herself.

Undressing in front of others had been a nightmare for her since middle school gym class. Most of the other pre-teen girls displayed developing curves while she still looked as if she belonged in a boy's gym suit. Of course that skinniness was long gone, replaced by generous curves before she reached twenty. But these days her mature-woman curves had gathered rumples she usually hid under clothing.

Ah, well. At least she was doing something new to open up a new life and, even if temporarily, wash away the darkness and agony of an unsolved murder.

They'd passed Melissa in the hotel lobby on the way to the gift shop and spa. At first, seeing the wedding planner in the hotel chilled Carrie, but then she realized Sergeant Trent must have already talked with her about the knife and the made-up gossip concerning the Mukherjees. And, indeed, Melissa's greeting to the three of them had been perfunctory rather than aggressive or threatening—a good sign. In any case, Carrie simply refused to worry about Melissa Donley right now.

Crack! The sound that had announced a bullet flying through the conservatory window invaded her thoughts. Why did she feel like some idea about that shooting was still lurking, hidden, inside her head?

The bullet missed everyone, but the police and Henry now agreed the gun it came from was only feet from where Ashur and Chandra stood. That meant the shooter prob-ably didn't intend to hit living flesh.

Why shoot at all, then?

That shot...all along she'd pictured Sonya and Jan in the darkness, Sonya with the gun. Kurt Gibson even told them Sonya was familiar with firearms, had taken her son Cody hunting last fall. Sonya...

Carrie sat up in the tub, splashing water over the edge. NO! Sonya was dead by then. Maybe not placed on the hillside yet, but dead somewhere.

Two people in the darkness. If not Sonya and Jan, then who?

WHO? Jan and...and...Melissa?

Melissa knew...knew...what did Melissa know? And why was she part of this at all? Surely it had to be for a reason more significant than receiving money to send flower business toward Owen.

Well, what, then?

Henry said people sometimes killed for reasons anyone else would see as trivial, but Melissa seemed far too intelligent and calculating for that. If she was involved in killing, it would not be for any trivial reason. Blackmail? Did Sonya know something bad about Melissa? Or was it Jan who knew... whatever?

What now? Oh! Sergeant Trent could research Melissa's past. She needed to talk with him right away.

Carrie lifted her head and squirmed in the slippery tub, looking around the small room. The terry robe she'd put on in the dressing area was on a hook by the door behind her.

Golly, she sure didn't want to leave this glorious whirl-pool. The attendant said she could be alone in the water for not more than twenty minutes.

Her cell phone was in a dressing room locker with her clothing and other possessions. *Oh, bother. Calling Trent could wait.*

She'd just settled back in the tub when someone came through the door behind her. Was the time up already? Before Carrie could turn her head, a powdery substance floated into the tub. What? Rose-scented bubble bath?

Then a red scarf drifted in front of Carrie's eyes, and before she could scream, red arms tied the scarf around her neck, cutting off any sound above a feeble duck-like squawk. The figure moved to the side of the tub and there, close enough to touch, was the bride dressed in red.

But the bride had no face. In place of the face, Carrie saw a hideous mask, made blurry and more evil-looking by the red veil that covered it. She began thrashing back and forth, trying to get her feet under her, to pull up.

Bubbles made the tub so slippery she couldn't move.

A red arm raised, lifting something that looked like a cigarette lighter in front of Carrie's own face. Then came the spray...

The coughing, heaving gags, gasps for air, were slowing down at last, and Carrie began to sense her surroundings. She moaned and tried opening her eyes. The glimpse she got through slitted lids told her there was no need to bother with the pain of open eyes because she lay in total darkness. Her face throbbed with heat, every breath was burning agony, but below the neck her naked body was so cold she vibrated with uncontrollable shivering.

"Oh, dear God, I need help."

The floor under her felt rough; her hands and feet were bound with some kind of wire...florist's wire? Did that mean she was dead, dying, or someone would soon kill her? Would she, too, become a body on a hillside?

NO! Do something. Fight. Use the strength God gave

you.

She tried to connect thoughts to body and eventually found the muscle strength to force herself into a sitting position. Ow! She must have been dragged here on her bare behind. Bracing scraped-raw flesh against what felt like a wood wall, Carrie inched up until she stood, propped against...hinges...a door?

Cold, so cold...oh, dear heaven. This had to be the mortuary refrigerator.

Well, thank goodness her hands were bound in front of her. She moved away from the door in tiny hops, arms straight out, until one bare breast hit the edge of a shelf, stopping her with a yelp of pain. Yes, there were the shelves! She lifted her hands, felt a plastic cylinder, and curved her fingers, pipe-wrench style, around it. She lifted the container and, without trying to pull out the roses it held, dumped the icy contents over her face, setting off yet another round of convulsive shivering. A second vase of roses and water went the same way; another and another were dashed into her face until the burning in her eyes, nostrils, and skin lessened, and her thoughts began to move in something beyond a body-conscious whirl of pain, congestion, and cold.

Since her wrists had been wired together in front of her, why couldn't she...yes, she could reach her feet when she sat her scraped and tender backside on the floor and bent her knees. In only a few minutes she'd removed the wire and her feet were free. Had that woman...had the red bride known how easy unwinding the wire on her feet would be when her hands were bound in front of her body?

C-cold.

She tried to picture the cooler as she'd seen it last

Tuesday morning. Heavy wooden walls, tongue-and-groove boards lined with insulation. Even if her voice was strong enough for yelling, would anyone hear her through these walls?

There was something made of cloth in here somewhere. She'd seen folds of it on one of these shelves last Tuesday, in...in a back corner to the right of the door. But she had no sense of direction now. There had been all those vases of flowers and—she concentrated—stacks of fabric on a shelf in a back corner.

She was on her feet again, moving, taking each step carefully, mindful of splinters and unseen obstacles. Once she'd located a shelf, she began sliding her bound hands along it, wary of splinters there, too. She bumped into a roll of paper, managed to rip off a wad, and lifting her hands, awkwardly mopped dripping eyes and nose.

Then she continued feeling along shelves, moving past what seemed like hundreds of flower holders until, at last, she came to a stack of stiff, folded fabric. She tugged at the top of the stack. A piece about the size of a bed sheet began unfolding until it piled next to her feet on the floor, raising dust that brought a sneeze. Well, at least the sneeze helped clear her head. She pulled again until a second piece thumped to the floor, still folded.

Sitting on the folded cloth, Carrie worked with her fingers and elbows until she managed to pull the first piece around her, blanket-style.

After that, time dulled to a stop while she sat motionless, brooding like some stoic Indian chief waiting for a pow-wow. *Well, I can be grateful I'm covered and the awful shivers have stopped,* she thought.

She wasn't going to cry, she w-w-wasn't.

Warm tears felt so good.

Snick, thunk. A squalling rasp of hinges.

Carrie tried to leap up, get on her feet. *If she could only make it to the side of the door, grab a vase, she could hit...* the fabric trapped her and she tumbled over on her side as Eleanor's voice said, "Carrie? Oh, my dear, what on earth are you do..."

The words stopped as Eleanor catapulted through the door, landing with her head in Carrie's lap, and Shirley fell against both of them. The door squawked, clunked shut, and Carrie heard three distinct groans at the same instant. "What?" was all Carrie could manage to say after they'd sorted themselves out and sat huddled together on a dry section of floor.

Shirley cleared her throat. "What's going on and where are we? It's like an ice box in here. Oh..." Her voice disappeared in a gasp.

Eleanor asked, "Why did that freak in red shove us? We were just looking for you, Carrie, and then, well, would you please tell us what's going on here? *What?*"

"Ghost," Shirley said. "We're in the mortuary cooler."

"Ghosts don't shove, Shirley. That was a solid person who pushed us in here. Who was it, dressed in that red get-up? Jan Owen? Melissa Donley? Why push us in here, for heaven's sake?" She wiggled closer to Carrie. "I'm freezing. Can you share a little of that blanket with us? Here, let me..." Eleanor gave a yelp of surprise as her hand touched bare flesh. "You're naked. How on earth...well, how did you get in here and where are your clothes?"

Carrie told them, described her bound wrists, and reached toward Eleanor until her friend felt the wire and removed it.

Shirley said, "Tear gas, for land's sake, you poor thing. It did smell peculiar back there, chemical-like, but I hadn't a thought what it might be.

"Anyway, here's what happened to us. When we got to the spa, the attendant was bouncing around like a wind-up toy, saying her client had vanished. Everyone was mad as the dickens because you left bubble bath suds all over your room. Soap is a no-no, clogs up the works or something. We were sure something was wrong because why would you put bubble bath in their whirlpool? So Eleanor and I decided to help look for you, of course, and since you'd told us about the hallway leading to a maintenance area and an outside door, we figured we'd try this way. When we started to look in here, the red person shoved us, and..."

Eleanor broke in. "We'll be missed eventually. Someone will come looking for us just like we came looking for you." She snorted. "I'd like to see that red freak try shoving Henry King if he's the one who comes."

She was silent for a moment, then her voice shivered a question. "Do you think that gruesome woman has a gun? Who is she? She reminds me of the evil queen in that ballet we watched on Public Television a few weeks ago. Remember her, Carrie? Alexa Vaskov danced the part."

The Red Queen Ballet! Of course. Enlightenment came like a burst of fireworks and Carrie almost laughed with relief in spite of their present circumstances. Now she knew the reason for the dancing red bride of her dreams, and it was nothing frightening at all! Except...except right now.

Coming back to the present and Eleanor's question, Carrie explained what she'd been thinking about in the spa tub.

"Blackmail? Yes, I see." It sounded like Eleanor was talking to herself, words following thoughts. "Ummm, someone is blackmailing someone, probably Jan blackmailing Melissa. But we don't have a clue as to what or why, do we?"

Now her voice sounded firm, even angry. "Girls, we have work to do and questions to ask. We've got to get out of this darn ice box."

"Shouldn't we start yelling?" Shirley asked.

"Doubt we can be heard through these walls," Carrie told her, "and besides, it's late afternoon. Most of the housekeeping staff has gone home. We might as well save our voices."

Shirley said, "They'll eventually look for us."

"Eventually," Eleanor said, "if the woman in red doesn't come back first. The spa staff might think we found Carrie, and rather than admit to putting bubble bath in their tub, she just headed for home with the two of us."

"What about Henry?" Shirley asked.

"And what about my clothes? If they think to look in the spa locker, everything I had on is there, right down to my bra and underpants."

Eleanor said, "Which does mean, since you're naked as a newborn, you're hardly likely to wander out of the hotel. Now, I think..."

A clunking sound from the general area of the door stopped her. After a breath of silence, Eleanor and Shirley began yelling their heads off while, forgetting bare skin, Carrie stood and felt for a vase to use as a weapon.

Chapter 29

Henry's ears identified the creak of leather and metallic jangle of belt equipment before Sergeant Lonnie Trent's voice said, "Impressive," from the Veranda Room doorway.

Henry, Chandra, and Ashur had just finished their work and were standing back to assess the effect. Chandra and Ashur, after a few tweaks here and there, smiled with satisfaction and, Henry was sure, more than a little pride.

As for what he thought? Well, the room looked like a garden rather than the blank interior space they started with only a couple of hours ago. It was okay.

"Finished?" Trent asked. "Can we talk?"

The Mukherjees turned toward him with looks that betrayed their continuing anxiety, and Henry was the one who said, "Yes, finished. These folks are artists, aren't they?" He hadn't planned his words and was surprised to realize he meant exactly what he'd said. Maybe Eleanor's idea about opening a flower shop wasn't cuckoo after all.

"Got some news," Trent told them. "Where are the ladies?"

"Down in the spa, being soaked and mauled."

Trent laughed. "Too bad, I'd hoped to see all of you at once. When will they be done?"

Henry looked at his watch. "I don't know, maybe thirty minutes. After that we were planning to get a bite to eat here in the hotel and head for home."

"Ahh. Well, in the meantime I'll bring you up to date. Do we need to get out of the way of a wedding?"

"It doesn't start for a couple of hours," Chandra said. "We have time."

"Okay, then, let's sit here in the last row and I'll tell you what's been happening.

"First off, Cody Wells and his dad came to the station at noon. Seems he'd found out somehow that the two of you," he nodded toward Chandra and Ashur, "definitely did not cause the death of his mother. That gave him a heap of hurt, not to mention guilt. He's supposed to be with a responsible adult at all times now and was working at Aunt Jan's this morning, but he told her he wanted to have lunch with his dad. When his dad picked him up, they came straight to the police station.

"He gave us his story about the bombing. Aunt Jan did a good job convincing him one of the Mukherjees killed his mom, and she suggested a small pipe bomb as a way to 'get justice for your mother' as he quotes her. She put the thing together using information from some book she has and assured him it was very small, would only cause a little smoke and bang. We may never know whether she believed that or not. Anyway, I think he pictured it as something like fireworks—says he was freaked out by what actually happened. Still, after Aunt Jan told him no one was hurt, he kept his mouth shut. When he learned you two had nothing to do with the murder, the whole thing came down around him. Soon as he could, he got his dad to bring him to the station." Trent stopped talking, looked toward the windows. "He's a good kid, really."

"Is he okay? What will happen to him now?" Chandra asked.

"Well, he *has* confessed, and there are witnesses..."

"You know, I've been thinking about that morning, and I could be wrong. I'm not sure he's the boy I saw."

Trent held up a hand. "Why am I not surprised to hear you say that, Chandra? Still, he did what he did and must take responsibility for it. It wouldn't be good for him to go without any punishment."

When she said nothing, he went on. "Even more interesting than Cody's confession, however, is what we've found out about Melissa Donley. Took some doing by Detective Wolverton, who's smart with computers, but we now know Miss Donley has a shady past. Once Wolverton found the first stuff in Nevada where Donley grew up, we were off and running. There's a juvenile record, and I'm betting it's related to when she worked as a motel maid during high school. Though we don't have access to those files, I suspect theft is what we'd find there. Doesn't matter, because more of Wolverton's computer work and a few phone calls got us plenty of additional information.

"Donley has worked in hotels several places, and at every one of them she was either questioned about suspected theft and let go, or left her job quickly for no recorded reason. Never convicted of anything, so she has no adult record. She does have a handgun permit, however.

"I called a few of the places where she worked. Managers and owners generally wouldn't say much—afraid of being pinned for libel, I suspect—but every one of them gave me a strong 'no' in response to my question about whether they'd write her a job recommendation or re-hire her themselves."

"Ah," Henry said, "do you have any idea if she's continuing or planning to continue her career as a thief here in Eureka Springs?"

"So far I've only asked a couple of general questions in this hotel. The management has had no complaints about thefts from guests and nothing appears to be missing as far as hotel equipment or money is concerned. I know the owners pretty well, and I'm sure if they'd heard about her past, they wouldn't have put her on the staff. She didn't change her name, but since she's never been convicted of anything, what's happened before doesn't get around generally."

Henry looked at his watch again. "I think I'll go see if the ladies are finished. They'll be glad to learn what Cody's done."

"Let's all go," Trent said. "I'd like to hear their reaction to what we've got on Melissa Donley now."

Everything about the spa reception area spoke of tranquility except the three people in it. A woman in a blue smock was screeching at the receptionist, gesturing wildly at the same time, while a second attendant stood next to her, fitting distress sounds in-between the fast-forward words of her co-worker.

Henry's brow scrunched. It wasn't a second before he sensed this ruckus had something to do with his Carrie. Confound it, would their life always be full of anxiety and turmoil? Where *was* she? All this noise...*was she okay?*

Lonnie Trent silenced the clamor. "Bluebird, Daisy,

Sky, what's going on here?"

The three women turned toward the newcomers and stared at them for a moment in the sudden silence. Finally blue smock said, "Three patrons. They..."

"Vanished," said the receptionist, who was probably Daisy, if the flowers woven into her pony tail meant anything.

Henry didn't wait to hear more. He headed through an archway that surely must lead to the hall where he and Carrie had seen whirlpool and massage rooms on Tuesday morning. He ignored Daisy's cry, "Wait, you can't go in there."

His nose detected a foreign odor and he stopped to sniff. Then, almost running, he followed the smell into a room with a still-stirring whirlpool that had spilled a good percentage of its bubbly contents on the floor. Faint enough to be almost imagination, he detected the scent of tear gas. In another couple of seconds he was back in the reception area. "Who was in that last room?"

"M-ms. McCrite," Daisy said.

"And the other two women?"

"They came in later and were supposed to be disrobing for the baths, but when Bluebird went to move their friend to the massage table and found her missing, they vanished too. Blue came here right away to see if I knew where her client was. The other two must have realized their friend was missing, because when I went back with Bluebird to look for Ms. McCrite, they were all gone. We searched the spa, but..."

"How about the maintenance area?" Henry asked. After getting blank looks from the three women he said, "Come on, Trent."

The maintenance area was empty, but when Henry

switched on the bright work light, he saw a puddle of water by the flower cooler door. A padlock secured the latch but it wasn't locked, so he yanked it out of the hasp and turned the handle.

The minute he stuck his head in the doorway something banged against his shoulder. Then water and flower stems splashed into his face, and a very familiar female voice said, "Oh-oh."

Henry grabbed a handkerchief from his pocket, wiped his eyes, opened them, and...

For a minute he was shocked speechless, then he managed a stutter. "C-Carrie dear, uh, no clothes...you're... uh—only a red scarf? I think you'd best join Eleanor and Shirley under that flag. Sergeant Trent is here, and I, uh..."

Carrie scurried away from the door and was just squeezing in between her two friends when Sergeant Trent's voice said, "Holy cow! I've heard of wrapping yourself in patriotism, but this beats all. Where did you ladies find that old flag?"

"I believe they store worn-out flags here in the cooler," Carrie told him stiffly, looking down at her wrapping. "You have to hold a special ceremony to destroy them, don't you? I imagine these flags are merely waiting."

She picked up one of the pieces of florist wire from the floor of the refrigerator and held it out to Henry. "This wire was around my wrists and ankles. See if it matches what you have in your pocket."

It didn't, and he gave the wire to Trent. "I'll bet it's like what bound Sonya Wells," he said, "and Owen's Flowers is probably the source."

After that, everyone did a lot of explaining. First, though, they found a robe for Carrie and checked her face and eyes for damage. Second, she had a necessary session with Daisy for splinter-removal from her behind. Then Bluebird made hot tea and everyone sat, Carrie more gingerly than the others, in the spa's reception lounge. Except for the fact that everyone wanted to talk at once, visitors would have accepted the gathering as a relaxed tea party.

When they ran out of accumulated facts, ideas, and discoveries to share, Sergeant Trent got in touch with the police station and asked that Melissa Donley be found and brought in for questioning. He'd just finished talking when Melissa herself appeared in the spa doorway.

"Hello, everyone," she said, speaking way too brightly for the look of weariness and distress apparent on her face. "I wanted to tell Ashur and Chandra that the Veranda Room looks heavenly, and the desk clerk said I'd find all of you here. The Wilsons will be very pleased with your creation, I know."

The minute he saw her, Trent called for an officer to assist him at the Crescent Hotel Spa.

Carrie said, "You look worn out, Melissa. Would you like to sit with us and have some tea?"

"I don't think..."

Trent was on his feet. He took Melissa's arm and said, "I think you'd better join us, okay?" He turned to Carrie. "Ms. McCrite, since I don't have a female officer here, would you please check Ms. Donley for anything concealed on her person that shouldn't be there? You don't mind, do you, Melissa? I'm sure we have your permission. Right?"

Melissa nodded wearily as he took her purse and handed it to Henry. "Okay if we look through this? If you say no, we'll get a warrant. We have enough information now to justify that."

"Do whatever you want," she said, looking at the floor.

"Fine. Major King, how about dumping the contents of this purse on the counter so we can all see what's there. That way Ms. Donley won't be tempted to accuse us of planting or stealing anything. I know you won't touch the contents."

Carrie got to her feet and, with a murmured apology to Melissa, felt along her arms, torso, and legs like she'd seen it done on television cop shows. She even stuck a finger under Melissa's bra between her breasts, where any number of small items could have been hidden. "Nothing unexpected here," she told the sergeant.

"She has a canister of tear gas in her purse," Henry said, "and here's a pill bottle with its label gone. I think the pills in it now are plain aspirin."

"Got something to tell us, Melissa?" Trent asked.

After a moment of silence passed, Carrie patted the cushion next to her on the couch. "Come, sit here with me." Moving like a robot, Melissa came to the couch and sat.

Carrie looked steadily into the young woman's face as she took her hand. "I know how upset you must be. Things kind of got out of control, didn't they? First, it was just sending floral customers to Jan. Then, as Sonya's pressure on Jan to close the shop increased, Jan's requests began to escalate.

"She knows about your past, doesn't she, dear? How did she find out?"

Looking only at Carrie, Melissa began to talk. "Almost a year ago a couple from Dallas came here on vacation.

They stayed at this hotel, saw me, and recognized me from Dallas. About five years ago, I...they..."

"You stole something from them in a Dallas hotel?"

"I...tried to, yes." Melissa lifted her chin. "They're wealthy. I didn't think it would bother them to lose a bit of money. I was only going to take part of it. They left it out in the room after all, and I needed every penny I could scrape together because I wanted to finish college. They came into their room and caught me."

Carrie patted her hand. "They mentioned this to Jan?"

"No, to Sonya. They saw me here working a wedding with Jan and didn't know she and Sonya were related. Worse luck, they decided to look for land in the area. Sonya ended up being their realtor. One thing led to another and they told her about Dallas. As far as Sonya was concerned, that was just one more reason for Jan to close down the flower shop. She'd stooped to working with a criminal."

Melissa's voice cracked, and she coughed, then was quiet for a moment before continuing. "So, of course, Sonya couldn't wait to tell Jan."

Carrie said, "And Jan saw an opportunity to take advantage of the situation?"

"Oh, you bet."

"Tell me about last Saturday night."

Melissa sighed, swallowed, and went on. "Jan said she wanted to scare the Mukherjees into leaving town because they were taking too much of her business. She knew I owned a handgun because I'd talked about going to the shooting range outside town a couple of times."

"And you shot at Ashur and Chandra. Were you supposed to miss them?"

"No. Originally I thought so, but at the last minute, Jan told me she wanted me to hit one of them. She said she didn't care whether they ended up dead or only injured."

"Yet you missed..."

"Believe me, if I'd wanted to hit either of them, I could have. I missed on purpose and told Jan my arm jerked."

"So then you stripped off the black sweats, changed to a business suit, and came back to the hotel?"

Melissa nodded.

Because she didn't want to break the almost hypnotic contact with Melissa, Carrie couldn't glance at Trent. She hoped he thought she was doing okay, because what she planned to ask next was only a guess.

"Why all the messing around, leaving roses, phoning me, playing the red bride ghost? Why the tear gas and flower cooler? Why the threatening talk with Rebecca?"

"Jan's crazy, out of control. After I learned she'd killed Sonya, I was terrified of what she might do to any of you. I hoped I could scare you into going away and staying away. Then maybe she'd calm down and everyone would be safe."

"You said she killed Sonya?"

"She told me early Sunday she'd mixed sleeping pills in her sister's drink Saturday before lunch so she could 'get her off my back,' as she put it. She gave me the empty pill bottle later and told me to throw it in with the hotel trash. I needed one, so decided to keep it instead." She pointed to the contents of her purse scattered on the counter. "That's it."

"Do you know where she killed Sonya?

"At the Wells house, I'm sure. On Saturdays they often sat together on Sonya's patio to eat lunch if the weather was good, so Sonya wouldn't have been suspicious. Both sisters have houses in the woods behind their business building, you know. Only those who come right up to a house would ever see what's going on. Jan could have killed Sonya using rocks from her own backyard. She knew Cody would be gone. He always hangs out with his friends on Saturdays and eats lunch with them."

"Why do you think she told you what she'd done?"

"She didn't tell me the whole story, I'm guessing some of it. But because she used my business card to keep the Mukherjees at the hotel Saturday night, she knew the police would eventually ask me about that and she wanted me to be prepared to back her up. I think she told me a few things because she was proud of how clever she was. She said she used one of the Mukherjees' own flower-cutting knives to point suspicion at them. And she laughed about that."

"I understand you didn't back her up. You told the police you hadn't put your card under the windshield wiper."

"That's right. I knew it was risky to cross Jan, b-but..."

It was easy to tell Melissa now struggled to hold back tears. Carrie had no doubt the younger woman was fighting to control her emotions.

She squeezed Melissa's hand. "You'd had enough of these awful things."

"Y-yes."

"After Sonya was dead, do you know what happened?"

"Jan has a black Mercedes as well as the van. After she planned our trip to the gazebo, she had Cody help her bring the car and leave it at my place. She wanted me to drive it that evening, but I had no idea why. When I got to the church parking lot, she was already there in the van. I'd guess Sonya was in the back of the van, or had been, and Jan used it rather than her car because no one would be suspicious if they saw it around the hotel."

"Why the wig?"

"I'm sure she wanted everyone to think the Mukherjees mistook Sonya for her. They had a stronger reason to kill Jan than Sonya, whom they barely knew."

"How did she get both vehicles home? Was there time for you to drive one for her? We saw you in the hotel about half an hour later. You were dressed for the wedding then."

"I have a tiny apartment off the main highway, not far from the hotel. She told me to drive the car back there. All I had to do then was change clothes, brush my hair, and drive my own car here. Cody already believed she'd loaned the Mercedes to me, and the two of them were to pick it up later that night. Of course he didn't know about his mother yet. Jan told me her sister planned to go shopping in Springfield on Saturday and I suppose Sonya had told Cody about her plans before he left to be with his friends."

Carrie squeezed the young woman's hand again and looked over at Sergeant Trent, who sat behind Melissa. "Do you have any questions, Sergeant Trent?"

He stood and walked around to stand in front of both of them. "Yes. Ms. Donley, where is Jan Owen now?"

Melissa jerked in surprise. She'd evidently forgotten she was in the room with anyone besides Carrie. Finally she said, "I don't know. But I'm so afraid she intends to hurt Rebecca and the baby next. That's why I wanted them to leave town."

In what seemed like less than a second, Lonnie Trent

was speaking to someone at the Eureka Springs Police Department. As he talked he waved a restraining arm toward Ashur and Chandra, who'd leaped to their feet and started for the door as soon as Melissa mentioned Rebecca.

A police officer Carrie didn't recognize appeared in the doorway, blocking it. Trent finished the call, then put his hand around Melissa's arm. "We're taking you into custody, Ms. Donley, and it's partly for your own safety, at least until we find Jan Owen. I assume you'll be ready to repeat what you just told Ms. McCrite for the record when you get to the station. This officer will take you to get a few essentials, because you'll be spending the night with us. I'll talk with you again in the morning."

He walked Melissa to the officer. "Ron, maybe you'd better put handcuffs on her to be safe, but leave by the employee entrance so she won't have to go through the lobby."

Melissa, looking like a rag doll whose stuffing had leaked out, said to Carrie, "Do me a favor? Call Tiffany and ask her to take my place at the Wilson wedding, and..." She looked into Carrie's face. "And I'm very sorry for what I did to you and for...for all of it."

Carrie nodded, then Melissa and the officer disappeared down the hallway.

Chapter 30

Trent turned back toward the six anxious, weary people left in the spa, but spoke first to the Mukherjees who were heading for the door again. "You folks stay here. We'll see that Purdy and Rebecca are safe. I can't risk having you out there too—you'd only be in the way. But, if you'll call their house on your cell phone for me, I'll tell them what's going on and ask them to double-check that all their doors and windows are locked and the blinds and curtains closed.

"Now," he said, taking a stab at sounding cheerful, "why don't all of you go have dinner upstairs while you wait for me. I'll report back as soon as I can."

They went to the dining room as directed, but when their food came, Carrie noticed everyone except Henry found more on the plates to stare at than eat, and not even the normally loquacious Eleanor was interested in conversation. What could they say to each other beyond fruitless speculation over whatever might be happening out there...

some place? Carrie herself felt dazed and half-awake, almost as if she'd been drugged. She guessed everyone else suffered from something like that.

All they could do was wait. And wait...

Finally Chandra, sitting next to Carrie, stood and murmured something about going to the ladies'. Carrie lifted her head, and a tickle in the back of her mind bounced to life. She was suddenly aware that an increasing tension had been radiating from Chandra's body while the two of them sat together, contemplating their plates. On impulse Carrie pushed her chair back and said, "I think I'd better go, too." She glanced at Henry, but he merely nodded, his thoughts obviously far away.

Chandra didn't look back as she hurried along the carpeted hall and Carrie trotted soundlessly after her.

When Chandra got to the side hall leading to the restroom, she didn't turn down it but continued straight ahead into the conservatory. The catering staff was working there, setting up for the evening reception. She ignored them, and no one paid attention to her. They were undoubtedly used to seeing her around the hotel during wedding preparations.

Instead of stopping, Chandra kept going until she reached the French doors on the other side of the room and went through them. Just then a uniformed waiter pushing a cart full of loaded food trays crossed in front of Carrie. When she finally got to the doors and went out on the gazebo walkway, Chandra had vanished.

She hesitated, trying to decide whether or not she should go back to the dining room and report what had happened, when she heard an engine start. The Mukherjee van? Feeling for the keys attached to a ring in her purse, Carrie began running toward the parking lot. Thank goodness Henry had insisted last Sunday that she begin keeping a copy of his car key with her.

There was no van, still or moving, in the parking lot, but Carrie had no doubt where Chandra was heading. She was a mother, full of fear for her children, and right now she wasn't thinking clearly. She must be stopped, not only for the safety of those children, but for her own safety as well.

How long had they been gone?

Henry looked at his watch and wished he'd thought of checking it when Chandra and Carrie left the room. *Seemed like too long for what they said was intended...*

He'd been asking Ashur about the flower business, partly because he wanted to take the man's mind off what might be going on at Rebecca and Purdy's house. But Henry was also genuinely interested in Ashur and Chandra's profession, and it was obvious Eleanor and Shirley were too. They'd been paying single-minded attention to every tidbit of information Ashur offered.

Finally, during a period of silence, Henry turned toward Eleanor. "Could you or Shirley check and make sure Carrie and Chandra are okay? They've been gone quite a while."

"Oh, sure," Eleanor said, not acting alarmed. Maybe she understood what women could be doing for long periods in a ladies' restroom—besides the obvious. Both she and Shirley stood, and Henry figured they were as eager for activity as he was. He'd been about ready to suggest a brisk walk up and down the hotel's main hall, no matter how strange that might look to others. Going outside for a real walk was out of the question, since Trent could return any minute.

When had Trent left? Nuts. What was the point of wearing a watch if you forgot to look at it?

Eleanor and Shirley disappeared through the dining room door, walking slowly, still casually unconcerned. For an instant Henry felt silly. He didn't want to act like a worrying old maid in front of Carrie's friends.

After another silence, Ashur said, as if speaking to himself, "I wonder if I should call Purdy and Rebecca again?"

Henry's ears heard the question but nothing directing action or a response transferred to his brain. It wasn't until he glanced at Ashur a moment later that he realized the man expected an answer to his question.

"Oh, sorry, Ashur. I was thinking...about something. I don't see how calling them could hurt anything."

That's when Eleanor and Shirley came back into the dining room, almost running. "They aren't in the restroom or anywhere around that part of the building!" Eleanor said, out of breath. "Caterers are setting up for a reception in the conservatory, and one of them says he saw Chandra come through there in a hurry about fifteen minutes ago. She went out the French doors. He doesn't remember seeing Carrie with her; he thinks Chandra was alone."

Three sets of anxious eyes faced Henry, and Shirley asked, "Where on earth could they have got to? And why?"

"Rebecca and Purdy's!" Henry and Ashur said in unison. Henry got to his feet, told the maitre d' where they were going, and asked him to give that information to any police officer who might show up. Then, after discovering both the Artistic Floral van and Henry's car were missing from the parking lot, they piled into Eleanor's car. She drove the curving roads much faster than the posted speed limit, throwing Henry and Ashur from side to side in the back seat as she said, "Where are the police when you need them? Wouldn't you know not one of them cares how I'm driving now?"

"Careful," Henry said, "we'd best approach the house quietly and slowly. Eleanor, switch your lights off just before you turn in. The security lights on the greenhouses will be enough to see by after that."

Eleanor did as he'd said, and they rolled to a stop at the first greenhouse, pulling in between the green van and Henry's car. "Guess we know where they are for sure," Shirley murmured, "and I pray God to protect them."

Next to Henry in the back seat, Ashur whispered a few words in a language Henry didn't recognize and, when he finished, Henry said, "Amen," without realizing he'd spoken aloud.

Carrie looked around the corner of the second greenhouse. *Surely Chandra wasn't going right up to the front door of Rebecca and Purdy's home!* She sucked breath in through her teeth, blew out. *If she could only have caught up with the woman in time, talked some sense into her. Frightened mother or not, what she was doing could put her children in more peril than they were in already. Jan Owen might be anywhere around, and if Rebecca or Purdy opened that door...*

Chandra rang the doorbell, and Carrie wondered if people inside the house had some way to see who was on the lighted porch. She'd heard Sergeant Trent tell Purdy not to open the door to a woman, and to be sure he could identify any uniformed police officer who knocked.

Where WERE the police?

Carrie heard a slight swishing sound behind her and, before she could turn to see what it was, felt something small and hard push between her shoulder blades. Jan

Owen's voice said, "My, my, what are you doing here? Come to visit the heathen?"

Carrie's thoughts grappled for an answer, but she couldn't think of anything sensible for the moment, so all she said was, "Hello, Jan."

Then she realized that, from where Jan stood, farther away from the corner of the greenhouse than Carrie herself, she probably couldn't see Chandra or the porch. Maybe it would be possible to distract her, keep her and the gun away from the house.

"Well, now, this is an odd place for us to meet. Jan, for goodness sake, point that gun somewhere else. It's just me, Carrie McCrite. I'm not any threat to you."

Jan gave a hiccuped, wild-sounding laugh, and the pressure against Carrie's back didn't ease. She tried a step backward, pushing against the gun, but just as Jan moved back involuntarily there was a distant clunk, the sound of a door opening, and Purdy's words coming clearly through the night air. "Mother! What are you doing here?"

Carrie was shoved forward roughly as the gun pressure went away and, realizing Jan meant to shoot Chandra, she twisted her body and fell sideways, hoping to knock the woman off balance. A hideously loud exploding sound came from above as she hit the ground. Then, almost at the same instant, another gunshot cracked. Someone tripped over her and, from a distance, she heard a woman scream, "*No!*"

Couldn't have been me screaming, Carrie thought. *That Owen woman has smashed down on top of me and I can barely breathe.*

Then everything faded away into silence.

"What can we do besides wait?" Eleanor asked as the four of them sat in her car, not moving. "It's totally quiet. I don't see anyone near the house or beyond the greenhouses. Where do you suppose Carrie and Chandra are? Is everyone hiding somewhere? Tell us what we should we do next, Major King."

Henry's whole body and heart wanted him to leap out of the car and run to find Carrie, but keeping his voice as calm as he could, he said, "I'm afraid to make any more noise than we already have just by driving in. It might alarm Jan Owen—if she's here—and put Carrie and Chandra in even more danger than they could be already."

His eyes struggled to see anything resembling a human shape in the semi-darkness. All those shadows... Finally he said, "Eleanor, would you switch off your door light for me. I'm going to get out and see what I can find. You three stay right where you are. Lock the doors after me, and I'd suggest ducking down in the seats as much as you can. No heads sticking up." He pushed the door open and slid out into the night, letting the door close slowly until it was almost shut, then giving it a push until it latched with a soft click.

For a moment he waited, crouched by the car door, listening and looking.

Nothing.

Bending over, he hurried to a shadowed area by the first greenhouse, then moved away from the Mukherjees' home along its length. If he could get between the two buildings he might be able to see if anyone was hiding there. As he remembered, the space between the greenhouses was clear except for one wheelbarrow by a side door.

When he had crossed behind the first greenhouse and was able to look around its corner, he saw two forms near the other end, one large, one small. Jan Owen, with her blond hair, was easy to identify. The smaller woman was too heavy for Chandra, so it had to be Carrie. What were the two of them doing? He had to get closer...

As he slid past the wheelbarrow, he saw that the greenhouse door was open. He stopped, held his breath, and was sure he heard breathing and a soft swish coming from the other side of the door. The police? Since Jan Owen was up ahead, who else could it be? Holding a hand in front of him, he stepped inside the dark building and touched the cloth of a shirt.

Trent swore, almost too softly to allow voice identification, before he whispered, "Are any more of you going to parade in here like an avenging army? How many civilians do I have to put up with tonight? You, at least, should realize what a mess this is making of things. If only all of you had stayed put."

Henry decided now was not the time for explanations, so he followed Trent and Gloria Wolverton as they began silently making their way toward the front of the building, moving between benches full of growing plants and flowers.

Some of the flowers were in bloom and Henry identified the heavy scent of gardenias, remembering it from long-ago prom corsages.

"Anyone in the next building?" he whispered, and Trent whispered back, "Kurt and Ron."

When they were in position not ten feet from Jan Owen, they crouched silently, unable to hear outside conversation through windows that were closed against the night chill.

But they saw clearly enough. As Gloria Wolverton knelt and rested her gun against the window sill, Henry could tell Jan Owen also had a gun, and it was pointed at the middle of Carrie's back, right where it would probably hit her heart if it went off. He stopped breathing.

Trent slowly cranked the window open, and the sound of Purdy's voice came through it clearly. "Mother! What are you doing here?"

Two shots. Carrie falling.

Henry couldn't tell if she had fallen before or after the first gun crack. He exploded through the front door of the greenhouse, hearing Chandra cry, *"No,"* as he ran to kneel beside the two women on the ground.

Jan Owen wasn't moving and wouldn't be. Detective Wolverton's bullet had hit her in the temple. Ignoring any thought of destroying evidence, he shoved Jan aside and bent his ear toward Carrie. She was breathing deeply, as if she were asleep. He could see dark splatters on her jacket, but they were probably from Jan. His hands searched, touching Carrie's body carefully, feeling for damage, breaks, or the moisture of bleeding. Nothing.

Then he pulled her into his arms, put his cheek against her forehead, and began rocking slowly back and forth in the grass.

"Ummm...Henry? You smell good...like gardenias and wet dirt."

An hour later it was all over. Jan Owen's body was gone, and, thanks either to poor aim or Carrie's fall against her, the bullet from Jan's gun missed both Chandra and Purdy, splintering a glass panel next to the door instead. There were glass cuts on Purdy's arm, and Carrie had a few scratches from her fall on the rocky ground, but the medical technician who cleaned them up said, "Good as new in a few days," and drove away in an empty ambulance.

"Well...guess things ended okay," Sergeant Trent said as they sat together in the Mukherjees' living room, "because not only did Jan Owen have that gun, there were two pipe bombs in her car. And you'll be glad to know Kurt and Ron found blood on the back floor of her van. We're sure it will prove to be Sonya's. I'm sorry we can't question Jan, but if we hadn't brought her down, who knows what might have happened next? Thank goodness Ms. McCrite fell out of the way so Gloria could get a clear shot."

Carrie asked, "Is Melissa still at the station? Does she know about all of this? About Jan's death?"

"Yes, she does. She'd already repeated for the record what she told you in the spa, and much more besides. She's sick over the mess she got herself into, says she'll cooperate fully with us. I'm sure that'll lighten whatever she ends up being charged with. Before leaving the hotel she took Ron to her office there and showed him a red dancing dress, some veiling, a gas mask, and her gun, all hidden in the back of her closet. She says she originally thought playing ghost would give her a good chance to steal from guests, but it turned out she likes this town, her job, and the people she works for. She'd already decided not to continue her career as a thief here in Eureka Springs. Says she hasn't been comfortable with it for a long time anyway."

"What about Cody Wells?" Shirley asked.

Trent smiled. "I've been thinking about him and talking with my wife. Our sons are gone from home now, one married, one in college. We thought we might keep Cody with us until the end of the school year, assuming the terms of whatever the legal system decides for him will allow it. Then, after graduation, maybe he can go to his dad in St. Louis."

"That's good," Shirley said, "and you're a good man,

Sergeant. Oh—you should know we've been talking about Cody—the three of us. We're not fully sure he's the boy we saw at the flower shop after all. We'd just pulled in, and..."

He looked at Shirley, then Eleanor and Carrie. "Funny thing, Chandra isn't sure now, either. You women must have poor memories for faces."

"And right proud of it," Shirley told him.

Chapter 31

Yes? No? Carrie looked at the jacket, tried to remember when she'd worn it last, couldn't, and stuffed it in the bag.

There hadn't been the teeniest thought about sharing space or sharing anything when she moved to her new home in the Arkansas Ozarks six years ago. This house was all hers. She'd loved that and had rapidly spread possessions through every room and closet. "Maybe I'll need it someday," was the rule that governed when it came to what got stored.

Now she was shocked by the number of "somedays" she'd found while clearing space for Henry. *Feng shui* it wasn't.

Thank goodness he'd rented furnished since his divorce. He didn't own much besides his clothes, a few tools, and his very large self. That's all she had to find space for in her—their—home. And she had only two more days to do it.

For the umpteenth time she felt the twinge of doubt that had shadowed her since she said yes. Would all her newfound independence be lost? Fear of that was like a grief that wouldn't go away, and she couldn't think of a single person she dared confide in, simply because it seemed so foolish and self-centered.

Hmmm. Well, there was God...*I will be with thee.* Sitting on the floor in her closet, she began a prayer.

The urgent banging of her door knocker came simultaneously with part of a verse from the first chapter of Genesis: "...male and female created he them." Getting to her feet she thought, *Well, if God can plan for two, I suppose I can manage it.* She felt downright cheerful when she opened the door.

And her heart sank into her wooly slippers.

Henry stood in the doorway looking sheepish.

Carrie stared at the pink and white striped box he carried, then at his dear, sweet face. Her own face flamed, she blinked, and said, "Ahhhh..."

For a minute, possibly influenced by her lack of verbiage, he seemed unable to think of anything sensible to say either, so he simply held the box toward her. "A gift," he said. "I chose it myself. For you. From Victoria's Secret."

"Oh, my," she said. "Come in. I can't imagine..."

But, the trouble was, she could imagine. She'd recognized the wrapping, and her mind immediately began racing through pictures of thongs and teddies and baby dolls in satin and lace. Chemise? Cami? Skimpy lace bits exposing all the curves and private places the models owned. On her, on Carrie Culpeper McCrite? Oh, golly. And Henry had undoubtedly bought whatever it was three sizes too small.

"You're crying," Henry said in dismay. "I wanted, well,

I wanted something really pretty for you...for our honeymoon." His voice faded away, and now he looked embarrassed.

Loving him in spite of whatever wicked, awful thing his gift box might hold she said, "It's just that I'm so... so very...touched." Swiping a hand across her eyes, she backed into the house. "Come in. I was, uh, just clearing closets and drawers to make room for your things."

FatCat jumped from her basket to the hall table and stared at them, her tail, with its peculiar end curl, waving in the air. While Carrie watched, the tail hit the angel sun catcher, causing it to rock.

Henry drew her attention back to him when he said, in a Christmas morning voice, "Don't you want to open it?"

The only answer to that would be cruel, so she sat. Her robot arms and hands moved, pulled at the black bow, lifted the lid, pulled back the pink tissue, and saw...

Teal blue FLANNEL? High ruffled neck? Long sleeves?

"The color looks like your eyes," Henry said, almost bouncing on the couch next to her. "And I liked the pink and white roses printed all over. Look, the buttons even have rosebuds carved on them."

She held the nightgown up, looked at the label. It did indeed say *Victoria's Secret*. She looked at the rosebud buttons. "There are a lot of buttons."

"Twelve. I counted," he said, grinning like a schoolboy.

"I love it, Henry. Thank you."

Susan, who was the tallest, lifted the circlet of ivory rose buds and set it carefully atop Carrie's white curls. The roses matched her dress perfectly.

Carrie couldn't say a word, but Shirley and Eleanor, reflected beside her in the mirror, filled the silence.

"Ooo, look at you, Carrie, you're beautiful."

"That dress is just perfect."

"We did good, if I do say it myself."

Thing was, she agreed with them. She'd never felt beautiful in her life, but now...oh, now, she was a bride, and she *was* beautiful.

Catherine and Susan, standing on her other side, smiled at her in the mirror. "We're all beautiful today," Susan said. "I, for one, love my dress, but Carrie...well, Dad is going to burst from admiration and love when he sees you."

It was the first time Carrie had heard Susan call Henry "Dad." Understandable, since the couple who'd adopted her as an infant were "Mom" and "Daddy" for thirty years. Now Henry would hear that blessed title for the first time in his life.

Their wedding day was proving to be a beginning for so many things. Carrie thought of how her son Rob and Henry's half-sister Catherine had laughed and talked and looked at each other during Thanksgiving dinner yesterday and at breakfast and lunch today. How they'd gone off for a walk after lunch holding hands, Rob's blond coloring such a contrast to Catherine's sturdy, dark beauty...

"It's time," Shirley said, interrupting her thoughts. "And Carrie McCrite, if you don't think you look better than all those stick-brides in the magazines, I'm going to whup you right here and now."

"You won't have to whup me, Shirley. And, *thank you!*"

After hugs all around, Eleanor opened the door. Rob was waiting outside the suite. Carrie took his arm and began her march toward Henry King and a whole new life.

"Henry, will you have this woman to be your wedded wife, to live together with her in the holy estate of matrimony? Will you love her, comfort her, honor and keep her, in sickness and health; and forsaking all others keep only to her..."

He promised, Carrie promised, and in a short and beautiful time, it was done. They were husband and wife for real and for ever. Today, right now, Henry was glad Carrie had said no to the courthouse wedding, and, what's more, he would tell her that. Later. Now he was going to enjoy all this good-looking food, even if he still didn't know what to call most of it. At least there was shrimp speared on the carved toothpicks he could point out to everyone, and plenty of his favorite fudge. Carrie, Eleanor, and Shirley had spent almost a whole day making that from Carrie's recipe. The crescent shape and powdered sugar dip they'd fancied it up with probably wouldn't hurt the taste at all.

Henry shut the door and turned to look at her. Their two-bedroom suite was next to the Crescent Conservatory, but it might as well be miles away. They were really, truly alone as husband and wife. As far as he was concerned, the rest of the group could party all night if they wanted to. He had his own ideas about how to finish the night, but still felt a twinge of worry about how...and even *if.*

He held out the huge fruit basket he'd brought in with him. "Can I tempt you with oranges, apples, almonds, pecans? How about a grape or two?" He put a grape in his mouth.

"I'll bet none of our wedding decorations end up in the trash, and Chandra made sure there were enough baskets for everyone to fill and take home. Smart, wasn't it? No waste. Pretty too, with the bows and gold nutcrackers."

"She wouldn't let me pay them a dime for the wedding decorations," Carrie said, then turned her back to him.

"What?"

"Your first duty as a husband," she said. "Unzip my dress, please."

"Oh, right..."

"And if I were you, I'd hang that handsome grey suit in the closet. Wouldn't want it to get wrinkled."

"Things don't wrinkle these days, do they? But I was planning to take it off, anyway."

"Meet you in the large bedroom," she said. "I'll undress here in the small bedroom. I won't need that bed tonight so I can smooth my dress out on it."

"Did you pack our special nightie with all the buttons?"

"Yes." There was a shiver in that one-word reply. He heard it quite clearly.

"You can have the bathroom first," he said.

She was sitting up against white satin pillows on the king-sized bed when he came in. Her eyes got very wide as she looked at him, then looked away. "Only undershorts?"

"It's quite warm in here, don't you think? I didn't need a night shirt."

He sat on the bed next to her, looked at the rosebud buttons for a moment, then, as she scooted toward him, opened his arms. He was right, it was warm. They kissed with increasing tenderness, then increasing heat before he pulled back and looked at her again.

Should she say something? "Henry, I love you so much, but this is all...new, and I'm...uh..."

"Me, too, Carrie, but we're together, I love you, and nothing matters but that."

He touched the front of her nightgown, stroked there gently, then went to the buttons.

"One," he said. "Two. Three." The count continued until all twelve were unfastened. His hands slid through the long opening and pushed the nightgown off her shoulders.

After a few glorious minutes she stopped him and lifted the gown over her head. He pulled off his shorts and slipped under the covers, swishing across the satin sheet until his body met hers.

"Welcome to our private world," he said, as he lifted on an elbow and looked down. "Cara, I think you are the most beautiful woman I've ever seen. Thank you for being my wife, little love, thank you."

She managed to get out a proper, "You're welcome," before his mouth cut off conversation.

In the silence that followed she heard a faint "swish-shh, swish-shh" that seemed to be coming from all around them. Glad for this final benediction, she began showing Henry how very welcome he was.

The beginning...

Carrie's Recipes

CARRIE'S CHICKEN PIE

1 16-ounce bag frozen mixed vegetables
2 refrigerated pie crusts
1 can cream of chicken soup
¼ cup milk
2 4½ or 5 ounce cans white chicken meat,
    cut into bite-sized pieces
½ tsp. pepper
½ cup chopped onion

Thaw frozen mixed vegetables in microwave. (About three minutes in a microwave container.) Mix all ingredients but milk and pie crusts together. Add amount of milk needed to make desired creamy consistency. Spoon the mixture into bottom crust, top with second crust. Pinch edges, cut vents. Place on baking sheet in 375° oven and bake 35-45 minutes, or until crust is golden brown.

Four to six servings.

CARRIE'S CHOCOLATE FUDGE

1 12-ounce package semi-sweet chocolate bits
2/3 cup sweetened condensed milk, such as Eagle Brand
1 tsp. water
1 tsp. vanilla extract

Melt chocolate pieces over hot (not boiling) water, remove from heat, add sweetened condensed milk, water, and vanilla. Stir (do not beat) until smooth and satiny. Drop from teaspoon on cookie sheet covered with waxed paper and cool. Before cooling, candy can easily be formed into balls or crescent shapes. Then, if desired, brush with additional melted chocolate and cover immediately with powdered sugar.

Makes approximately thirty ¾ oz. pieces.

About the Author

Award-winning Arkansas writer and journalist Radine Trees Nehring and her husband, photographer John Nehring, live in the rural Arkansas Ozarks near Gravette.

Nehring's writing awards include the Governor's Award for Best Writing about the State of Arkansas, Tulsa Nightwriter of the Year Award, and the Dan Saults Award, which is given by the Ozarks Writers League for nature- or Ozarks-value writing. The American Christian Writers named Nehring Christian Writer of the Year in 1998, and the Oklahoma Writers Federation, Inc., named her book *Dear Earth* Best Non-Fiction Book and her novel *A Valley to Die For* Best Mystery Novel. *A Valley to Die For* was a 2003 Macavity Award nominee for Best First Novel.

Research for her many magazine and newspaper features and her weekly radio program, *Arkansas Corner Community News*, has taken the Nehrings throughout the state. For more than twenty years Nehring has written non-fiction about unique people, places, and events in Arkansas. Now, in her Something To Die For Mystery series, she adds appealing characters fighting for something they believe in and, it turns out, for their very lives.

OTHER BOOKS BY ST KITTS PRESS

A Treasure to Die For by Radine Trees Nehring

When Carrie McCrite and Henry King attend an Elderhostel in Hot Springs, Arkansas, they suspect that illegal gambling money from the '60s is hidden in the hotel. When Carrie disappers in steaming water, Henry goes hunting.

LIBRARY JOURNAL "Lovers of cozy mysteries with colorful characters will want this third title in Nehring's 'Something to Die For' series (after *A Valley To Die For, Music To Die For*)." (REVIEWED BY TAMARA BUTLER)

THE OZARKS MOUNTAINEER "The mystery is as hot as Hot Springs' springs, and the characters are as natural and well-drawn as a hot bath in one of the town's historic bathhouses." (REVIEWED BY JIM VERITAS)

MIDWEST BOOK REVIEW "Nehring puts together a very entertaining whodunit in *A Treasure to Die For*...A good read." (REVIEWED BY SHELLEY GLODOWSKI)

OZARKS MAGAZINE "...a fun read."

I LOVE A MYSTERY "I enjoy seeing older protagonists, and the author makes the area so intriguing I want to go see it for myself. RECOMMENDED." (REVIEWED BY EDEN EMBLER)

THE PILOT "...features 'regular' people...The characters are likeable...the books tell an interesting story as well as offering well-researched historical background...Nehring has hit on a good combination." (REVIEWED BY FAYE DASEN)

GRAVETTE NEWS HERALD "If you haven't read Radine's first two books in the series, you're missing a lot. Get to know Carrie and Henry and don't miss this third book." (REVIEWED BY GAYLE WILLIAMS)

THE BENTON COUNTY DAILY RECORD "Along with good, tight story-telling, the writer highlights some of the most interesting locations in Arkansas where her stories take place." (REVIEWED BY TONYA MCKIEVER)

PATRICIA SPRINKLE, 2004-05 PRESIDENT OF SISTERS IN CRIME, BESTSELLING AUTHOR OF THE THOROUGHLY SOUTHERN MYSTERY SERIES "Nehring's delightful novel features history and romance with murder thrown in. Who would have imagined an Elderhostel could be so dangerous?"

J.M. HAYES, AUTHOR OF *PLAINS CRAZY*, *PRAIRIE GOTHIC*, AND *MAD DOG & ENGLISHMAN* "The treasure here is Radine Trees Nehring and her plucky crime solver, Carrie Culpeper McCrite."

DR. DOJELO C. RUSSELL, PROGRAM COORDINATOR, UNIVERSITY OF ARKANSAS ELDERHOSTEL PROGRAMS IN HOT SPRINGS, ARK. "The characters are as alive as present-day Hot Springs."

Music to Die For by Radine Trees Nehring

Carrie McCrite goes to a tourism convention at the Ozark Folk Center State Park and finds murder and kidnapping. Sparks fly again as Carrie and Henry King search for the missing child, the daughter of famous country musicians.

LIBRARY JOURNAL "As inviting as an episode of *Murder, She Wrote*, this follow-up to Nehring's Macavity Award-nominated

A Valley to Die For delivers a good, old-fashioned whodunit that should please any fan of Christian cozies."

THE OKLAHOMAN "The Ozark Folk Center...is the setting for the second in a series of 'to die for' mysteries by a former Oklahoman who obviously loves the Ozarks..." (REVIEWED BY KAY DYER)

THE TULSA WORLD "...hooks [readers] with a story they can't put down." (REVIEWED BY JUDY RANDLE)

MIDWEST BOOK REVIEW "...[leaves] the reader sighing in satisfaction." (REVIEWED BY SHELLEY GLODOWSKI)

MYSTERY SCENE MAGAZINE "A nicely woven cozy by a writer who knows both the music and the hill people of Arkansas." (REVIEWED BY MARY V. WELK)

COZIES, CAPERS & CRIMES "In this character-driven story, heroes have their values straight and fight for what they believe in." (REVIEWED BY VERNA SUIT)

I LOVE A MYSTERY "Highly recommended." (REVIEWED BY EDEN EMBLER)

OZARKS MONTHLY "Happily, rumplyness takes nothing away from the cleverness of gray-haired heroine Carrie McCrite..." (REVIEWED BY LEE KIRK)

GRAVETTE NEWS HERALD "Action, plot twists and wonderful characters..." (REVIEWED BY GAYLE WILLIAMS)

THE BENTON COUNTY DAILY RECORD "...Nehring's specialties— intrigue and suspense, unique characters and situations—all set in the gorgeous Ozarks."

AMI ELIZABETH REEVES, AUTHOR OF *NEXT OF KIN* "With an ear for dialect and an eye for the beauty of her natural surroundings, Nehring brings a strong sense of place to the twists and turns that ensue while searching for the child."

JOE DAVID RICE, ARKANSAS TOURISM DIRECTOR "...a compelling read."

BARBARA BRETT, AUTHOR OF *BETWEEN TWO ETERNITIES* AND, WITH HY BRETT, *PROMISES TO KEEP* "...murder and mayhem in perfect pitch!"

JULIE WRAY HERMAN, AUTHOR OF THE THREE DIRTY WOMEN GARDENING MYSTERY SERIES "Endearing characters make you want to come back to visit soon!"

MARY GILLIHAN, HARMONY MUSICIAN; PARK INTERPRETER AND ELDERHOSTEL COORDINATOR, OZARK FOLK CENTER STATE PARK "It was such fun to read about our Ozark Folk Center and picture where *the murder* took place."

A Valley to Die For by Radine Trees Nehring

Carrie McCrite and her neighbors are fighting to save their beloved Ozark valley from becoming a stone quarry. But when someone decides that one of them should die, Carrie must uncover and destroy the darkness swirling in the valley.

LIBRARY JOURNAL "With flair, Nehring, an award-winning Arkansas writer, launches a cozy series that will appeal to mystery readers..."

THE TULSA WORLD "The skill...the character development, the place, the pace and the action tell the true story." (REVIEWED BY MICHELE PATTERSON)

SOUTHERN SCRIBE "...a warm and enchanting tale. Carrie is charming as a woman who wants to be recognized as spunky, independent, and a hero. Casting the book in the Ozarks is... well, icing on the cake." (REVIEWED BY ROBERT L. HALL)

FORT SMITH TIMES RECORD "...a delightful mystery with appealing characters fighting for a cause. Throughout the story I grew all the more attached to Carrie, marveling at her strong faith and silently chastising her for her stubbornness. A...bonus is Carrie's cooking." (REVIEWED BY TINA DALE)

GRAVETTE NEWS HERALD "...kept my heart pounding...a page turner with no easy stopping places." (REVIEWED BY GAYLE WILLIAMS)

THE BOOKWATCH "...a smoothly written novel that grips the reader's attention from first page to last, and documents Radine Trees Nehring as a mystery writer whose imagination and talent will win her a large and dedicated readership."

I LOVE A MYSTERY "The suspense is grabbing, but the book is as relaxing as living alone in the forest... Very highly recommended." (REVIEWED BY EDEN EMBLER)

JANE HOOPER, PROPRIETOR OF SHERLOCK'S HOME BOOKSTORE "Weeks later, I'm still thinking about the book and characters. I can't wait for the next in the series."

CAROLYN HART, AUTHOR OF THE DEATH ON DEMAND AND HENRIE O MYSTERIES "A pleasure awaits mystery lovers."

DR. FRED PFISTER, EDITOR OF *THE OZARKS MOUNTAINEER* "It's great to read fiction about the Ozarks that rings true."

MIKE FLYNN, PRODUCER AND HOST OF THE *FOLK SAMPLER*, HEARD WEEKLY ON PUBLIC RADIO "...a fascinating mystery that gets better and better as the pages roll."

Dear Earth: A Love Letter from Spring Hollow
by Radine Trees Nehring
The unforgettable chronicle of a couple who traded secure jobs and the rat race for a life of simplicity and quiet joy.

BOOKLIST "Read it and dream."

MIDWEST BOOK REVIEW "This compelling story traces their

transitional experiences, presenting an endearing account."

DR. NEIL COMPTON (CONSERVASTIONIST AND PULITZER PRIZE NOMINEE FOR THE BATTLE FOR THE BUFFALO RIVER) "An engrossing account of the ups and downs of a couple who cast aside the big city life for life in the hills. Nehring's book is a must!"

MIKE FLYNN (PRODUCER AND HOST, "FOLK SAMPLER," NATIONAL PUBLIC RADIO) "You should give this book to everyone you love, particularly to the young, so they can learn the things that Radine and John learned on their journey to the Ozarks."

MARVIN BAKER, PH.D. (PAST REGIONAL VICE PRESIDENT, SIERRA CLUB) "There is inspiration here for all who contemplate making a change in living that brings one closer to the natural world."

DAVID T. NOLAN (PRESIDENT, NORTHWEST ARKANSAS AUDUBON SOCIETY) "An interesting adventure in moving, not of physically moving the body, but of moving the mind."

A Clear North Light by Laurel Schunk

Petras Simonaitis is a struggling Lithuanian artisan. When his sister dies, perhaps at the hands of a cruel Baron, Petras must try to protect Rima, the woman he loves, from the same fate. But is he strong enough?

LIBRARY JOURNAL "Schunk solidly launches a new 'Lithuanian' trilogy, following one family's triumphs and tragedies through the generations."

BOOKLIST "Schunk, author of the well-regarded coming-of-age story *Black and Secret Midnight* (1998), drops back to 1938 with *A Clear North Light*, the first installment of her Lithuanian Trilogy."

NWSBRFS (WICHITA PRESS WOMEN, INC.) "...notable as much for its excellent character development as for its story line...Good reading..."

GRETCHEN SPRAGUE, AUTHOR OF *MAQUETTE FOR MURDER*
"...dramatically illuminates the effect of deadly global politics on the private lives of all-too-human individuals caught up in events not of their making."

JAMES D. YODER, AUTHOR OF *LUCY OF THE TRAIL OF TEARS*
"...pulls one into an historical drama with excitement and moral persuasiveness as Petras fights and searches for faith, meaning, and love..."

Under the Wolf's Head by Kate Cameron

All Callie Bagley wants is to be left alone to garden. But her plans for solitude are interrupted when a dead body shows up nearly on her back step.

GRIT: AMERICAN LIFE & TRADITIONS "You'll laugh at the sisters' relationship and grow to love the two women just as Callista's plants grow through her loving care."

PUBLISHERS WEEKLY "The gardening tips seeded throughout the narrative are a clever ploy, echoing the inclusion of cooking tips in the ever-popular culinary mysteries..."

LIBRARY JOURNAL "Plenty of gardening filler and allusions to inept local law enforcement lighten the atmosphere, as do the often humorous sisterly 'fights' and the speedy prose."

NORWICH BULLETIN "Schunk in the past has tackled child abuse and racism; her first gardening mystery provides a message about ageism and the value placed on elderly lives..."

THE CHARLOTTE AUSTIN REVIEW "Highly recommended." (REVIEWED BY NANCY MEHL)

ABOUT.COM "...a wonderful new release..." (REVIEWED BY RENIE DUGWYLER)

THE BOOKDRAGON REVIEW "...evokes in the reader an understanding of the atmosphere of a small town, where everyone is important and interesting." (REVIEWED BY RICHARD ROYCE)

NWSBRFS (WICHITA PRESS WOMEN, INC.) "...a quick and pleasant read..."

JAMES D. YODER, AUTHOR OF BLACK SPIDER OVER TIEGENHOF "Kate Cameron brings this murder mystery to a finale, murders solved, villains implicated and captured, with the added bonus, protagonist Callie Bagley discovers new love in her life."

Death in Exile by Laurel Schunk

The Regency is noted for its gaiety, but sometimes the sparkling repartee covers darker things, like murder. Lord Wentworth and Anna Kate work to save their friend Diana from death in exile.

LIBRARY JOURNAL "What could have been a straightforward Regency romance is elevated by apt social commentary in this offering from Schunk..."

THE PILOT "Schunk is a good writer who has a good grasp of story and character."

THE CHARLOTTE AUSTIN REVIEW "This beautifully written Regency novel...will throw you into another time, and you won't want to leave." (REVIEWED BY NANCY MEHL)

MURDER: PAST TENSE (THE HIST. MYS. APPREC. SOC.) "Laurel Schunk is a masterful storyteller."

Black and Secret Midnight by Laurel Schunk

Murder in the South in the 1950's. Are Beth Anne's innocent questions about racism precipitating the murders?

LIBRARY JOURNAL "Beth Anne's appealing child's-eye view of the world and the subtle Christian message should make this appealing to fans of Christian and mainstream mysteries."

PUBLISHERS WEEKLY "Beth Anne is at times touchingly naive..."

SMALL PRESS BOOK REVIEW "...a memorable picture of racism that is variously stark and nuanced."

THE PILOT "...a good look at racial relations in the south...with a mysterious twist."

MURDER: PAST TENSE (THE HIST. MYS. APPREC. SOC.) "The story is so gripping that I worried [Beth Anne] would be killed before the end."

NWSBRFS (WICHITA PRESS WOMEN, INC.) "...Schunk's adult novels are serious, skillfully crafted works."

THE CHARLOTTE AUSTIN REVIEW "...a light in the darkness and a novel to sink your teeth and your heart into." (REVIEWED BY NANCY MEHL)

AMAZON.COM "...a great regional mystery that will excite fans with its twists and turns." (REVIEWED BY HARRIET KLAUSNER)

DOROTHYL "...skillfully mixes a story of segregation in the South and deep, dark family secrets with the plot of Shakespeare's 'MacBeth' in a very unique way." (REVIEWED BY TOM GRIFFITH)

SANDY DENGLER, AUTHOR OF *THE QUICK AND THE DEAD* "MacBeth and mayhem in the 50s. What a mix! I love Ms. Schunk's characters, and I remember the milieu all too well. It was the era you love to hate, beautifully brought to life."

LINDA HALL, AUTHOR OF *MARGARET'S PEACE* "Indicative of life in the South in the 1950s when racism and bigotry were around every frightening corner, *Black and Secret Midnight* is a great mystery with plenty of foreshadowing, clues, and red herrings to keep you reading far into the night."

The Voice He Loved by **Laurel Schunk**

Paige Brookings has traded her career as a New York model for a less glamorous life in Wichita, Kansas. Now she's being stalked. Can she protect herself from an anonymous madman?

THE CHARLOTTE AUSTIN REVIEW "...a masterful tale that reaches into the inner workings of a bruised and battered psyche, while keeping the plot moving at a breathless pace." (REVIEWED BY NANCY MEHL)

The Heart of Matthew Jade by **Ralph Allen** (available only from St Kitts Press)

As Matthew Jade ministers to the lost and broken, three inmates die. Who is the killer, and who will be the next victim in the cages of Coffin County Jail?

PUBLISHERS WEEKLY "...a compassionate view into religious, familial and romantic love..."

KEVIN PATRICK, CNET RADIO, SAN FRANCISCO "Fabulous!"

THE MIDWEST BOOK REVIEW "...an obliging and magnificently written mystery which is as entertaining as it is ultimately inspiring."

THE EAGLE "...Allen's book will inspire many who believe in the power of faith — and enjoy a good story."

THE CHARLOTTE AUSTIN REVIEW "...an eye-opener. *The Heart of Matthew Jade* is a compelling novel that will stay with you long after you put it down." (REVIEWED BY NANCY MEHL)

THE BOOKDRAGON REVIEW "...this novel's strength is in the behind the scenes glimpses of faith behind bars." (REVIEWED BY MELANIE C. DUNCAN)

THE LANTERN "...destined to become a classic. Its mixture of love and hate, religion and fallacy grabs readers from the very beginning and never lets them go."

LAUREL SCHUNK, AUTHOR OF *BLACK AND SECRET MIDNIGHT* "This compelling story chronicles the faith journey of a simple accountant from his sanitized office building into the maw of Hell as chaplain in a county jail."

Hyænas by Sandy Dengler
(available only from St Kitts Press)

Gar, shaman of his clan of Neanderthals, must discover who killed a rival clansman. And a mysterious stranger with the heart of strength of a hyæna follows him every step of the way.

LIBRARY JOURNAL "Highly recommended."

INTERNET BOOKWATCH (THE MIDWEST BOOK REVIEW) "...a terrific murder mystery and a work of unique, flawless written exploration of prehistoric antiquity."

THE CHARLOTTE AUSTIN REVIEW "Dengler has crafted a masterpiece. *Hyaenas* proves that there are still new slants to the mystery genre." (REVIEWED BY NANCY MEHL)

AMAZON.COM "For anyone who wants something a bit different with their mysteries, *Hyaenas* is the answer, hopefully with future novels starring Gar and company." (REVIEWED BY HARRIET KLAUSNER)

DOROTHYL "...I had a hard time putting the book down when I needed to do some work." (REVIEWED BY TOM GRIFFITH)

PAT RUSHFORD, AUTHOR OF THE HELEN BRADLEY MYSTERIES "Dengler is masterful at creating characters that come alive in any era."